HEIRS OF BAYWATER
Love & Lust

J. T. Scott

American Literary Press
Baltimore, Maryland

Heirs of Baywater: Love & Lust

Library of Congress
Cataloging-in-Publication Data
ISBN 1-56167-874-0

Library of Congress Card Catalog Number:
2005902482

Published by

American Literary Press

8019 Belair Road, Suite 10
Baltimore, Maryland 21236

Manufactured in the United States of America

Contents

PART ONE

PART TWO
Baywater Estates

This book is dedicated to my cousin, "The Lollipop Kid," Jerry Maren, the munchkin who performed with Judy Garland in *The Wizard of Oz* and has appeared in many movies and television programs.

This article appeared in Monday's *Sayr's Point Tribune.*

Taurus Worthington, 85, inventor of an electrical device and owner of Baywater Estate, died Saturday in his home after a recent illness. His housekeeper, Emma Brown, was there at the time of death, as was James Treadwell, his attorney and longtime friend, and his great niece, Janet Blake Henderson, wife of local attorney Charles W. Henderson. Mr. Worthington, born in New York City, had traveled all over the world and brought back many valuable objects d'arts to Baywater. Many famous persons visited Mr. Worthington at his palatial home. He leaves his entire estate as follows: $5,000 token of appreciation to Emma Brown; 20 acres of the estate, most of it on the bay, to his great niece Janet Blake Henderson; the remaining 10 acres and mansion to his great niece Lenore Akton Morgan. If Lenore Akton Morgan does not want to occupy the mansion, then Janet Blake Henderson may have lifetime use of it, and on her death the house, together with the one acre immediately surrounding it, will revert back to Lenore Akton Morgan. All of his remaining funds and personal possessions are to be divided equally between the two great nieces.

Part I

Baywater Estates

1931–1963

PROLOGUE
SPRING 1963

The minister's voice broke through Lenore's reverie. "Lord, thou who has made this man, allow his soul to rest in peace." She watched as the ropes lowered the coffin gently into Taurus's final resting place and thought, what a beautiful day to end a wonderful life! The crocuses were pushing their way up through the ground and the warmth of the sun and soft sounds of the birds gave evidence of the coming of summer.

"Ashes to ashes, dust to dust," and the minister sprinkled earth over the casket as it descended farther into the grave. It was over. Two remained still, while the others dispersed.

"It's been a long time, Lenore."

"Yes," her voice was wistful. "I should have come back to see Uncle Taurus. I've had five years to do it. He never saw Robbie."

"He must be big now. Did you bring him?"

Lenore smiled at Janet, perceptive enough to sense that the question was filled with curiosity. "No, I didn't."

Janet wondered if something was wrong. The question on the tip of her tongue was about Peter, but Lenore's attitude stopped her. She saw Charles with Treadwell, waving to her beside the car, and took Lenore's arm. "We'd better go. Charles has to get back to the office."

The limousine came around the bend, and when they stepped in, Charles directed the driver to his office. The drive to town was silent. When the limousine stopped, he quietly asked Janet, "Where can I reach you later?"

She suggested to Lenore that they go to Baywater. Lenore nodded. Treadwell agreed, "That's fine, I can pick up my car there and leave you two

1

to make up for lost time."

The limousine started up again and headed for Baywater. As it passed landmarks familiar to them both, the women's thoughts turned to the distant past. Memories began to crowd in. Baywater seemed all it had been long ago, a tranquil sanctuary giving solace to two shattered young lives. The massive lions, poised on the concrete monuments, challenged one to push beyond their gigantic jaws. The chauffeur stopped and pushed open the huge spiked gates, and the limousine rolled toward the old mansion of a bygone era. Lenore stared at the lions and recalled the last time they had come here together. How young they had been then, and how long ago it seemed now.

Janet was ten and Lenore fifteen when Treadwell had brought them to Baywater to live in torment from the impact of the terrible tragedy that had changed the course of their lives. It was only two weeks before that their parents had taken off in the plane headed to the Rockies for a happy holiday. Taurus Worthington, their great uncle, had been like a father to their mothers, and after the disaster, he disrupted his bachelor's way of life to give the girls his protection, care, home, and love, hoping that in some measure the girls would temper his own grief. Now, even after death, he provided them with a home and security by leaving them his estate.

Her thoughts were interrupted when the car door opened. Janet slipped her hand into Lenore's as they walked toward the steps. Someone was standing on the porch. Treadwell said, "I took the liberty of having Mrs. Brown put the house in order. She can stay on for a while, if you need her."

Lenore ran up the steps and hugged the little old lady. "Emma! It's good to see you."

"My dear girl," she sobbed. Her voice broke and she took a handkerchief from her apron pocket to dry the tears that were rolling down her cheeks. "We've missed you, Lenore." Lenore stood back, aware of the toll the past seventeen years had taken. The once sturdy figure had deteriorated into a frail, thin, bent woman.

"I know, I know, Emma, and I've missed you, and Baywater." There was

silence as Emma dabbed her eyes, then she moved toward Janet. "I've made some sandwiches and chocolate."

Janet thanked her and kissed her on the cheek and they followed the old bent form into the house. Treadwell stopped in the doorway. "I'm sorry I can't stay, but you know where to find me if you need me."

The women conveyed their appreciation for all he had done, and when the door closed they went to find Emma in the kitchen preparing a tray.

"We'll stay here and have our sandwiches and chocolate with you the way we used to," Janet told her.

The warmth of the kitchen relaxed them as they sat together, reminiscing. The heat from the ornate wood-burning stove spread through the entire room. The patina of the oak trestle table contrasted sharply with the pale yellow wainscoting of the walls. Watching Emma putter around the kitchen was pleasant; it was as if nothing had changed through the years. After a while, with effort, Lenore pulled herself out of the tranquil, quiet mood and said, "This has been nice Emma, but I must check on my husband. Janet, would you like to accompany me into the library while I call Peter? He's at the motel resting, tired and uncomfortable."

They entered the mahogany paneled library, the somber gloom of the room unrelieved by the shaft of sunlight beaming in from the solarium. Janet asked, "Is he sick? Is there anything I can do?"

Lenore gave her a wry smile and squeezed her hand. "There's nothing to do. Peter likes being ill, and most of it's imaginary."

Having shared a new confidence, the years fell away and the bonds that had drawn them close as children were renewed.

"I hope you're back to stay Lennie. It would be good company to have you close. Do you think Peter would like living here?"

"Perhaps. Peter doesn't care where he lives, but we're concerned about Robbie. A change might be what he needs. I'll fly back to California and arrange to sell the house. School will be over in a month and I'll bring Robbie back then. Meanwhile Peter can stay here and get acquainted with your people and his new surroundings." She picked up the phone and

dialed the motel. After a short discussion she gave Peter the directions to the house.

They settled down in the brown leather chairs. "This room reminds me of Uncle Taurus, solid and comfortable, always ready to stand between us and the world." Lenore stroked the arm of the chair.

"When you came back from India, why didn't you come here?"

"I knew Peter and Uncle Taurus wouldn't get along. Uncle Taurus was brimming with life, an extraordinary man whose friends were remarkable people, and by then Peter was overly neurotic about his illness. It never would have worked."

"How does he get along with Robbie?"

"Fine. He's good to him, and Robbie, in return, is tolerant about Peter's pills and pains. They're fond of each other. But, how about you and Charles? Does he like this country life, or does he miss the city?"

"Perhaps he misses the city a bit, but we had planned to move out here in time." Janet bounced out of the chair and pulled Lenore by the hands. "Look, before Peter arrives, let's take a quick tour of the house. Aren't you anxious to see your room?"

"All right. We can talk up there. Are there rooms prepared for Peter and Robbie?"

Janet stiffened. Separate rooms. Things must not be going well.

Lenore read her thoughts and as they climbed the stairs she explained bitterly. "My life with Peter is very different from your marriage to Charles."

"Oh?" Janet pondered about that for a moment. "Maybe Charles . . ." She stopped. Lenore wasn't listening to her. She had swung the door to her room open and stood there looking back into time. Nothing had changed. As she stepped inside, it was like seventeen years ago, as though she had never left.

Janet, sensing her thoughts, whispered, "Even your clothes are in the closet."

Lenore turned abruptly, suppressing her tears, and as she gazed across the hall to the opposite door, Janet crossed in front of her and turned the porcelain knob. "Wonder if my piano is in tune."

Lenore followed her inside. The room had been completely redecorated. The old chintz arm chair had been replaced by a colonial love seat, matching the blue damask draperies. The sturdy canopied bed had been recovered in blue toile; the gingham of her childhood was gone. Janet walked past the antique chests, opened the lid of the piano, and ran her fingers across the keyboard. She sat down and played. Lennie hummed along, her mind swirling with memories, when suddenly her thoughts were disturbed by a ringing telephone.

Janet stopped playing. "Bet that's Charles," and she went into Taurus's room.

Without a greeting Charles asked, "What have you decided?"

"Peter should be here any minute. They're going to stay at the house. We . . ."

He interrupted her, "I haven't much time between clients. Pick you up at six, and we'll all have dinner at the Club. Call and make reservations for six-thirty. See you later." He hung up.

Janet stood holding the receiver for a moment, then slammed it back on the cradle. It would be nice for once if he would ask her what she wanted to do. Then she shrugged. There was no use getting upset. Maybe it was better that they go out the first night. She phoned for reservations and returned to her room.

Lenore wasn't there. "Lenore?" There was no answer. "Lenore, where are you?" She called in a louder voice.

"In my room."

Lenore was standing in front of the open casement windows listening to the waves lapping against the beach. Janet went over to the windows. The swimming pool was empty, the beach house sadly in need of paint and repairs, the grounds were unkempt, the flower beds matted with dead leaves, even the beach was covered with masses of seaweed. An aura of decay hung over the whole estate. The once proud heritage had been brought to its knees by spiraling taxes, fantastic suburban development, high wages, and medical bills that had eaten away at the Worthington money. Their anxious eyes met. It would cost a small fortune to restore Baywater.

To avoid a discussion of the problem, Lenore asked, "Was that Charles?"

"Yes, he's stopping to pick us up at six. We're going to the Club for dinner. That's all right with you, isn't it?"

"Of course, Janet, whatever you think best."

She was going to say that it hadn't been her idea, but changed her mind. A car pulled into the driveway, and seconds later the gong announced a visitor; they heard the murmur of voices, and Emma called, "Lenore, it's Mr. Peter."

"We'll be right down." Lenore's voice was cool and reserved.

Janet hurried down the stairs, anxious to meet her cousin's husband.

"Hi Peter, I'm Janet."

Peter, who had been standing in front of the hall mirror smoothing down his long grey strands of hair, turned and extended his hand. "Hello, my dear."

Janet grasped his hand and pulled him toward her. "I've finally met Lenore's husband!" She gave him a kiss on his cheek.

Peter blushed, looked over his shoulder and observed Lenore at the bottom of the stairs watching with an amused expression. "Good afternoon, my dear. Your charming cousin has introduced herself." He paused for a moment. "Did everything go smoothly?"

Lenore approached him. "Yes, Janet and Treadwell had taken care of the details."

"That was thoughtful," he responded.

Janet smiled. "It was nothing. We only live ten minutes away." She looked from one to the other. "Why don't you take the bags upstairs, Peter? Emma has prepared your rooms and you can freshen up before dinner. Charles called. He's picking us up at six for dinner at the club."

Peter grasped the handle of Lenore's heavy suitcase and picked it up with effort, leaving his behind. Walking toward the wide staircase he studied and admired the beauty of the carved walls with their myriad faces and figures, intricate in design. The luster and richness of the wood gleamed from many hours of polishing. He stopped at the head of the staircase to catch his breath, and then as he continued to follow Lenore, he

observed that these exquisite carvings covered the length and breadth of the hallways.

Lenore indicated the doorway to her room and he placed her bag inside. "Your rooms are down the hall; bedroom, bath and sitting room. Let me show you." She started toward his suite but changed her direction and instead crossed the hall and stopped in front of the open door to Janet's room. "This is ideal for Robbie. Taurus' suite is next to my room, and the other guest rooms are in the west wing." A few moments later she left him at his door saying, "When you're ready, come downstairs. If you need anything, ring for Emma."

Peter nodded understandingly. He stood listlessly for a moment, then remembering his bag, went down to the front hall. Carrying it up the stairs he became aware of the quietness. Not a sound penetrated from the outside world at that moment. He understood how the stillness and comfort of this great old house could provide a wonderful refuge for anyone within its walls. His rooms were spacious and the heavy oak furniture had been given the same care as the paneled hallways. He pulled open a dresser drawer and marveled at the condition of the fine antique. After he unpacked, he went downstairs in pursuit of company. He followed the sound of voices.

Emma and Janet were in the kitchen talking. "So you found us." Janet called to him as he appeared in the doorway. "How about a drink?"

"Ah, I was going to ask for one."

"Come my good man, and we'll find something," she teased. She went into the sitting room and opened the liquor cabinet. "Voila, help yourself," and she stood aside while he selected a bottle of sherry. As Janet poured two glasses she heard someone calling. She went to the doorway.

Charles came down the hall. "Is everyone ready?" He brushed by her as he entered the sitting room, went over to Peter and thrust his hand out. "Hello there, I'm Janet's husband. You must be Peter."

"Yes, I am, and you're Charles, the attorney. How do you do?" He responded brightly to the conversation.

As Janet handed Charles her glass of sherry, she replied to his question,

"We're waiting for Lenore." She moved toward the cabinet to get herself a glass.

"Aren't our reservations for six-thirty? Where is your cousin?" He was irritated.

"Right behind you," a droll voice commented.

Charles spun around, unaccustomed to being taken unawares. "Lenore!" He took a step near her. "Welcome home. Good to see you, even though distressing circumstances brought it about."

"Yes, it was unfortunate." Her cool eyes surveyed him and he was strangely disconcerted. He put his glass down briskly and said, "If everyone's ready, let's go."

Janet picked up the glass and rubbed the damp spot it had left on the table, annoyed at his thoughtlessness. She moved the glass to a coaster and was the last to leave the room.

The station wagon was parked under the portochere and they climbed in. Once on their way, Charles turned his head toward Peter. "Did you have trouble finding the house?"

"No, not at all. Lenore's directions were accurate."

Charles commented, "Baywater is one of the last old estates left in the area."

"Is that so?" Peter asked nonchalantly as his attention wandered.

Janet sensed a distant attitude between Peter and Lenore, and attempting to bridge the gap between them blurted out, "You'll both love the food at the club. The chef comes from the West Indies and anything he touches is pure delight." She leaned forward from the back seat, placing a hand on Peter's shoulder. "What kind of food do you like best?"

"I have to be careful of what I eat, so many things disagree with me."

Before Peter could elaborate about his health, Lenore interjected, "How much further is it Charles?"

Charles's eyes met hers in the rearview mirror. "About half an hour." He felt uneasy. Her personality disturbed him. He couldn't fathom her and his scrutiny did not affect her composure.

Lenore was aware of his reaction; it was a familiar one. As the car sped on her mind wandered back to the past. Her father had done her no kindness in her younger years. After the death of her older brother, she had taken the place of the lost son. By the time she was ten, he had taught her to sail, swim, shoot, and even fly with some degree of competency. He took her along whenever possible and made her face the things that frightened her, keeping her at them until familiarity dulled fright. She was encouraged to work with him as she became older, and spent many hours watching and learning. He bought her a camera and she began to copy his work at sports events. Her father's name in the field of sports photography was high on the roster of fame. Lenore had flair for the work, learned fast, and it wasn't long before he recognized her special talent and ability. On one of his assignments he handed her his camera and had her shoot for him. When they developed the pictures that night, he was delighted with the results and gave her full credit for the work. After that they often worked together, and before his death he had the pleasure of seeing Lenore's name beside his in several magazines. He passed to his death knowing his daughter had successfully penetrated a field of work reserved for men.

Lenore and Janet had been uneasy when their parents left on that fateful vacation, but nothing they said had altered the plans.

Lenore had been stoical during the trying days that followed the tragedy. Janet turned to her for comfort through the agonizing period they had to face. The funeral was an ordeal neither one would ever forget. Mr. Treadwell moved them to Baywater; there was nowhere else to go. At first it was a world of emptiness. Although they had spent many wonderful vacations with Uncle Taurus, living with him was very different.

Lenore had packed her father's equipment, copies of the magazines with his work, pictures of his plane, photographs that she had received from famed athletes, and her clothes. Uncle Taurus had promised that she could go on with her work and had a darkroom set up for her. The girls became closer to each other, a bond that would never be broken. Taurus Worthington opened his house and heart, and Emma Brown, the housekeeper, lavished them with attention. Janet behaved as he expected, but

he could not understand Lenore. Where he wanted to give protection, she sought freedom; when he tried to keep the world out, she went to meet it. During the war, private flying was grounded and Lenore could not satisfy her love of excitement in the air. There wasn't enough gas for boating, so she went sailing. She was reckless and would race off into stormy weather, coming back like a drowned rat. Janet was terrified, afraid she would lose her too. When Lenore was a little older, she fought with Uncle Taurus about attending the USO dances. He finally allowed her to go because the dances were chaperoned. Lenore, sensing his disapproval, simply became more secretive; only Janet knew where she went and what she did.

At eighteen, Lenore, tall and slim, vibrant and adventurous, went to work at a local newspaper. Her excellent background in photography was an asset. Her copper hair glistened, and her hazel eyes focused behind her camera at any event worth filming, and when possible, she sold her pictures. She secretly felt she had to keep the memory of Gary Akton alive; she was grateful for the legacy of talent. One evening she met a good-looking young fellow at a USO dance and they fell in love. At twenty, she ran away with him and they were married. He was only nineteen and his parents had the marriage annulled on the grounds that they had both lied about their ages. The young soldier put up very little fight for his marriage, then was sent overseas, and Lenore never heard from him again. She retreated into a shell, stayed alone more than ever, and her eyes had a distant look. Lenore refused to stay at Baywater. The war was over, one of her father's friends found her a job that would enable her to travel. Before she left, she confided in Janet about her pregnancy. She traveled continuously, left the country to follow every major sports event as long as she could, and then went to Florida to have her baby.

Janet wrote, begging her to return and bring her son with her. Taurus wanted her home, unaware of the existence of a child. But she wasn't through with grief, the boy was born a hemophiliac and needed extensive care and supervision. She returned without the baby, Robbie, to petition Treadwell for money from the trust fund left by her parents. Even though she had a good income from her position, she wanted to insure the child's well being; he wouldn't be able to travel with her, but would need constant care. The few days she spent with Janet and Taurus went swiftly; again she

confided only in Janet about Robbie's condition. Treadwell agreed to the amount and she was able to make arrangements for her son's care.

Once more, her work became more important than ever and she drove herself mercilessly. Janet imagined that she lived an exotic life meeting fascinating men, whirling from one social activity to another, but ironically, though opportunities to meet men were unlimited, she was still scarred by a short marriage, and possessed a driving ambition which was a deterrent to romance. No longer satisfied with the range and scope of the sports field, she searched for new interests. A writer was assigned to her and it wasn't long before Taurus and Janet began to see illustrated articles by the team in magazines and journals. She had personality and confidence; coupled with good looks and ability, she easily obtained interviews with prominent figures from all over the world.

She had met Peter Morgan several times during her travels. He was a forty-two-year-old conservative, steadfast businessman, prosperous and unmarried, well-mannered and gentle. Lenore was twenty-five and had received the rest of the trust fund. Her own income was considerable, but she wanted Robbie with her. Peter asked her out to dinner and found himself enchanted by this enigmatic woman. He knew that Lenore regarded him as a friend only, and was not romantically interested. During the times he saw her, he probed a little and learned of her son. She acknowledged that she missed Robbie. He was five and she felt she might safely take him along with the proper help. Peter proposed, willing to accept her friendship for him as a basis for marriage, and was agreeable to having her son with them. They were married in Paris after Robbie's arrival. Since Peter did a great deal of traveling, Lenore planned to continue her career; both incomes were more than adequate to provide constant care for the boy. Although she had many reservations, she resolved to inform Taurus about Robbie and her marriage. It had been a hard letter to write, but Taurus answered that Lenore would be welcome at Baywater any time and it would always be her home. He had been true to his words.

Peter's import business took them to strange places of the world. For five years, they were constantly on the move. Robbie had a tutor whom he liked and a mother he adored. He couldn't live a life of adventure, but could

share one vicariously through Lenore. Peter was proud of her accomplishments and never objected to her assignments. The young man she worked with was an excellent writer, equally ambitious and dedicated; he respected her abilities and strove to meet her standards.

Peter had to go to India and Lenore speculated that she might find interesting material there to absorb her. It wasn't long after they arrived when Peter was stricken ill and hospitalized. He had an operation that took part of his stomach; for months his condition was precarious, and then came a long, slow recovery. His mind was directed only to himself, his own state of health, and nothing outside of the hospital and his own well-being concerned him. Lenore stayed and waited, the days tedious, the inactivity hard to accept. After his release from the hospital, he refused to assume any responsibility. Lenore persuaded him to sell his business and retire to his home in sunny California.

Once in California she could not endure any further idleness, so she bought a small plane and went back to her career. Since Robbie's physical condition hampered his own activities, he spent a great deal of time with Peter while Lenore pursued her own interests. To keep herself in good condition she practiced yoga, and finding people interested, conducted classes at home. At thirty-seven she was slim and graceful, and possessed an awareness beyond average. Very little escaped her, and she was more aloof and reserved than ever before.

It had been a long time since she had written Baywater; and she resumed communication with Janet only weeks before the death of Taurus. Peter, never having been to Baywater, was anxious to go, but when they had arrived at the motel, he was extremely tired and preferred to rest rather than accompany Lenore to the funeral services.

As the car moved along she wondered about Baywater and its future. Glancing up she caught Charles's eyes on her in the mirror. He looked away hastily and she turned to view the scenery.

The dying rays of the setting sun vanished behind the horizon and gradually dusk engulfed the naked trees along the old road. The car passed a lake; the branches along the water's edge stood stiffly silhouetted against the sky creating a charcoal sketch on a grey canvas. A covey of

ducks swimming across the lake broke the glassy surface with gentle ripples.

"Look at the ducks! I wish we could feed them," Janet cried gaily.

Charles answered, "We don't have time to stop."

Peter gazed at the ducks, then turned toward Charles curiously. Sensing this, Charles elucidated coldly, "When we lived in New York, Janet was forever at the park with the animals. You'd think there was no one else there to care for them."

Janet laughed. "Just think how lucky you are, dear, with no zoo around here." Her voice was filled with sarcasm.

Peter smiled. It didn't take much to get her excited. There seemed to be a great difference between the two cousins. Lenore was cool and serene, and Janet was full of exuberance and gaiety. She was shorter than Lenore. Her hair was dark auburn, but the eyes had the same hazel coloring. He knew she was thirty-two and must have been quite young when their parents died. He found himself wondering about her life and how she had adapted to her home with her bachelor uncle Taurus.

The noise of a plane overhead made Janet wince. Hearing the sound above brought to mind her parents' last vacation. The two couples had not been on a trip together in years, and Gary Akton was determined to fly them on a cross-country journey. On the day of their departure, the girls, along with the Akton housekeeper whose charge they were to be in those few weeks, went to Roosevelt Field to wave good-bye. It was sunny and warm as the young cousins stood watching the little plane take off. It circled the field once, dipped its wings before it headed west, then became a tiny speck in the vast blue sky.

The girls waited anxiously for the call on Friday night, and when it came they were relieved. On Saturday night Janet had awakened from a nightmare and cried out for Lenore. Both girls were troubled not hearing from their parents. Early Sunday morning the police stopped by to tell them the bad news. Janet was inconsolable; the funeral left her shattered.

Taurus had quarters prepared for them, and when they arrived, Janet saw her mother's piano, music, and photographs in her room. She cried as she touched the keys with her small fingers.

During the first few months she found it hard to adjust; she hated

13

to be alone. In the fall Taurus took her to study with Claude Phillipe, one of the best teachers in the area, and she showed enough interest so that the distinguished pianist encouraged her to consider a career in music. As the girls grew older, Lenore was home less, so Janet took refuge in her music. Sometimes she would practice late at night while waiting for Lenore to steal into the house.

Janet was the first to sense that Lenore's restlessness would drive her from Baywater, but she knew that nothing would stop her. After Lenore had gone, Janet occupied herself in advanced music studies. The local church invited her to become its organist, so Taurus had a home organ installed in the library for her to practice on. Then she began commuting to the city and studied piano and organ at the Janieson Preparatory School of Music for two years. Playing at church recitals and local functions stimulated her interest, and in the fall of 1947 she went on to study at the Julliard School of Music. Five years later she obtained her degree, and at twenty-two and in search of a career, moved to the city with Taurus's approval. He had now, in a sense, lost both girls, although Janet came back to Baywater some weekends.

During the holidays Janet was the featured guest artist at a Legal Aid Society Dinner. Charles Henderson was there and he found himself attracted to the young performer. He had studied law in New York, and at twenty-six was working at his first job with the firm of Ellis, Symington and West. One afternoon shortly before closing time, his secretary informed him that a young lady was in the outer office with a problem concerning a lease. As he shuffled some papers aside on his desk waiting for the secretary to usher her in, the door opened. To his surprise, Janet walked in. She needed advice on her existing lease as she wanted to move, and after promising her that he would look into it, invited her to dinner. A few days later he took her out once more, and after that they dated regularly. It took him three years to convince her to marry him, and once married he found himself resenting her career. She had been playing piano in some of the better supper clubs in the city, but Charles was possessive and did not want her performing publicly. It was about this time that he first became aware that the position he had would not take him far.

After a few years of marriage, he decided to look for a job on Long Island. Sayr's Point area was growing and the firm of Brown and Bennington needed another attorney on its staff. Taurus introduced him to the partners, old friends of his, and Charles joined the legal staff. They moved to a little village west of Sayr's Point and Charles plunged enthusiastically into his new position. Janet was restless, so to occupy her time became choir director and organist at a large church. Even that wasn't enough to occupy her, and she looked for some other activity. Property and houses had always held a certain fascination for her, so she became a part-time real estate sales lady. She worked at this for two years, but gave it up when Taurus became gravely ill, and spent any spare time she had with him.

During the years that Lenore was away, Janet never failed to write her each week. Though she didn't always receive an answer, she was certain that Lenore expected to hear from her. Janet had anticipated that Lenore would come during Taurus's illness, but Taurus died suddenly and there wasn't time to do anything except telephone the news and wait.

Charles knew the girls had been close, but to him, Janet's excitement about Lenore's arrival seemed out of proportion. He had expected to meet Lenore and Peter at the airport, but their plane was delayed so they went by limousine directly to a motel. Lenore arrived late to the funeral by cab, and there was no immediate opportunity to find out what had happened to Peter.

As the car rolled on, the smell of salt air drifted in through the open window. Janet reflected, "You've never been here, have you, Lenore?"

"No, with gas rationing during the war, it was impossible." She didn't continue.

"We came here a lot after you left. And since Charles and I have moved back to the island, it's become one of our favorite spots."

The station wagon pulled into the parking lot. They could hear the roar of the ocean, and walking toward the club a few second later, they could see it. The waves were rolling and crashing up on the beach, sending spray high in the air. Janet took Peter's arm. "Come, let me show you

around. The tennis court is over there, and there's a pool on the other side of the clubhouse. They do a tremendous business here once summer comes. The courts are crowded as is the pool . . . there's even a wading pool for the children. Isn't this marvelous?"

Before Peter could answer, Charles commented, "Come on Janet, you have the same thing at Baywater; the ocean, a pool, tennis and a beach house."

Janet weighed his statement, then squealed, "Charles do you know what you said? We do have all that at Baywater! What a great beach club it would make!"

Charles looked about. He pulled his jacket tighter around himself. "Let's go inside to talk. I'm cold."

While walking into the club, Janet evaluated the size of the property. It was smaller than Baywater. Charles ordered drinks at the table then asked, "What in the devil are you doing?"

Janet was rummaging in her handbag. "I need a pencil and some paper. Oh, here's some."

They watched her. She had the blueprint in her mind and could envision an entire project. Swiftly she pencil outlined Baywater. She drew in a location to pinpoint the property which was hers. She said excitedly, "You know, we could put about sixteen houses in here, and Lenore, if we cut a road a little further, they'd have access to the pool and we could enlarge the beach house. With the tennis court, we could have a club and an exclusive development. What do you think?"

"It would cost a lot, wouldn't it Jan?"

"Yes it would, but don't you think it would be worth it, in the long run?" Lenore didn't answer, trying to evaluate the pros and cons of the situation.

Charles interrupted her thoughts. "It could be prosperous. There's nothing in our area that would lend itself as ideally to a beach club and I don't think it would take very long to make a tidy profit on that and the houses."

"I have the money in my trust fund," Janet coaxed.

"Peter won't be working again, and with expenses for Robbie and

the house, I don't think I'd want to gamble with what we have, even if I can resume my career. Of course, selling the place in California is a help, but you have to remember that while Charles's practice will grow and his income increase, we don't have that to look forward to."

"If we use my money and property, and you put in your property, we can figure something out." Janet's pleading eyes searched Charles's face. "Can't we?"

"Certainly, it can be done, but how do you feel about it, Peter?"

The waiter approached the table and silently served their drinks.

Peter waited until he had finished, coughed and cleared his throat, as though making some momentous decision. "This is more in your line than mine, but Janet's ideas seem to make sense and with you behind the girls, how can the project fail? It sounds good, but I'll let you three decide."

Janet perked up. "Now Lennie . . . what about it?"

"We'll have to go into it more thoroughly, naturally, but it seems feasible on the surface, and we could use the money for the future."

Janet continued to sketch and make notes, and in no time she had drawn an entire plan. As it was passed around, they studied it.

"What's on the other side of the property?" Peter asked.

"Wetlands, owned by the state. Why?"

He pointed to the sketch. "You might be able to put in a marina over here. People could be induced to buy property more readily if they had a boat dock."

"That's a great idea," Janet bubbled.

Charles lifted his glass. "You've hit on something girls! Is a toast in order?"

They agreed unanimously and solemnly lifted their glasses high and toasted the success of the venture. Then Janet said cheerfully, "I know this will work," paused, and turned to Charles, "perhaps we could take a waterfront lot for our new home."

Charles ignored her suggestion as he drank his cocktail.

It was late when they finished dinner. The spring air felt refreshing and cool after the smoky dining room. The drive back to Baywater was

quiet and relaxing. When Peter stepped out of the station wagon, Janet moved into the front seat. They said their good-byes and waited while Lenore went up the stairs with Peter. As Charles drove away Janet yawned. "We accomplished a lot," she said. Then she leaned her head on Charles' shoulder, thinking, planning and wondering what the future would hold for Baywater and themselves.

It was a little after nine the next morning when Janet drove to the estate. Lenore was standing by the empty pool and waved as Janet pulled up. "Hi, lovely morning, isn't it? How did you sleep, Lennie?"

"Fine. As though it were years ago! I've been up an hour and have gone through the house and decided the changes I want. Emma mentioned that her nephew in the building business might be able to help with renovations. Do you remember him? He used to do odd jobs around here."

"I vaguely remember someone, but can't think of his name."

Emma was waving from the porch. Lenore acknowledged the gesture.

"Breakfast is ready. Let's go in. Maybe she can call her nephew to come over today and go over my ideas for the house. I want to break through the wall and have a door put in between my bedroom and Taurus' suite; Robbie's and Peter's rooms need a few improvements, and there are a few other things."

They went inside and while they ate, Emma phoned her nephew, Dan O'Quinn, and he agreed to come at once. Lenore explained what she wanted, and while he was estimating the cost, he overheard the cousins talking about their plans for Baywater. Dan hinted that he would be most interested in doing the building, but Janet suggested that he complete the changes in the mansion first so they might have some idea of the quality of his workmanship. Then they might discuss the future of Baywater with him.

Later, the two women strolled about the estate, chatting and planning. Peter found them near the pool and asked Janet if she would follow him in her car while he returned his auto rental, then drive him back to the house. She was obliging, and when they came back from Sayr's Point, Lenore informed them she had called Robbie in California and was flying back the next day.

The following morning Janet drove Lenore to the airport and then went home to begin the ambitious project of building Baywater into a profitable enterprise. She was elated about the prospect and confident about the outcome.

Part II

Baywater Estates

1966–1969

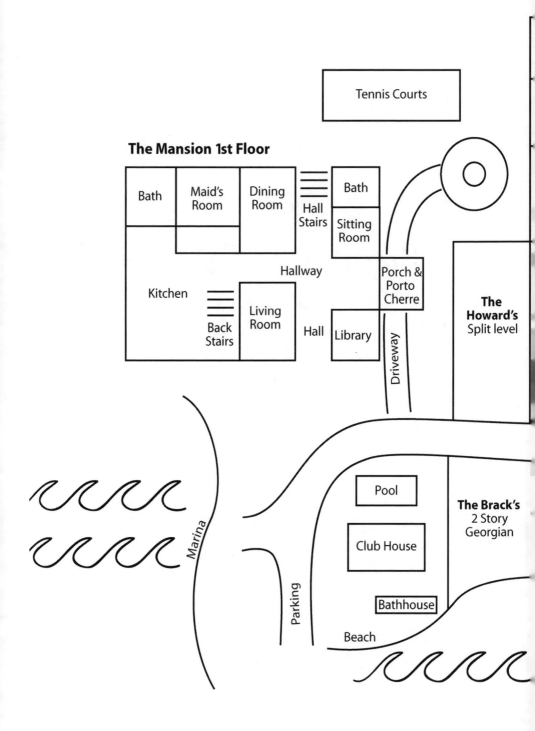

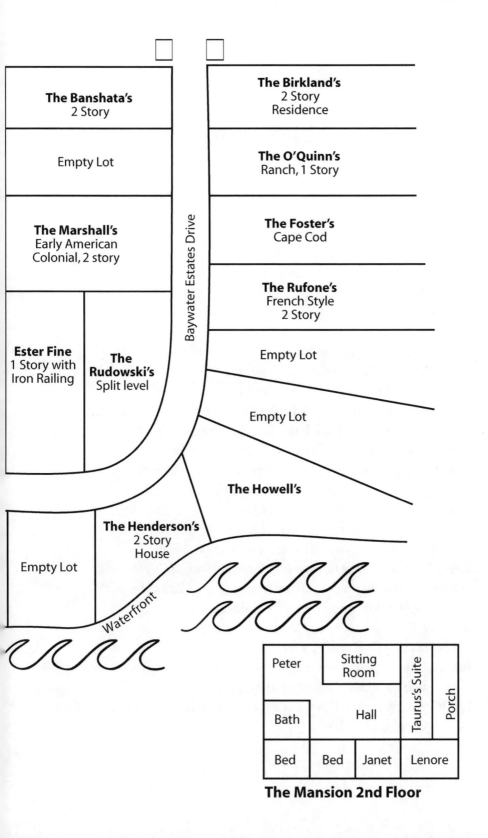

The Banshata's
2 Story

Empty Lot

The Marshall's
Early American
Colonial, 2 story

Ester Fine
1 Story with
Iron Railing

The Rudowski's
Split level

Baywater Estates Drive

The Birkland's
2 Story
Residence

The O'Quinn's
Ranch, 1 Story

The Foster's
Cape Cod

The Rufone's
French Style
2 Story

Empty Lot

Empty Lot

The Howell's

The Henderson's
2 Story
House

Empty Lot

Waterfront

Peter	Sitting Room	Taurus's Suite	Porch
Bath	Hall		
Bed	Bed	Janet	Lenore

The Mansion 2nd Floor

CHARACTERS

Taurus Worthington – bachelor; great-uncle of Lenore and Janet; owner of Baywater Estate

Mr. Treadwell – Taurus's lawyer

Emma Brown – housekeeper for Taurus, helped raise the two great-nieces

Janet Blake Henderson – great-niece of Taurus and an inheritor of Baywater Estate

Lenore Akton Morgan – great-niece of Taurus and an inheritor of Baywater Estate

Robbie – her son, a hemophiliac

Peter Morgan – Lenore's second husband

Charles Henderson – Janet's husband and attorney

Dan O'Quinn – builder of houses at Baywater, married to Dottie
    Children: Michael, Patrick and Katherine

Dr. William Blossom – friend of Charles

Phil Robbins – Charles's law partner, married to Stephanie

Willis Gant – Charles's law partner, married to Mary Lou

Toby Marshall – Baywater resident; a pilot married to Meg
    Children: Donald, Lawrence, Andrew and Kenneth

Reverend and Mrs. Richard – residents of Sayr's Point

Kerry Richard – their thirty-two-year-old son from Virginia

Stanley Rudowski – a contractor who moves to Baywater with his wife, Gloria, and their five children

Tony Di Pasco – lawyer and Democratic County Attorney

Pat Seymour – Di Pasco's secretary

Joe Banshata – businessman, resident of Baywater with his wife, Jenny, and daughters Beatrice and Mary

Dr. Vincent Rufone – Baywater resident with his wife, Ann, and their daughter Lucille

Ray Dowling – elderly school principal, married to Ethel
      Son: Austin
Sally Kendrick – art teacher
Professor Mark Harrison – Math Department at the University
Priscilla Flemming – a date of Mark's
Thompson Brack – handsome Baywater resident, in the boat business,
      married to Kim, a very beautiful and talented woman; they
      have one son, Jerome.
Harry Williams – a pianist and music director
Warren Birkland – Baywater resident, owns a stationery store; wife,
      Marion; children, Henry and Adele
Gordon Foster – insurance agent; wife, Ruth
Stephen Howell – wealthy retired businessman, resident of Baywater,
      married to Linda, an alcoholic
      Children: Sue, Marianne and Terry
Russell Howard – former professional baseball player, married to
      Claudia. Children: Edwina and Andrew
Rudy Mayer – Chief of Police
Carol Mayer – Chief's daughter
Ester Fine – single woman resident of Baywater
Sam Bernstein – her attorney
Bob Sutton – well-known songwriter residing temporarily in Palm Beach
Lou Sbarglio – syndicate boss
Al – his driver
Marco – his bodyguard
Christopher Lane – well-known writer; former partner of Lenore
Harry Boyd – Republican County Chairman
New residents – the Smiths, Cloughs and DeNicols

CHAPTER 1
SPRING 1966

"Get that tractor away from that God damned tree!" Dan O'Quinn yelled. "It's not marked to be knocked down!" He shook his fist furiously at the laborer running the machine and thought, damn him, if it were his job he'd be more careful. "That's the trouble with help today. You've got to watch them every minute or you'd lose your shirt," he muttered to himself. His curly black hair fell on his forehead. He brushed it back and wiped the seat off with the back of his arm.

A white Chevy convertible stopped, and a beautiful, slim, dark-haired young woman jumped out. "For heaven's sake Dan, what's the rumble? I could hear you all the way down the street to the house. What's wrong?"

"Nothing much, hon, but that stupid jerk on the tractor wants to take down some of the trees I intended leaving on the lot."

Dottie's blue eyes surveyed the situation. "It will be as lovely as the others when it's finished, so don't get your Irish up. She tugged and smoothed her white slacks.

"Hey, what are you up to?"

"When are you breaking for lunch?" She hesitated, "I thought I'd get some golfing in. Your lunch is ready, it's in the refrigerator, so would you mind?"

Dan patted her shoulder. "No, go ahead. I don't know when I'll break away. The lot has to be cleared today so we can start the foundation tomorrow."

"Jan and Charles are having a party at the club tonight. Buffet and

drinks, so save some energy to dance with me." She hopped back in her Impala and drove off before he could answer.

Dan grinned and shook his head. He remembered how tough things were three years ago. It was a stroke of luck that morning when Emma had called. After he'd finished the changes on Lenore's house, he had convinced them that he was the man to help build Baywater into an upper middle class development with tennis courts, club and marina. He was aggressive but not pushy, and conscientious about his work. Jan and Lenore had treated him well and Dottie was thrilled when they had been able to buy one of his own houses. It was a long way up from River Street, near the docks. He thought about Dottie in those form-fitting white slacks.

Dottie parked, took out her clubs and handcart, and went to the clubhouse. Usually she had to wait in line to get started, but today she teed off immediately. It was a good shot, and she was in good form.

Before her marriage, she had worked in the mountains at a fashionable resort where they had golf, tennis, swimming and horseback riding. And in order to help keep her job, she became fairly adept at these sports. On one of her visits home she'd met Dan, fallen in love with him, and was married shortly after. She often wondered if she had waited awhile longer, whether some handsome bachelor with a fine social background and wealth might have come to the resort, met her and wanted to marry her.

Her sixth hole was played par. As she was heading for the seventh tee, she noticed two men. "Hi there," she called. "Charles, is that you?"

Charles W. Henderson had completed his tee off. He turned his agile body to find the lovely, slim, dark-haired girl headed in his direction. He waved at the exact moment that his guest, Dr. Blossom, asked, "Who is that divine creature?"

Charles blushed. "She's one of our neighbors."

Dr. Blossom, who lived up to his reputation of being a connoisseur of women, was eager to meet her. Dottie noticed that Charles's distinguished-looking companion was dark with grey at the temples, in contrast to Charles's fair complexion and blond hair. After the

introductions, Charles invited her to play along with them.

"That's a splendid idea. We can have a drink later," Dr. Blossom suggested, obviously interested. She wondered if there was a Mrs. Blossom, and suspected if there was, she hardly ever saw this smooth and handsome Lothario. The Doctor hit his drive; Dottie bent down to put her tee in the ground, drawing attention to her fine figure. Charles noticed the outline of her panties and bra under the white slacks and sweater. While most women were complaining about their body and weight, this girl had a small waist, well-curved hips and firm breasts. She must be active to have this kind of figure, he thought, and Charles became aroused. Dr. Blossom had been scrutinizing her, and it bothered Charles that this dirty-minded man would be having more detailed ideas.

"That was a good shot, Dottie. You play very well," Charles complimented, adding to himself, "for a woman," and they continued their game.

As each went their own way to play, Dottie was conscious of these two distinguished men watching her. Dr. Blossom was one of the best plastic surgeons in the county, and Charles Henderson was earning himself a reputation as one of the most reliable and smartest attorneys in the county. She was flattered being able to play with them, and more flattered with the attention they lavished on her.

Charles finished his ninth hole with a score of fifty-one, and wasn't pleased. Dr. Blossom was irritated that he had lost a few good balls over the fence. As they headed to the clubhouse for a drink, a voice from a loudspeaker announced, "Dr. Blossom, please come to the phone."

Bill Blossom said, "I may have to go immediately, so if I don't come back, I'll call you tomorrow to discuss the Pierson case. Thanks for the game." Then he directed his attention to Dottie, "I hope we'll meet again soon, my dear, it's been a pleasure. Lucky dog Charles is to have you all to himself for that drink!" He waved as he walked away and called back, "Be seeing you both."

Charles was miffed at the implication and to cover his embarrassment said, "I'm thirsty, how about you?"

She shook her head, "Thanks anyway, but I'll have to take a rain

check. The kids are home by now and if I don't get there soon, the place will be a shambles."

"I'm sorry you can't join me, but I understand. You are coming to the party tonight, aren't you?"

"Yes, see you then," and she left him standing alone.

He watched her walk away and thought how fortunate Dan was to have her as his wife. She was concerned about her family, didn't drink much and was athletically inclined. He wished Janet would be involved in sports so he would have a partner and companion. If she wasn't preparing a recital, she was busy buying and selling property, and the last couple of years she had used much of her energy in making Baywater a success. He could understand her need for challenges but it bothered him that she was so successful; it dimmed his light. Yet he had to admit that her success and popularity had been an asset to his practice, and he knew that her easygoing nature made it possible for her to tolerate his tensions and their way of life. "Left the money on the bar, Sal," he called after the last swallow.

As he drove down the street, he glanced up at the lions ahead. The gates were permanently open. Off to one side hung a sign reading "Baywater Estates." The lions on the monuments had become a symbol of success to the residents. The houses had cost at least $45,000, and with inflation most of them were in the $50,000 to $75,000 bracket. What had once been a driveway was now a paved road, with three quarter-acre or more sized parcels and magnificent homes. He could see Joe Banshata picking up fallen branches from the lawn. He waved and called out something as Charles passed. Charles returned the wave but couldn't hear what he'd said, probably something about the party later. He looked across the street, a little farther down, and saw a light go on in the O'Quinn's house. He didn't see any sign of life, but as he passed the driveway he heard a bellow from the house. He shook his head and went around the curve to park in his own driveway. It seemed that Dan couldn't talk in anything less than a shout. To Charles, he was a loud and boisterous bore.

Back at the O'Quinn's, Dottie hurried into the kitchen to see what

the commotion was about. Dan had Patrick by the back of the neck and was slapping him.

"Dan, what on earth are you doing to the child?"

Patrick, holding a pair of grass shears in his hand, sobbed, "Kathy wanted her hair cut and I couldn't find the scissors."

"Ye gads, you didn't use those to cut her hair, did you? Where's Katherine?"

"In her room." The youngster tried to back away from his father.

Dottie ran to her daughter's room, flung open the door and saw Katherine with unevenly chopped hair, playing with a doll. She leaned against the door to catch her breath. She would have to take her to town to have the mess straightened out.

Katherine smiled up at her. "See what Patrick did? Now you won't have to take me to the hairdresser and spend money." Dottie sighed. Katherine must have heard Dan objecting about their going to the hairdresser to have her hair set and Kathy's cut. Dan had grumbled that it was an unnecessary expense. She went back to the kitchen. Dan and Patrick were sitting talking. Patrick's face was streaked with tears. Dan asked, "Is it bad?"

Dottie nodded. "Honestly, those kids. Her lovely curls are gone and it will need recutting. She heard you complaining about the expense of a haircut, so Patrick volunteered to do the job and save you money." Her voice was filled with anger.

Dan directed Patrick to go find Michael and call Katherine for dinner, and after the boy left the room, he went over to her to put his arms around her. But she pulled away. "Aw, Dottie, I'm sorry, but we have to save our money. The mortgage and taxes are high, and we have to cut someplace. The things you like cost, and living in Baywater ought to be worth some sacrifice. Or, would you rather be back on River Street?"

Dottie winced. That was always his argument whenever he wanted to make a point of her extravagances. River Street. He went into the living room and flipped on the TV., then yelled for a cold beer. She took him one and suggested, "Dan, it's early. We have a long night at the party, and I don't want to be embarrassed."

He took a gulp of the beer and waved the can at her, "I'll drink all I want. Seems to me you've gotten a little high and mighty since we moved here. And that reminds me, don't forget my dinner. If you think I'm waiting till 9 o'clock to fill up on those silly crackers, you're crazy." He belched and continued, "Make me a decent meal."

Dottie went back to the kitchen, cursing at him under her breath. What right did he have to treat her like that, and why did he have to be so damned crude? He was getting worse instead of better, but she was afraid of him so made a stew. A car door slammed and she looked at the kitchen clock. It was after six and she assumed it must be Vinny Rufone home from his medical office.

The children came in and Katherine set the table. Michael spoke up, "I hear Pat made a boo-boo."

Patrick twisted his feet and made a face at his older brother. "Are you mad at me, Mom? I only wanted to help."

A wave of tenderness swept over her. She pulled Pat to her and hugged him. No honey, I understand. It'll be alright." She gently rumpled his hair.

Then she turned to her other son, "How was your day at school, Michael? Anything special happen?"

Michael glowed. He loved school, was an avid reader, and had good marks. At twelve, he was beginning to resemble her brother Phil. "I found a great book in the library room . . . about Babe Ruth. I'm going to read it tonight."

Dottie was pleased. She wanted Michael to grow up to be a cultured man, a scholar, one who used his brains, not his hands like Dan. She would cringe whenever Dan spoke of developing a big building business so that eventually Michael could take it over. She wanted her son to become a lawyer or doctor—anything professional. She had high hopes for Michael. Patrick was slower in school and would never measure up to Michael, but she reasoned that he was only nine and possibly in time he would bloom.

Dinner was ready and Michael called his father. Dan came down the hall whistling. It was the smallest house in Baywater, but he appreciated

it and felt fortunate that Jan and Lenore had let him have it at a lower price than it would have brought. It was a long rancher with three bedrooms, two baths, a living room, dining room and family room. The first six lots on their side of Baywater Drive backed up to a fence, while the ones farther down past the curve were on the bay, and far more expensive. Theirs was the second lot past the gate on the left side. The lots on each side of them were still empty. Farther down was Dr. Rufone's house, past that more empty lots, then the Henderson's. At the very end of the drive on the same side, before the clubhouse, was the Brack's huge Georgian waterfront home.

Katherine came into the kitchen with her father and they all sat down at the table. Dottie preferred to eat dinner in the dining room, but Dan objected and said the dining room should be reserved for holidays and special occasions.

His manners were atrocious. He loaded his plate and demanded another beer, which Michael fetched for him. Studying Dan across the table she wondered why she had ever fallen in love with him. It was true that he had a boyish grin, was good-looking, and most women found him attractive. He possessed a rugged masculinity; but, unfortunately, he was abrupt and rude. However, most women rarely became offended because he was almost childishly irresistible and had sex appeal.

He broke into her thoughts, "I think the new people who are buying the corner house will be at the party. Maybe that's the reason Janet is giving this shindig." He had both elbows on the table, and when he spoke, waved his fork about.

"Dan, please don't do that . . . you might stab one of us."

The children laughed and watched him in adoration. He could be amusing and they were impressed not only with his humor, but with his ability in building Baywater estates. Dottie had wanted to divorce him, but she knew that the children would be heartbroken if she did.

She stood up to clear the table and said, "Take your shower while I clean up in here, and then I'll come in and get dressed."

"Okay baby, I won't be long." He patted her backside as he left the table, which upset her. She had asked him not to do that in front of the children. She finished clearing and put the dishes in the dishwasher. As she went into the bedroom she could hear the water from the shower, Dan

sloshing about. She took her robe from the closet and started to undress as he came out draped in a towel. He came up behind her, squeezed her breasts gently, and ran his tongue around her ear. She could feel his breath quicken.

"Dan, we'll be late for the party. He thrust her toward the bed, pulled off her bra and threw the towel aside. She turned around to face him thinking she could move away easier, but he leaned over her and she fell back. Looking up from the bed she could see his face red with anger.

"What's the matter doll, not interested?"

"We don't have time."

"How the hell long do you think it's going to take?" He dropped down on her, kissing her eyes and throat. "I'll get you in the mood." He felt the lack of response and raised his head. "What's the matter, the old man not good enough for you?"

"That's not true, and you know it. Don't use that expression."

"Yeah, well, I remember the times it didn't bother you what I said or did. Come on, I'm hot, give. I've been waiting all day for this, since I saw you in those tight white pants." His hand moved to her thighs and he started stroking her, tenderly first, then he began to get rough. He was perspiring, his tongue darting in and around her mouth, his knee pushing her legs apart.

"You're hurting me, Dan. Besides, later on we won't have to hurry, we'll have all night."

He rolled off her, "Well, how about that? It's been a long time since we went the night. Okay, but remember, it was your idea."

She hurried into the shower thinking that maybe later he'd be tired and she could put him off. At least he wasn't angry. "How long are you going to be?"

"Only a few minutes."

He was wearing a blue checkered, cotton sport shirt and cheap gray slacks. He wouldn't spend a little more for anything better. She put on a light blue knit dress that hugged her body; she was sexy and vibrant in a clean, athletic sort of way. The dress went well with her large blue eyes, and her dark hair in a feather cut created a soft effect around her face. She wanted a mink stole but Dan wouldn't buy her one, so she wore the white angora

stole she had made the previous winter. The hours spent weren't wasted; it was becoming.

Dan made her account for every nickel. She was afraid to buy things unless they were on sale. With spring here she needed money for golf balls. Dan had had a fit when she joined the golf club and they'd had a bad row. When she refused to resign from the club, he packed some clothes and left the house. Two days later he returned and told her he'd gone to New Jersey, tied one on and the next morning found himself in bed with a "Broad." That was just like him, direct and to the point. He finally relented and allowed her to go on with these sports, but she knew that it was his guilty conscience that prompted him to agree. What could she do about him, she wondered? Most husbands had flings, the only difference was that she knew. Most people didn't get divorced over a one-time drunken affair, and for the most part he was true and a good father. She reasoned that if she hadn't made such an issue about the golf club he probably wouldn't have gone off like that.

She smiled at herself in the mirror. "This is the stole I made last winter. What do you think?"

"You're beautiful. See what you can do when you try? I'd love to see you make a dress for yourself some day." He wanted her to learn to sew; enough compliments in that direction might influence her.

She beamed. "I'm ready. I'll check on the kids."

"Okay, I'll get the car started."

Dottie looked at herself once more in the mirror. She wanted to look special tonight. The stole was soft and the white angora set off her dark hair. She reflected proudly on Dr. Blossom's reaction to her. She wondered if Charles found her as appealing . . . he seemed kind and gentle. She opened the blinds for a moment and looked out. The spotlights were on at the Hendersons. She tightened the cord, shut off the light, checked on the children and left the number of the club with Michael. As they drove by the Hendersons, she thought about Janet and Charles's lives together. She wondered what the two of them did with that great big house. "Must be great to find peace and quiet in a big house like that," she muttered to herself.

Dan asked, "Did you say something?"

"No, I was thinking."

Dottie was a nice girl but not very bright. She should have realized that Charles might prefer coming home to children rather than a cousin by marriage who dropped by frequently.

When he'd pulled in the driveway after the golf game, Charles saw Lenore's car. "Those two are inseparable," he groaned. Janet had loved Lenore and depended on her emotionally after her parents' death, but he wanted to be the exclusive interest in Janet's life. He went through the back door and walked through the kitchen filled with trays and bowls with delicious contents. He heard voices in the living room and went in. Janet was glad to see him home early and gave him a kiss. Lenore looked at his clothes and chuckled. His face grew red and he explained, "I finished a case earlier than expected, so I decided to play golf for the remainder of the afternoon." He knew he should have called home and told Janet where he was going.

"How nice dear," Jan responded, not thinking about it any further. "Emma was here helping for the party. The kitchen has been a beehive of activity all afternoon!" Then she added, "Lennie stopped in on her way home from shopping."

He looked at Lenore. She smiled knowing that he resented anyone who took time or attention away from him.

"Guess I'll get along home and get ready. Nice seeing you Charles. See you both at seven." She kissed Janet on the cheek and left.

"I'm tired from all the preparations. I'm going up to take a short nap."

"Go ahead. I want to take a shower and have a drink before I dress. By the way, how many people do you expect?"

"About twenty. The Rudowski's will be there. They're moving in soon. He's a builder."

"How is Dan going to react to that competition?"

"Rudowski doesn't build houses, just big projects like hospitals or shopping centers. He liked the last house we built; in fact, he said that Dan had done a fine job.

"How much did the house cost?"

"Don't you remember the contract? With the extras it came to $75,000. He must do well as he took a very small mortgage. Mrs. Rudowski is sweet. Did you know that they have five children? Should liven things up around here. I expected the closing should be within the month. You must have it on your calendar."

They went upstairs and Janet undressed except for her bra and panties. She stretched out on the bed, feeling both tired and sexy simultaneously. Charles went into the bathroom, turned on the shower, then came out for his robe. He stopped for a moment and looked at her on the bed, relaxed and inviting. She was watching him through partially closed eyes. "Why don't you relax with me for a while?"

He was ruffled. "I need a shower. Get some rest, you're going to be on the run tonight," and returned to the bathroom.

She pulled a quilt over herself thinking they seemed busy with other things and never had time for sex. She was afraid to approach him about it, sensing he would be shocked and irritated.

After his shower Charles went back downstairs, mixed himself a drink and carried it to the side porch. Their house was on a curve, and from the front lawn and porch he could see most of the houses in Baywater, including the mansion which was set back from the road farther than the rest.

Rudowski was moving into the new split level across the street on the corner of the bend. Behind the split level toward the gates was the Marshalls' house. Joe Banshata had the first house on that side, closer to the gates. Those were large, choice lots other than the waterfront. So far, only he and the Bracks had built on the waterfront parcels. The O'Quinns and Dr. Rufone were on the same side of the street as his house, around the bend toward the gates. Those lots were smaller and backed up to a fence and undeveloped property. He couldn't understand why Dr. Rufone had wanted an inexpensive parcel. His accountant was a close friend of Vinny's and indicated that his income was substantial, yet Jan had mentioned that Ann had never completed decorating the house, that it was sparsely furnished. Charles concluded that Rufone preferred to invest his

money rather than spend it in his home.

All the houses along the drive were beautiful and well-landscaped. Rufone's house was French Provincial design and the second-floor roof came down to the first with the windows cutting into the roof. The O'Quinns had a long rancher and the Marshalls had an early American. The house seemed to suit Meg Marshall, a soft-spoken Southerner, slim and pretty with a tiny waist and model's face. She reminded Charles of Vivian Leigh, the actress. He noticed that Toby's car wasn't in the driveway and concluded he must have a flight. Toby had a regular run between New York and Seattle. Charles liked him. Toby had a high I.Q., was in the Mensa Society, and his mind clicked like a machine. He could make rapid, clear-thinking decisions, the way a lawyer ought to. It was unfortunate that Toby was at the far end of the United States tonight and they would miss the party. But, one thing in his favor, Charles mused, was the fact that Toby could sleep or read on his quiet evenings away from home without being disturbed.

An empty glass and a glance at his watch indicated he should get ready. He went upstairs and woke Jan. "I'll help you put the trays in the car after I'm dressed, dear." Janet was surprised but appreciative. She was even further astonished when she came downstairs and found that he had already loaded the car. He flipped on the spotlights and they drove away.

CHAPTER 2
THE EVENING OF THE PARTY

Dan and Dottie heard piano music as they entered the door by the bar. It was a large room with a bay window that overlooked the water. Dimly lit crystal chandeliers looked like candies, and light reflected in the mirrors onto the cream-colored walls. Near the long table set with trays of food, several guests were standing, plates in hand, gazing through the windows to get a glimpse of the waves. The party had begun but as yet, no one was dancing to the old, familiar tunes coming from the piano at the far end of the room. Janet broke away from a few guests and greeted them. "I'm glad to see you two. Help yourselves to drinks, then say hello to everyone."

Dan looked around and recognized some people. "Thanks, getting a drink first would be a good idea. What do you want, Dottie?"

"I don't care, Dan, whatever you choose." Dottie noticed Charles standing at the side of the room with his law partners, Phil Robbins and Willis Gant, and their wives. "I'll wait here."

Janet and Dan ambled toward the bar. Dottie wished Charles would stop talking long enough to see her before Dan returned. Charles was caught up in his own thoughts and continued his discussion. "Johnson made a smart decision when he took Weaver as a cabinet member."

"Sure was a brilliant political maneuver," Phil agreed.

Stephanie Roberts added, "Say, the pentagon released figures showing that in proportion to their numbers, more Negroes have died in Vietnam than military personnel of other races. It's time we had a Negro in high government office."

"True," Mary Lou Gant replied, "and I don't think it was strictly a political

39

move, but the decent thing to do."

There was a lull in the conversation and Charles turned around. He saw Dottie and flushed with excitement at her loveliness. "Will you excuse me? We have more guests. Help yourselves to another."

Dottie's eyes glistened as he came nearer. She felt her heart beat faster.

"So, you came. How about a drink, my dear?"

"Dan was on his way to get me one, but he and Janet are busy talking and I'm the forgotten lamb."

"If they're talking about the new houses, you don't stand a chance. What's your pleasure?" And he gave her a big smile that lit up his entire face.

"An orange blossom. What are you drinking?"

"Scotch is my usual." He took her arm, guided her toward the bar and ordered. "Let me take your stole so you'll be more comfortable." He gently removed it from her shoulders, taking note of her breasts and shoulders, and had an unexpected urge to run his fingers over them. He placed the stole on a chair, handed her a drink, picked up a refill, and motioned toward the piano. They walked slowly across the room. Dottie preened, savoring the attention he was giving her.

"That was a good golf game, for a woman. Strange I never noticed you out there before."

"I enjoy it," she purred. "Do you play often?"

"Not as much as I'd like. It's difficult to get away from the office and even more difficult to find a partner on the spur of the moment."

"I know. I usually end up playing alone," she hinted.

"Golf is like alcohol. If you like it, you can't ever get enough. Dottie, would you mind if I called you to play with me sometimes? Janet doesn't appreciate the game." He sipped his drink.

"I'd like that Charles, but won't you get impatient with me?" she purred in an effort to appeal to his ego.

Before he could reply, Janet walked up. "Did I hear my name mentioned, dear?"

"I was telling Dottie how you dislike golf. Since she plays I was attempting

to persuade her to join me."

Dottie held her breath for a moment, waiting for a hostile remark, but instead Janet said, "What a fine idea!" Meg Marshall had come up behind Janet and tapped her shoulder. She pivoted, "Why Meg, nice to see you. Where's Toby?"

"In Washington, so I'm footloose and fancy free tonight," she replied in an exaggerated, soft, teasing southern drawl. They laughed.

Dan overheard her. "In that case, how about a dance with me?" His eyes swept over her body clothed in a simple, tight-fitting black lace dress.

Dottie's face tightened as Meg and Dan headed toward the dance floor. Janet sensed the tension and suggested, "Why don't you two dance? I have to check on the food."

Charles took Dottie's arm, and without saying a word, moved to the dance floor. As they started the step he said, "You're light as a feather. Does your dancing equal your golf game?"

She relaxed in his arms. "Just wait till I step on your foot!" And they laughed.

The music was romantic and the dim lights enhanced the mood. Charles was exhilarated. Dottie's supple body close to his stirred his sexual response. He looked around to see if anyone was noticing and saw Reverend and Mrs. Richard come in. Meg and Dan danced by and he heard Meg giggle. Then Dan patted her bottom and she reacted indignantly, moving away from him off the dance floor. Secretly, Meg savored the attention. It made her feel young and in demand again. Toby didn't have much time for her and the boys, and her sons were a handful. She was rarely allowed to have anyone sit as Toby believed a woman's place was in her home, and tonight was one of those infrequent instances when he agreed. Dan looked to see if Dottie was still dancing with Charles, watched them for a moment, then followed Meg.

"Hello Reverend. Nice to see you Mrs. Richard. This is Dan O'Quinn, our neighbor," and Meg touched Dan's sleeve.

"How do you do, sir? My wife and I are Catholics and haven't attended your services, but I hear you preach some mighty strong sermons!"

The Minister chuckled. "As long as they don't scare away my congregation, I can stay in business." They laughed.

Meg asked, "How are you feeling, Mrs. Richard?"

"Better. Thank you, my dear. This is my first evening out since my operation, so we won't stay long. And besides, it isn't good for my husband's image to spend much time at cocktail parties." She winked and had a twinkle in her eye.

Meg chuckled, then sighed. "I don't suppose it is, but it's good to get out once in a while. With Toby gone so often and my being home with just the children, I feel penned in."

"Mrs. Marshall, we're in need of another teacher at Sunday school. Do you think you could help us out, since you're a member of our congregation?" Reverend Richard's eyes met his wife's and she nodded. He continued, "We're planning a play for the children and could use some help. You might like to bring your boys."

Meg lit up. It would be an ideal way to get out of the house and Toby would agree to a sitter if her time was for the church. "I'd love to try, although I've never been involved in anything like that before."

"Then it's settled," and Mrs. Richard smiled.

Dan wandered away slightly bored. Janet excused herself and went over to see how the Rudowski's were doing, chatting with Mrs. Tooker.

"Mrs. Tooker is telling us about her daughter. All the while she was showing us houses, we thought she had no family." Gloria was vivacious. "Did you know her daughter lives abroad most of the time?" She addressed her question to Janet.

"Yes, I've known Susan since we were little girls. She's a darling."

Mrs. Tooker, a dumpy, heavy-set woman, beamed and straightened up. Her greatest pride was her daughter, a mediocre painter, and second to that was the money she had so shrewdly accumulated over the years. She had dominated her husband to the point that he had no self-esteem left, and that, coupled with his daughter's extravagances, had driven him to suicide.

One morning, unable to cope any further, he hanged himself on the front porch. Mrs. Tooker had discovered the body, along with a letter he had

left near his body, but she had never revealed the contents in the envelope to anyone. Susan had begun her trips to Europe and rumors of her activities had drifted back to Sayr's Point. The high school Spanish teacher had looked her up one summer while in Madrid and found her living with a bullfighter. He told a few teachers, who told a few other people, and the story had leaked out. But Mrs. Tooker treated Susan like an innocent child, unaware of her flagrant affairs.

"I'd like to meet her on her next visit home," Gloria said, then added wistfully, "She must have an exciting life traveling all over the continent."

"Enough about Susan," Mrs. Tooker stated proudly, holding her bosoms high as she spoke. "When are you two going to move into the new house?"

"Although the closing is set for two weeks from now, I have to complete a project in Hollis. When that's done, in three or four weeks."

Stan Radowksi was a self-made man who came from a very poor family. He had met Gloria, a salesgirl in a Rochester department store, while on vacation. She was anxious to leave her job and move away from the windy city, so when Stan proposed, she accepted, elated at the prospect of starting a new life on Long Island. Stan was a mason but he was ambitious, and Gloria encouraged him. It wasn't long after their marriage that he went into his own building business, and in the Long Island boom, had done so well that these days he only took big jobs, large institutions that resulted in handsome profits. He had accumulated considerable wealth and when they needed a larger home to accommodate their growing family, he had approached Mrs. Tooker to find a suitable home for them. Stan realized that she was a "grass rooter" in the area with well-to-do connections, that she had invested wisely in real estate and made money in stocks. And in spite of her personal problems, she could lend a certain amount of prestige to her dealings. Mrs. Tooker possessed a good sense about what people required and shrewdly reasoned that Stan would want the Baywater image, Charles might obtain a new and wealthy account, and Stan's family would approve of all that Baywater offered. She showed him the large split level on the corner across from the

Henderson's. He liked the house and thought it was well designed and constructed, and wanted to buy it immediately.

As Charles approached them with Dottie and Dan, Stan directed his next words to Charles. "We'll be seeing you shortly for the closing, Mr. Henderson."

"That's fine; the name is Charles. Glad to have you in the area."

"Dan did a wonderful job on the house," Gloria said excitedly.

Dan ginned and grabbed her wrist. "Well then, you owe me a dance, beautiful." He pulled her to the dance floor. Stan glared at Dan as they left. He was insanely jealous of his wife and insisted on knowing her whereabouts every moment, going so far as to have a telephone installed in his car so that he could check up on her. Her life revolved around the house and five children, and she had little time or energy for herself. She worried about Stan constantly, knowing he carried large amounts of the cash payroll with him when he stopped for drinks. She worried that someone would see the money and kill him to get it. Then she'd be left with next to nothing as he'd told her his will left everything in trust for the children and she would only get a small pension. He was "afraid some gigolo" would marry her to get his money. Gloria felt humiliated by this, and trapped. Her survival depended entirely on Stan. Dancing with Dan, she watched her husband nervously and felt shaky inwardly.

Dottie engaged Stan and Mrs. Tooker in conversation. Charles had gone to the bar to join Tony Di Pasco, who had just come in and was talking to Janet, Joe Banshata and Vinny Rufone as they were walking toward the bar. He heard Tony tell Janet that he had been working late at the office and thought it would be easier to stop by en route home. Tony said he hoped they didn't mind him bringing his secretary, Pat Seymour, with him, but that she had worked till late and deserved a drink! Joe mumbled to himself, "Damned fool to bring his secretary with this crowd. A politician should bring his wife."

Ann Rufone was talking with Jenny Banshata. She wondered who the girl was but continued her conversation. "Lucille has finally adjusted to kindergarten."

"That's good. Time flies so fast. Beatrice will be graduating from high

school soon, and going to college in the fall. It will be lonely without her in the house. Enjoy your daughter while you have her with you."

Ann nodded. "You'll still have Mary though, so it won't be too bad."

Mary was Jenny's younger daughter. She had been born with a heart defect and Jenny made a vow that if the Lord let her live, she would name her after the Virgin Mary and dress her in blue for seven years. Jenny had kept her vow.

Ann, an attractive, petite girl in her thirties, had brown hair and a kindly disposition. She envied Jenny's contentment and dedication to her home and family. Her own life lacked complacency. Vinny was at the office or hospital most evenings, and if he came home early, the phone would call him away on emergency. He worked hard for his income. He gave her very little money, explaining that he hadn't much left after office expenses, taxes, and the cost of living, and since he had a bad temper, she didn't dare question him much. Since living in Baywater, she had become friendly with Jenny and felt that the friendship had done a lot toward keeping her peace of mind. Her attention drifted back to Jenny, who was still talking about her daughters. She changed the subject. "I saw you putting in some shrubs the other day, Jenny. What were they?"

"Azaleas. I replaced the ones the frost killed."

"It was an awful winter, but at least we didn't get the thirty-foot drifts they had upstate." She was watching Pat over Ann's shoulders. "Janet is coming over with Tony Di Pasco and our husbands."

Janet introduced Pat to Ann and Jenny, then the talk turned to politics. Joe looked at Tony. "There's a rumor around that there may be an opening for a Democratic judgeship in November. Any truth in that?"

Tony chuckled. "Well, we haven't made any deals yet, Joe, but you're on so many boards and committees in town, you ought to know. How come you can't tell me?"

They all laughed and Tony turned to Charles. "Say, when are you going to take a political job? We need men like you."

"No thanks, Tony." Charles took a sip of his drink. "I like my practice. It's interesting, and the income is good. Besides, Jan needs me around to advise her and she hates it when I'm out late. I'll leave the politics to you professionals."

The Gants and Robbins had joined them and Willis Gant chimed in, "Your party should gain by the U.S. Supreme Court ruling last month where they upheld the 1964 Voting Rights Act."

"What's that?" asked Janet.

He continued, "It affirms the power of Congress to suspend literacy tests and authorizes registration through Federal examiners." Willis was born Republican like so many people in the surrounding towns of Baywater. He didn't respect Tony and took this route of reminding him that this area was predominantly Republican, mostly old-timers, and Tony, more than likely, wouldn't get a judgeship.

Tony bristled. "There is a majority vote of middle and lower income class in this county. It was proved by the Kennedy and Johnson wins. One day soon the Democrats will rule out here. With all the developing going on, they're moving from the city to the country. I don't think it will take long."

Charles was afraid the conversation was getting out of hand, so he suggested to everyone they join the dancers on the floor. Reverend Richard and his wife came over to say good-bye. As they left, Ray Dowling, the school principal, and his wife, Ethel, followed by Professor Harrison and a date, came in. Meg joined Jan and Charles while they exchanged greetings with the newcomers. Ray Dowling was about fifty-five and his wife looked close to that. Ethel was timid, but very sweet and agreeable. Ray was outgoing, popular in the community, and a well-respected educator, but he seemed restless. He smiled genially at Harrison. "Where do you find such lovely dates, Mark?"

Mark took the girl by the arm. "This is Priscilla Flemming. Our hosts Charles and Janet, Mrs. Dowling, and the appreciative gentleman is Ray Dowling." He looked at Meg inquiringly, and Janet introduced her.

Meg smiled at Mark. "So, you're the professor from the math department at the university. We've heard a lot about you." Her flirtatious eyes and teasing

manner indicated that she found him handsome and attractive, as most women claimed him to be. He was tall, had light brown hair and warm brown eyes that radiated a sincere interest in people.

"I didn't know I was a celebrity." He had a winning smile.

Priscilla teased, "I feel very superior being with a celebrity this evening."

"Where's Lenore?" asked Ray.

"Near the bar, with Peter," replied Charles. "Let's go over and have a drink."

At the bar, Janet introduced Mark and Priscilla to her cousin and her husband. As the drinks were passed around, Janet glanced at the dance floor. The party was in full gear. Tony Di Pasco was dancing with his secretary, and Dan was still dancing with Gloria. Jenny and Joe were dancing, as well as the Gants and Robbins. Meg was chatting with the Rufones and Stan Rudowski. Their guests seemed to be having a good time. Mrs. Tooker and Dottie joined them at the bar and Janet guided Charles's eyes to Dan on the floor. He picked up her signal and asked Dottie to dance again. Mrs. Tooker began to boast about Susan while Lenore stifled a yawn. For a moment Janet worried that Lenore might make a pungent remark about Susan to quiet Mrs. Tooker, but she relaxed as Lenore turned her attention to Ray Dowling.

"How has Robbie's work been progressing?"

"Very well. He'll be through this year, don't worry."

Peter placed his hand on Janet's arm. "We can't stay long."

Lenore continued, "Emma doesn't like to stay up late and I don't like to leave Robbie alone once she's in bed."

Mark asked, "How old is your son?"

"Nineteen."

Ray Dowling caught Priscilla's startled look and Mark's puzzled expression. "Mark, Robbie is the young man I mentioned to you the other day. He's a hemophiliac and doesn't attend school."

Mark asked, "Isn't he the young chap who plays chess so well?"

Janet chirped, "He certainly does. If you like to play you've more than met your match."

"Would your son accept a friendly challenge?"

"I'm sure he would. Feel free to call whenever you like."

Stan had walked back to the bar, and now he stood, drink in hand, glowering at his wife on the dance floor. Janet deftly distracted him for a moment. Unfortunately, Dan and Gloria chose that time to join them. Dan clapped Stan on the back and said, "Nice wife you have, a good looker too. Anytime you want to trade wives for a weekend, let me know." He was jesting.

Gloria blushed, but Stanley was livid with rage. "You keep your wife and I'll keep mine. No, I wouldn't be interested."

Mrs. Tooker broke the tension. "Dan, you're so boyish and say such cute things, but some day someone will take you seriously. We all know that you love Dottie and wouldn't share her with anyone else, and I'm sure Stanly knows you're joking." Everyone breathed easier and Janet smiled at Peter.

"Peter, we don't mind if you leave. Just slip out. I'll see you and Lenore tomorrow." She went off to look for Charles. The party was getting noisy and the room was filled with smoke. "I'll have to open a window," she mumbled.

The piano stopped abruptly and everyone turned. The pianist was staring at the bar door. Their eyes followed his and suddenly there was a hush in the room. The Thompson Bracks were standing in the doorway, a picture straight out of a magazine. Thompson was tan already, his lithe body and good looks set off by a Brooks Brothers blue suit. Kim, motionless beside him, was wearing a strapless white chiffon, draped to accentuate her figure. A long scarf, clipped to her throat with a diamond pin, flowed across her shoulders and fell softly behind her. The pianist whispered, "Wow! This has got to be one of the most beautiful women I've ever seen."

Janet greeted them and turned to face the room. "These are our neighbors Kim and Thompson Brack." There was a murmur of greeting and the party resumed its noisy pace, but the pianist kept his eyes glued on Kim as she moved across the room, her long, pale-blond hair bouncing gently against her shoulders.

"I'm sorry we're so late, Jan, but Thompson got delayed showing a boat

and just came home."

"I understand. Business comes first. My, you both look magnificent. I should have introduced you as the beautiful people who have everything. How's about a drink?" She guided them toward the bar. While they were waiting for the bartender to prepare the drinks, they noticed Dan O'Quinn listing from side to side, heading their way.

"Beware of Baywater's wolf, Kim," she said softly.

Dan came up and nudged Thompson. "You're a lucky dog, Brack." He stared at Kim. Thompson stared at his wife, eyebrows raised, and perceived that Kim wanted to get away from Dan. The pianist started to play a cha-cha and Thompson asked Kim to dance. They excused themselves and went to the dance floor.

Ann Rufone smiled at her husband, "Wow! They dance like professionals, don't you think?"

Vinny agreed, entranced by Kim's beauty. He thought he would like to give her a physical examination sometime. The ladies he treated were usually homely and fat. He wondered about her body; it was very inviting. When the dance was finished, they joined the Rufones and Banshatas, and Thompson explained why they were late. "Yes, they gave me a deposit on a twenty-eight-foot flying bridge. The season has begun."

Vinny said, "It must be great to get away from it all whenever you want."

"Dr. Rufone, with your busy practice you could afford a yacht! You ought to consider one, think of all the pleasure you and your family would get."

Vinny hesitated, watching Thompson, whom he liked, then replied, "Perhaps, later on. Ann wants to finish the decorating first." He turned to Kim. "Do you like boating, Mrs. Brack?"

"To a degree, but there are other pleasures I pursue. Music, for instance."

"Do you like dancing?" he asked teasingly.

"I most certainly do."

"In that case, may I have this dance?"

They watched as Vinny led her to the dance floor. Then, Jenny and Ann went to the ladies room, while Janet took Thompson's arm and guided him toward Mrs. Tooker, Dan and Lenore. The Rudowski's sauntered and she introduced them to Thompson. "They're going to be our new neighbors, Thom, we expect them to move in soon."

"It's a pleasure to meet you both." He directed his attention to Gloria, who blushed. "I think you'll both like Baywater."

"We expect to. Dan has built us such a lovely home." She was flustered. The charm and poise of this handsome man attracted her. She was unaware that Stan noticed her blush. Stan realized that Gloria's black hair and pale skin were good, but her nose was too long for her face, and by comparison to Kim, she would be considered homely. He was completely caught off-guard when Thompson asked her to dance. Kim was such a beauty that he wondered how Thompson could look at another woman. He concluded that Brack was being polite and neighborly, so he told them to go ahead and enjoy the music.

Kim and Vincent Rufone had wandered over to the piano to join Professor Harrison and Priscilla, then the Dowlings walked over too, and they all stood forming a circle around the piano. The pianist looked up at them. "Why don't you join in? Everybody knows these numbers." One by one they began to sing, other members of the party came over and joined in. Kim Brack stood there watching until the pianist went into a blues song. Her rich, lush voice floated through the room, capturing everyone's attention. They stopped to listen, and when she finished, they clapped and begged her to sing some more. She agreed and continued with a show tune. She finally tired and sat down beside the pianist, humming as he went on playing. Ann Rufone joined Vinny and they danced. He looked over at Kim. She gave him a wide smile. He thought to himself that he'd like to spend just one night in bed with her, but he knew she'd be shocked if he even dared make a pass. "God, she has a beautiful body," he said to himself.

"What's your name?" Kim asked the pianist.

"Harry Williams."

"Hello Harry. I'm Kim."

"You have an exciting voice Kim. And you dance beautifully. Have you ever done any theatre work?"

"No, but I studied dance and voice for some time."

"Did you know we have a summer workshop out here? We were planning to do *Gentlemen Prefer Blonds* but the lead is moving. Her husband was transferred and we haven't been able to find anyone to replace her."

"What do you do with the group?"

"I'm musical coach, direct the chorus, teach people their music and so on. Look, why don't you try for the part? You'd be great. We have lots of talented kids who come from the city to work with us in the summer. They want a chance to be seen, perhaps be discovered. I think you'd like them."

Kim thought for a moment. "I'll discuss it with my husband and get in touch with you. Where can I reach you?"

He took a card out of his pocket. "I have my own music studio, call me there." Then he added, "Anyone as lovely as yourself, with so much talent, should be on stage where everyone can see and hear you."

"Thanks Harry, I'll be in touch." She walked away and joined her husband at the bar. She spoke to him for a few moments, obviously about the show. Thompson glanced briefly toward the piano, a smile flashed across his face, then he turned away with a slight shrug and handed Kim a glass.

Mrs. Tooker said her good-byes and left, and Janet started toward the piano to see if Harry wanted to take a break and eat. Before she reached him, Harry Williams broke into a wild rock number. Dan O'Quinn let out a whoop and latched onto Gloria Rudowski. She tried to pull away, but Dan wouldn't let her go. "Come on baby, let's dance." His voice was thick and blurry. He started to dance with her; as the music got faster he lost control of himself and began to grind his body into hers, holding her tightly. Stan Rudowski ran over and grabbed his shoulder, in an effort to stop him. "Come on Dan, I think you've had a little too much. Besides, this is my dance." He was angry but diplomatic.

Dan wrenched himself away from Stan's grasp. "Knock it off Rudowski.

Don't want anyone else to dance with your wife? Can't keep her all to yourself, man." He had loosened his grip on Gloria, but still holding her hand, began to make obscene movements toward her. "Come on baby, swing it, you've got it."

Gloria was frightened. Stan was livid with rage. He yelled, "Leave my wife alone!" Everyone turned and Harry stopped playing. Stan pulled Gloria away from Dan and stood in front of her.

"Listen, you bastard!" Dan shook his fist at Stan. "Get out of my way or I'll deck you."

"You drunken bum, why the hell don't you dance with your own wife, or can't she stand you either?"

Dottie and Charles started across as Dan roared, "You son of a bitch, I'll kill you!" He went toward Stan, swinging wildly; Stan stepped aside, Dan's fist whistled by his head, then Dan lost his balance and fell flat on his face.

Dottie was embarrassed beyond words. She accepted the napkin with ice cubes someone handed her, and trying to revive Dan, said in a low voice, "Dan had too much to drink. I'm sure he won't remember anything in the morning. Please accept our apologies and excuse him."

Charles was beside her, trying to get Dan on his feet. Vinny Rufone came over and helped them. They half carried and half dragged Dan outside to the car. Charles remembered Dottie's stole and went back inside to get it. Janet caught his eye and shook her head. She had never seen Dan behave like that and the whole episode shocked her. Charles brought the stole out to the car, and when he came back took Janet by the arm. "Come on honey, relax. Let's dance."

The party ambled along, calmly. Mark and Meg danced by them and Meg leaned toward her and said, "Janet, Mark Harrison plays tennis. How about proposing him for club membership so I can have a partner?"

Janet replied, "Fine, I'll send you an application Mark. We'll vote on it right away, if you want."

"Yes, I'd like that." He pulled Meg closer to him and danced off.

Janet felt sorry for Priscilla, who was sitting bored beside the pianist. One by one, the remaining guests took their leave, complimenting Janet

on the party, avoiding any discussion about Dan. It was ten o'clock when the last guest had gone. Charles paid the pianist and Janet had the bartender close up. She and Charles disposed of the leftover food and locked up the clubhouse. On the way home she sighed. "So many things happened tonight and I realize how little I know my friends and neighbors, Charles."

Charles didn't answer. He was thinking of Dottie and the humiliation she must have suffered.

After Charles had brought her stole to the car and gone back to the party, Dottie sat by the wheel, her eyes blurred with tears. She fumbled for a handkerchief in her bag. Dan struggled to sit up, mumbling incoherently. He tried to focus his eyes on her but the effort was too exhausting, and he slumped back on the seat staring out the window. "What's the matter? What are we doing here? What happened?"

"Dan, how could you make such a fool out of yourself and embarrass me like that?"

"What the hell are you talking about?" he rubbed his eyes.

"You made a scene with Stan and almost got into a fight."

"I don't believe you. Dan fights if he wants, and he beats the shit out of the other guy!" he yelled.

Dottie shrank at his language. "You were vulgar with Gloria and you insulted Stan. In fact, you drank so much, you were disgusting all night!" She began to cry and narrowly missed bumping into several cars as she backed the car out.

Dan roared, "So, I'm vulgar and disgusting, am I?" he continued to bellow as they drove down the drive headed for home. Dottie was having trouble holding the car straight. Her shoulders shook and tears coursed down her face.

"I only had a few drinks. What did I do wrong? Danced with some of the girls, gave them a few compliments, that's all."

"A few compliments? You wanted to swap me for a night with Gloria and you were absolutely crude about Kim Brack."

He reached out and squeezed her thigh. "You know something? I think you're jealous."

"Jealous?" Dottie was stunned.

"Yeah, you're just sore 'cause I didn't dance with you. Maybe your nose is out of joint because you're not as gorgeous as Kim. You've got nothing to be jealous about. At a party a guy has to pay attention to other women. Don't worry, baby, I love you." He squeezed her thigh again.

Dottie pulled in the driveway and shut off the ignition. "I'm not worried, and I'm not jealous!" She was furious at his remarks.

"Heck, you don't have to be. Come on over here and I'll prove it to you." Dan grabbed her by the back of the neck and pulled her to him. She slid across the seat, not expecting his attack, and was pinned easily against the back rest. His mouth crushed her lips, and he slipped his hand under her dress, pushing his thumb up hard. A trickle of saliva ran down her chin from his mouth and Dottie fought to get away. He lifted his head and growled, "Now what's wrong? Thought you felt horny. You're the one who wanted to go the night . . . remember?"

"You're hurting me!"

"That's what you always say; are you made of glass or something? Come on." He was pulling at her clothes.

"Dan, for heaven's sake, not in the car."

"What's the matter with the car? It's not the first time." He flung her stole into the back seat, and with one hand pulled her dress zipper down. She struggled, but he laughed and pulled at her bra, then leaned over and sucked a nipple sharply. Dottie held her breath from the pain and grabbed his hair. He let go and she wriggled loose, reaching for the door handle. Dan grabbed her stomach and twisted his fingers into her abdomen. With the other hand he reached for her legs and began to draw her toward him.

Dottie started crying. Suppose someone drove by or the children heard them. "Stop it, have you gone crazy?"

"Gone crazy? I'm hot for you, you bitch."

He pushed his door open and started to slide Dottie under him. She muffled a scream and slapped him. Dan stopped immediately, stunned, and she squirmed away at the chance. She jumped out of the car before he collected himself, pulling her dress around her. "I'm sorry Dan, but not like this."

"Oh, go to hell, you're not so great anyway. But, you're going to get it for hitting me." He was holding his hand on his face where she had slapped him.

She ran into the house and tiptoed into the bedroom; then hurried into the bathroom to wash and undress before she went to check on the children. She prayed Dan wouldn't start fighting when he came in.

Meanwhile, Dan sat in the car cursing. Then he zipped his trousers and threw himself across the seat. In a few second he was sound asleep snoring noisily.

The same night. . .

Young Terry Howell unbuttoned his jacket and raised the bottle. "Hey now, you are really beautiful and you and I are going to have a fine time for ourselves." He chortled with delight, for if there was anything Terry enjoyed, it was drinking any time, any where, and he was totally indifferent to what he drank as long as it was liquor.

Tonight he had been lucky, having located a bottle of scotch. First he tried the club at Baywater, but they had a bartender on duty. Since his parents were planning to move there, he couldn't afford the risk of asking the bartender to sell him one or to get caught stealing one. He had headed to town and waited near the liquor store for an opportunity. Then someone walked out, put his purchase in a car and walked farther down the street to the delicatessen. Terry nonchalantly strolled over to the car and took the bottle from the bag on the seat. Too bad that Jimmy couldn't get out tonight, but he appreciated his tossing his motorcycle keys to Terry. "Better than walking," he muttered. He wondered if Jimmy was trying the drug scene and was making an excuse. "Well, who cares?" he said to himself.

On his way to his favorite spot in the woods he whistled merrily and drove carefully to safeguard the precious possession under his coat. Now, sitting on a tree stump, he smacked his lips and let out a wild scream. The first taste went down smoothly and he savored the warmth of the taste joyously. A few more swallows set him off and he jumped up and hit a

nearby tree with his fist. "Hey, you stupid, oversized toothpick, you don't know what you're missing. All you do is stand there and wave at the sky. How about a drink, dummy?" As he poured a little scotch on the tree, his attention was caught by a flash of light. There was a car moving down the road to a little cottage near the lake. Being curious, he made his way down to the cottage and hid behind some small pines. The car stopped in front of the house, doors slammed, and he heard the mumble of voices. He couldn't see the two people clearly, but it was obvious they were going into the cottage. The moon glistened on the lake, the silence broken by the gentle rustle of the wind through the branches. They were so engrossed in each other that they didn't notice Terry's shadow in the background.

"Did you have any trouble renting?" the man asked. "This is just right."

"No, I told them it was for my mother from the city."

"You couldn't have done better. It's quiet and far from the other houses. We won't be recognized. Where's the key?"

She handed him the key and they walked to the door. "How heavy are you?" he asked teasingly.

"Why don't you find out yourself," she purred.

He unlocked the door and picked her up easily. "Let me carry you over the threshold. This will be our part-time home over summer, might as well do it right."

She kissed him on the cheek as he put her down. Then he closed the front door. He followed her into the kitchen and said, "I must admit this is a good set up. I doubt any of the other cottages are occupied so early in the season, but you haven't shown me the most important room, the only one I'm interested in tonight." He turned her around and pushed her toward the closed door. The window shade was up and the moon streamed into the room.

Terry couldn't see clearly, but it was obvious they were inside the cottage, so he skillfully made his way closer. The car was familiar and Terry wondered what was going on. He moved around the cottage until he found a window. The couple was standing in a bedroom. Terry couldn't hear them, but he watched intently. They were busy and didn't notice him peeking

through the window.

The man kissed her gently. Her response was passionate, stirring him to further impatience. A light from the living room outlined them. The man kissed her eyelids and ran the tip of his tongue down her cheek toward the edge of her mouth. She sighed and leaned on him. He knew the longer he waited, the more eager she would be, and he wanted her to be wildly eager and excited. He took his time, caressing her with his fingers, stroking her face and neck, and brushing her hair away from the curve of her cheek. He pulled her dress zipper down and slid the dress from her shoulders. It fell to the floor. He picked her up effortlessly and lowered her to the bed. She twisted her body invitingly, arching her back slightly. He slipped his hand behind her, unhooked her bra, swiftly pulled it away, and stripped her panties off. Looking at her in the moonlight, he thought how cleverly he had planned this. His wife thought he was at the Henderson's and her husband was away at sea. He knew she was in love with him and he found her attractive enough. Their arrangement made it easier to have an affair without his wife finding out. She smiled up at him. A quiver went through her as she watched him undress. Then he lay down on the bed, kissing and fondling her. Although the moon was brilliant, they didn't see the young face pressed close to the pane. Terry watched Tony and his secretary, their bodies naked on the bed.

Terry wasn't impressed with Tony's choice. Pat wasn't a pretty girl and, coupled with being demure, most men overlooked her. Alfred, her husband, was in the merchant marines and away for such a long period of time that she got lonely. He didn't make much money and wasn't anybody important. Working with Tony had been good from the beginning. She was occupied and it gave her extra money. She worked diligently, and when he began to take a personal interest in her, she was flattered.

Tony had a modest law practice, but he still earned twice the income her husband did, and she considered the possibility of improving her status. Pat liked the power and prestige Tony had as a county political leader. True, his party was not the "in" group, but in time it might be. And if this happened, Tony would take a judgeship or maybe eventually be State Democratic

Chairman. He had never told her he loved her, but his advances in the office were enough at the moment. And after tonight, anything might happen. She thought she'd like to be a judge's wife. She knew that as long as she kept him pleased and interested in her, she was safe, but there was always the fear that since so many women liked politicians, someone else might catch his fancy. Tony's caresses drove everything else out of her mind and she responded with a passion that delighted him.

Terry watched studiously with a grin on his face. "Look at the old goat bang her. That Di Pasco acts high and mighty in town, and here's the horny bastard fucking his secretary."

As he moved, a twig cracked and he ducked below the window, but their passion blotted out the crackling sound. He remained huddled long enough to assure himself they hadn't heard him, then he walked back up the hill to his bottle, settled down on a log and took a swig, thinking about the scene he had witnessed. He stuck his tongue into the neck of the bottle and worked it around, sucking gently as he pondered. He could think of a better place to put his tongue. He held the bottle in the air. It was half empty.

The call of nature interrupted his reverie and he put the bottle down beside a tree. His hand fumbled as he unzipped his pants. "Curtain time," he called, but his fingers felt cold on his penis. He flexed his muscles to make it move and stroked it gently. "No cunts for you, fella, but how about a little piss?" He stood up, staggered slightly, and straightened up to guide the stream and hit a leaf. The leaf cringed and he laughed; he changed his direction and the stream struck a distant branch. When he had finished he pulled at it, and it hardened. Terry was thinking about the beautiful blond woman he had seen through the window at the club earlier this evening. "Boy, what I could do with her now!" His penis was alive in his hand and he began to sing softly, "For the want of a cunt, a screw was lost," and he continued with his manipulation.

His bleary eyes focused on a nearby tree; a branch and trunk formed an inviting "V". Terry moved near the trunk. He wrapped his most prized possession in his handkerchief and bounced gleefully against the tree. When he felt a tingle, he unwrapped himself and completed the job by hand. He

held himself taut, waiting for the pulsation to subside. Suddenly, he pulled his clothes off and laughed uproariously as he addressed the tree. "It'll be standing up soon enough, baby," and he gently manipulated his penis again. He worked up to a furious pace, remembering the times he had pushed a girl up against a tree to fool with her. He wrapped it once again and decided to alter his position, sprang to his hands, and pounded the tree upside down. His head felt dizzy and he fell to the ground. He didn't hear anything except this own crazy laughter, and felt nothing but his excitement, not even the scratches on his thighs and abdomen. He pulled at himself and ejaculated on the tree.

His bottle spilled, and some of its contents emptied on the ground. He picked it up and downed the remaining contents. He lay there for a while trying to bring the world in focus. The branches above him were grotesquely twisted, and the trees loomed eerily in the moonlight; they seemed to be falling on him. He sat up, but everything was a blur, whirling like a kaleidoscope, crashing around, then reeling away, spinning in the distance. He struggled to his feet, trying to stabilize himself. Slowly the world stopped its frenetic motion and he could see again. He had knocked over the motorcycle and he groped his way over to where it lay. The gasoline cap had come loose and gas was trickling out. He propped it up and took a cigarette from his shirt, which dangled from a small shrub. He reached for the matches and an idea prodded his brain. The car was beside the cottage and the wind had shifted. A slow, blissful smile grew on his face. He tilted the bike, shaking some of the gasoline out. He donned his shirt, tossed a few lighted matches toward the wet leaves and jumped onto his motorcycle, careening wildly through the woods, calling, "Have fun, you bastard!"

The flames caught quickly; the wind fanned the small blaze and the leaves rustled into colorful life. Soon a blazing inferno danced toward the cottage. Safely out of reach of the fire, Terry rode along the edge of the woods with nothing on except his shirt, but he knew of a spot where he could hide. Then, he could work his way home through the back roads and unfenced yards. At that hour his mother would be fast asleep, and he could sneak into the house.

Back in the cottage Tony stiffened.

"What's the matter?" murmured Pat.

"I don't know. I thought I heard something. Sounded like a crackle . . ." He looked out the window. "My God." The fire had spread and was roaring toward the house. "Come on, let's get the hell out of here." He pushed Pat from the bed, thrusting her clothes at her. She started to dress but he stopped her. "Never mind that now. We can dress in the car. That fire is moving fast."

Pat scurried out the door with Tony close behind. They raced to the car and leaped in. Tony had the engine started before Pat could close the door, and she struggled to get it shut while he tore up the dirt road. She scrambled into her clothes, then held the wheel while Tony tried to get into his. When they made it to the main road, they heard the fire suck up the cottage and shoot sparks high in the air. The fire engines were coming from the opposite direction and they sped away, hoping to avoid any encounters.

Baywater. . .

Just as Nero played his fiddle while ancient Rome burned, most of Baywater's residents slept, oblivious to the commotion and raging fire at Lake Constance. Few lights twinkled and the occupants of the dark houses were comfortably tucked away in bed.

In the old mansion, Lenore sat at her bedroom table looking into the mirror, brushing her hair. As she stared at her reflection, the same unanswered questions poised in her mind, "Who am I? Where did I come from? I'm so different."

As she studied her image, her face changed and an eerie, white vision with a strange mouth and small ears appeared. Her breath quickened. Then that image disappeared. Slowly, gradual changes formed in her face once again, and she found herself looking at yet another face. Her hand shook as she put her brush down. She asked, "Who are you? I know you somehow." As she studied the image, she sadly began to feel she had journeyed through time and different places, and that these images were her

own being from lives ago.

The mirror became a blur. Lenore struggled to get up and walked to her bed. Did she hear a voice? Her eyes swept the room and lingered a moment on the mirror above the table. In the dim light another image appeared, the plastic, white-looking flesh twisting and turning; then it took the shape of a strange face with small, dark, luminous eyes that gazed into her own. She watched intensely. Seconds passed. "It's been a long time, Lenore." She attempted to direct herself to get up and touch the mirror, but her body wouldn't respond. Was she dreaming? There were footsteps, but no one walked. Was she hallucinating? In an instant he floated across the room, and a feeling of passion and longing swept over her. He seemed to read her thoughts. His hand caressed her body. He spoke, yet he didn't make a sound. It was as though she was able to read his mind. "I haven't forgotten our life and love. It is I who watches over you and makes sure you produce magnificent pictures. Haven't you ever wondered?"

Lenore was breathing heavily and moaned a weak sigh as a strange sensation overwhelmed her. This creature had engulfed her body, yet her body felt warm and light. She reached out to stroke his strange face, this alien ghost from another life. Her body climaxed, and the anxiety turned to serenity. He pulled back as she reached further; he was fading away.

"Don't go," she cried.

In a whisper he responded, "We'll be together again." Then there was silence and he completely disappeared.

Lenore turned in her bed half awake, half asleep. What had happened? What was the meaning of this dream or encounter? Was it real? She heard distant sirens but paid little attention. She gazed at the mirror, but all there was to see was a reflection in the dim light. No one was there, yet . . . "My pictures, always good," she mumbled and she fell asleep.

Later that same night at Baywater. . .

Meg Marshall was sitting at her dressing table setting her hair, listening to the local station, when the news came over about the fire raging at Lake Constance, three miles away. She was thinking about the party and had an urge to call Toby in Washington and tell him all that had taken place. She wasn't sure where he would be staying, but she could find out. She placed a person to person call to him at the pilot's lounge; they would have a number where she could reach him in an emergency.

"I'm sorry," the girl at the other end said. "Mr. Marshall has a confidential number and does not wish to give it out."

Meg cut in ahead of the operator. "This is Mrs. Marshall and it's urgent that I get in touch with him."

After some persuasion, the girl released the number. "Very well, you can reach him at Palm 4-7655. Do you wish to put the call through?" asked the operator.

"Yes, please," and Meg sat down on the bed waiting to hear Toby's voice. She knew he would be surprised. He told her never to call long distance and spend the money for toll calls, but tonight she wanted to tell him about the party. The number was ringing. She was distracted by a scream. The baby was crying. "Never mind, operator, I'll call back later."

She put the number in her address book and hurried to Kenneth's room. He was wide awake, sitting up in bed, screaming at the top of his lungs. Meg picked him up and began to croon softly. It took a long time to quiet him and by the time he fell back to sleep, it was much too late to place her call. She walked into the living room and turned on the TV. She moved to the windows and opened the drapes, looking out at the lovely moonlight. There were lights on at the Rufone's, and as she watched, the downstairs plunged into darkness and the hall lights upstairs flicked on. Then, shrugging her shoulders, she closed the drapes and curled up to watch a late movie on TV.

Ann Rufone went into the bathroom as Vinny came up the stairs. She didn't like to undress in front of him. A few seconds later Vinny was walking around in the bedroom, banging drawers shut. Then there was stillness. She took as much time as she dared, anticipating that he would be asleep shortly.

She slipped the pink nightgown over her head and crept into the bedroom. Vinny was sitting on the side of the bed, deep in thought. They'd had coffee when they came home, and talked about the scene Dan had created and about Kim's chance to do a show.

Having coffee had been a mistake; he was wide awake and the conversation about Kim had stimulated him. He couldn't get her out of his thoughts. He wondered what it would be like waiting for her to come out of the bathroom, instead of Ann. That business of Ann's undressing in the bathroom was ridiculous; after all, they had a child and were married seven years. She should have overcome her shyness by now. "Good Lord," he thought, "after all the women I've seen naked, what does she think she has to hide?"

The sound of Ann's slipper shuffling on the carpet brought him back to reality. She walked over to the bed, lifted the sheet, and climbed in. He talked to her as he went in to wash; he didn't want her to fall asleep, not yet. He was horny and hoped she'd be more responsive to him if he was casual and talked for a while first.

"Did you have a good time?" He stopped brushing his teeth to hear her answer.

"Yes, but Janet's parties are always fun, aren't they?"

He mumbled into the towel, dried his face quickly and came back into the room. "Yes, Charles is a good host too, but that husband of Lenore's is an oddball."

"I suppose since he's not well he can't be himself. Do you know what's wrong with him?"

"No, the times I've been there to see Robbie, Peter was usually in his room. I hardly know him."

"I feel sorry for Robbie. Can't anything be done for him?"

Vinny took her hand and stroked it. "Not much. He's fortunate to be close to a hospital and get all the transfusions he needs. The Hemophiliac Foundation is working on a clotting factor, but how soon it will be available is another question."

"It must be hard for Lenore having a hemophiliac son and a husband like Peter."

Vinny kissed her cheek lightly. "See how lucky you are? A healthy child, a healthy husband who is too busy most of the time to bother you. How about rubbing my back?" He tossed the bedclothes aside and lay down on his stomach. As Ann rubbed he became aroused, and the image of Kim burned in his mind. He turned quickly and reached for her. She didn't resist, and he pulled her close, then kissed her tenderly. He knew he'd have to move slowly for her to respond. He shut his eyes so the picture of Kim wouldn't be dimmed. It wasn't Ann at all, it was Kim in his arms. He pushed his tongue through her lips and slowly explored her mouth, at the same time sliding her gown up and over her head. He cupped her breast in his hand, squeezing lightly. He pushed his tongue into her mouth further and felt her stiffen, changed tactics, and moved down to her breast. She made a small sound that he took for pleasure, and it encouraged him. He kissed her throat and her breast, again and again, then moved to her stomach. She didn't protest, so gradually he increased his ardor. His fingertips caressed her, then slipped in between her thighs, and when he felt she was sufficiently simulated, he lowered his head and slid his tongue in to replace his fingers. She was moist. If he could show her pleasure, she might return the favor. She twitched under his mouth and he moved into a more convenient position, so both could partake in the same kind of love making.

Suddenly she arched her back and grabbed his head with her hands, "No more Vinny, please don't."

"What is it Ann, can't you go along for once? Won't you try to please me?"

"You know I hate to do it that way. Why do you keep insisting?"

Vinny sat up, his face a deep red; she was frightened and started to cry. "I can't, I can't!" She turned away and pressed her face into the pillow.

"Ann, it's nothing," said Vinny softly, controlling himself with great effort. "It's nothing abnormal; you know I wouldn't ask you to do anything that was."

"I hate it, it seems so, so . . ." she hesitated, "dirty."

The phone rang and he picked up the receiver. His answering service was making its nightly check. There was nothing important.

"I understand, alright, I have it." He put the phone back down and

stood up. "I have an emergency. I'll try to get back soon. I'm sorry, Ann, I didn't mean to upset you. We'll forget about it."

"Do you mean that? You won't try again? You're not angry?" She was sobbing softly.

Vinny stroked the top of her head. "No, I'm not angry," he answered. "Go to sleep. I'll be quiet when I come in, and if it's very late I'll sleep on the studio couch in the playroom."

He dressed and went downstairs. He picked up the extension in the playroom and dialed. A girl answered. "It's Vin. You alone? I need you."

"Sure," the husky voice replied with a chuckle. "Come on over."

Vinny put the phone down and reflected, remembering the strange circumstances that started their relationship. On his way home from the office one evening, he noticed a young woman standing at a corner bus stop in the pouring rain. She looked like a drowned rat and his heart went out to her. He pulled his car over to the curb and offered her a ride. Surprised by his gesture, she acted frightened, mistaking him for a rapist or crazy man, terrified that no one would save her from him. He convinced her who he was, going so far as to show identification, and he explained that he had only meant to be helpful and to excuse him. She hesitated and then, perhaps because she either believed him or was fed up waiting for her bus in the downpour, got in the car and went with him. By the time they pulled up at her address he'd found out that she was a model and salesgirl in Sayr's Point Department store, lived alone, and was single.

She insisted that in appreciation for his "being Sir Galahad," he join her for a drink. When they got inside her apartment, a small but tastefully furnished third floor walk-up, Vinny mixed the martinis while she went to change her wet clothing. When she returned to the living room clad in a thin black robe, with her wet hair piled high on her head, he noticed she was very pretty and had a lovely figure. She looked inviting, and as he drank his cocktail and they chatted, he had a desire to pull the tie on her robe and stroke her breasts.

She insisted he mix a second, then another, and by the time he had finished his third drink, she was in his arms on the sofa and they were kissing. She paused, then unzipped his trousers, leaned over his lap and kissed and sucked

65

him. She ran her tongue around and around, stopped, pulled, licked from top to bottom, bottom to top. Vinny was deliriously happy . . . he'd found a woman who was eager and ecstatic to play his game. He had never known anyone to compare. She knew when to stop, how to control him; it was a gift of timing. He'd relax and she'd start all over. She quickened her pace and at the height of his excitement, swallowed the liquid he had released. Then he subsided.

When he left that evening he'd found a ticket on his car, but he went back to her whenever he could, always phoning first to be sure she was alone. She pleased him in any way . . . and he made sure he had a pocketful of money when he visited her. They played a game. If he was one hundred percent satisfied, he left seventy-five dollars on the bureau; if he wasn't very pleased, he left whatever seemed fitting at the moment. They never argued about the amount. She was appreciative of his kindness, and she never nagged about marriage the way most women did when they were having an affair. Lately however, she appeared cool toward him and he suspected there was someone else in the picture, some other competition.

Vinny headed the car down the driveway, and as he turned onto the street, saw headlights in the rearview mirror. He recognized Thompson Brack's Continental. "Maybe he's out of cigarettes," Vinny pondered. But he couldn't imagine leaving Kim home in bed for a pack of cigarettes. As he drove through the gates he noticed a red glow in the sky, but as his thoughts turned to what lay ahead of him, he was oblivious to the raging fire and distant sirens.

Thompson recognized Vinny's car as he passed through the gates. He must have an emergency, he thought to himself.

After the party he and Kim had had a drink and talked about the possibility of her doing the show, then he asked her if she'd mind his going out for a while.

"No, go ahead, dear," she replied, neither asking for nor expecting an explanation.

That was the way a marriage should be, he thought. Kim never asked him what he did or what he spent, and of all the marriages he knew, he considered his to be one of the best. Or as Janet had said at the party, "the

beautiful people who have everything." Kim was one of the most beautiful women he had ever met. Her background was shabby, but no one suspected where she came from or what she had done prior to their marriage. Perhaps that was why she never questioned him; she was grateful for what he had saved her from.

Her father, a train conductor, had died when she was a young girl, leaving her mother penniless. Her mother tried to support them, in vain, and when she found she couldn't get a decent job, had turned to whoring in a small, dusty Ohio town where they had lived. As Kim grew, her awkward legs became beautiful limbs. She filled out and there were signs of a budding beauty by the time she was fifteen. Her mother was seeing one of her clients, a widower, on a regular basis. Occasionally he would stop in on his way home from work, or drop by in the evenings. One night her mother had gone to a movie with the lady next door and there was a knock on the door. Kim explained that her mother had gone to the movies, but the man insisted on coming in. He sat down in the kitchen and drew her into conversation, telling her he might be her new daddy. As Kim put her arms around his neck, excited that she would finally have a new father and life might be easier for them, the man pulled her to his lap. He had had a strange, glassy-eyed stare on his face, and suddenly he shoved his hand up her thigh under her dress. It was at that moment her mother came in, horrified at what she saw, and decided to send her daughter off to a relative.

Kim was shipped off to the back woods of Montana. When she arrived she'd found that she had a cousin a few years her senior with whom she had to share a twin bedded room. Her Aunt and Uncle treated her well, but her cousin hardly spoke to her. Kim thought she was rather strange. Letitia was a big bosomed girl of seventeen who liked to horseback ride and go logging with her father. She always wore the same dirty work pants and blouse, which revolted Kim.

One night, about six weeks after Kim had arrived, they had received a call informing them that her mother had died in an auto accident. Kim had taken it very hard, and one night as she lay in her bed crying softly into her pillow, Letitia came in, went over to her and held her in her arms, stroking her

tenderly. She quieted her, and the next moment undressed and snuggled up to Kim under the covers, telling her that she had the most beautiful body in the world.

From that night until the day she left that house, Kim was Letitia's prisoner. But her cousin was attentive to her needs and bought her pretty things from her logging salary. This went on for two years without her Aunt and Uncle suspecting.

One night the family drove into town to see a movie. During intermission Kim went to the ladies room, and on the way back to her seat, the young manager stopped her, asked her name, and asked if he could see her some time. She was afraid Letitia would notice and they'd have a fight over it, but it was her Aunt who walked up to them. Kim was seventeen and lovely, and the young manager persuaded her Aunt to allow him to call. And seeing this as the only escape from Letitia, Kim dated him, and a little later, married him.

After the wedding she settled down to cooking and cleaning, but that alone bored her so she took singing lessons, and her young husband paid the bill. Her music teacher encouraged her to take dancing lessons; they were spending every pay check and did not prepare themselves financially for the day when he lost his job. The lessons stopped, things went from bad to worse, and Kim learned what it meant to be poor again. They fought, each blaming the other for their circumstances, and finally, unable to cope anymore, she left him.

Thompson had gone to Montana on vacation and Kim was waiting on tables at the resort where he stayed. He noticed her poise and facial beauty, and suspected more beauty under the loose-hanging uniform. He wanted to take her back to New York, and convinced her to get a divorce, which he arranged and paid for. Once in New York, he passed her off as a well-to-do young lady from the west whom he had met at a vacation resort. Before the wedding, Kim had confided in him about Letitia and the kind of life she had led as a child, but even that didn't disturb or dissuade Thompson. Kim knew she'd never go hungry, and she was deeply indebted to Thompson for all he had done.

In the days that followed, she found he wasn't an ardent lover. Their

sexual encounters were fast and furious, but she never complained. Then one day she realized she was pregnant and she would be able to proudly present him with a child.

CHAPTER 3
SUMMER 1966
THE COFFEE KLATCH

Spring wove subtly into summer and the threads of the warm days created a pattern of mosaic activity. Lawn mowers buzzed, jet sprinklers whirled merrily, and flowers were coaxed and cajoled into bloom. The lives of the Baywater residents merged as the club hummed with activity. The season's opening party, a July 4th celebration, started with an enormous barbecue, followed by magnificent displays of fireworks on the beach. During the festivities an emergency occurred, an event that drew the families closer together, as near tragedies will. Robbie Morgan was hemorrhaging. Fortunately, Vinny had been at the party, and some of the men who had volunteered blood raced the boy to the hospital. Robbie pulled through, but the other mothers sympathized with the cross Lenore had to bear, and marveled at her strength.

The number of children in the area increased and they played boisterously and unceasingly. Janet arranged classes in swimming, tennis and sailing to occupy the children's time so their parents would be free to pursue their own interests. The pool was a Mecca for the women; the men preferred swimming in the bay, but evenings drew everyone to the club for partying and dancing. The bar lounge was opened daily and the summer theatre held frequent rehearsals at the club, to the delight of the residents who were regular observers. Baywater was humming as July whirled into August and the long awaited summer season came full flower.

Kim Brack worked hard in the lead of *Gentlemen Prefer Blonds*. Besides her regular rehearsals, Kim had convinced Lenore to hold Yoga classes and proved to be her most avid student.

71

Gloria Rudowski was busy decorating the new house. She was happier living in Baywater. She found the community almost self-contained, and there were enough supervised activities to keep the children busy. Stan had stopped phoning from the car to check on her whereabouts, and Dan O'Quinn had apologized for his behavior. (Dottie's refusal to sleep with him had coerced that.) Stan accepted the apology graciously and made light of the matter, and they were on friendly, neighborly terms.

Janet and Charles spent one weekend upstate, but for the most part stayed close to Baywater. Charles was busy at the office but found time to play golf, sometimes with Dottie.

All the gardens in the area were attractive, but none compared with the Banshata's. Joe and Jenny spent a lot of time caring for their property, and it was no surprise when the Banshata's won the Sayr's Point "Garden of the Year Award."

It was a hot and muggy day and Janet pushed a wisp of hair from her face. She was almost sorry that she had invited her new neighbor, Ruth Foster, over for the afternoon. A blast of warm air struck her as she came out to the porch carrying a tray of iced coffee and cookies. Ruth was laying on a chaise lounge, fanning herself with a magazine and appraising Baywater and her new home.

"My you look comfortable."

"I feel like a contented cow, now that you mention it. Can I help with anything?"

"Everything's under control, thanks anyway." Janet offered her a glass of the iced coffee.

"Our house is what I've always wanted, a perfect Cape Cod, and our early American furniture looks as if it belongs."

Janet offered her a cookie. "How's Gordon? We never see him around."

"Oh, fine, he's awfully busy selling insurance. His father is completely bowled over. Sometimes we can't believe he's the same Gordon. Perhaps making him a junior partner in the firm helped. He's been working like a dog to prove himself and even had time to finish the beautiful chest he's making for the entry."

Janet noticed a car pulling in the driveway farther down the block. "Oh, I think that's Meg. I'll call her and maybe she can join us." As Janet left the porch to go inside, she heard a voice calling.

"Hi, anybody home?"

"Would you see who it is, Ruth? Sounds like Kim. Let her in."

"Right you are," and Kim strolled up the steps. "Say, you look cool and I'm bushed!"

"You may feel bushed, Kim, but you don't look it. Janet will be right out. She's calling Meg. Want some iced coffee?"

Kim sank into a chair. "That sounds great."

Janet came back to the porch. "Meg will be right over." She sat down next to Kim. "How are the rehearsals going?"

"Wild. Everything is in a state of confusion and some of the scenes need a bit of polishing . . . We open this weekend and I'm a nervous wreck."

"From what I've seen at the club, you should top Carol Channing." Ruth smiled. "You have opening night jitters."

Meg Marshall tapped lightly at the screen door. "Hi, what's doing?"

Kim got up and unhooked the door for her as Janet poured another glass of coffee. "We're talking about the play. I'm bushed from the rehearsals. What have you been doing?"

"Oh, gracious, haven't you heard? I'm the dean of children at the church, in charge of the up and coming production of . . . hold your hats girls . . . *The First Thanksgiving*, due to open in November," and she bowed.

They laughed and Janet said, "Be sure to save us opening night tickets. We don't want to miss your production either." She handed her the glass as Meg sat down, then passed the cookies. "How's your tennis partner?" she teased.

They laughed and contributed comments about Mark till she protested. "He's a darned good player, and I admit he's a nice guy, but I'm happily married, and he IS a gentleman."

They hooted at her and ended up giggling as Meg added, "Confidentially, it keeps Toby in line."

73

"Well," said Janet mischievously, "I guess if you have to look over a net at a tennis partner, it might as well be a good looking male."

"And, if it helps keep a husband in line, I'm all for that," added Ruth Foster as she took a cookie.

Meg leaned forward in her chair. "Say, I hear that Reverend Richard's son is going to visit him soon. Lives somewhere in Virginia."

"Oh?" Janet poured more coffee for the girls. "If that's all the gossip we can come up with, we're wasting this coffee klatch." They laughed again and she continued, "Did I tell you we're getting some more neighbors?"

Kim piped up, "You sold the other two houses?"

"We have a deposit on the two-story from the Birklands, who own a large stationery store in Bel Harbor, and we'll close soon on the waterfront next door. The Howells bought that one."

Meg asked, "Which Howell?"

"The Stephen Howell's. They have three children, two girls and a boy. One girl is in grade school, and the other two are in high school."

"Oh, no!" Meg wailed. "She's a pip. Drinks like a fish, and screams after those kids. Her husband's not much better. You could set your watch by him, every afternoon at the Sayr's Point Inn Bar."

"What do you mean?" Kim asked.

"I hear he reels in every day at 4 o'clock on the button for before dinner cocktails . . . he has unlimited credit . . . and last week he was so drunk that he fell off the bar stool and his son Terry had to come get him."

Janet sighed. "I didn't know that. I guess they're spending all the Howell money the family accumulated for generations. They wanted a lot of costly extras in the house, and when Dan asked them if they wanted an estimate, they said they trusted him and to go ahead. Are you sure about their drinking?"

"She has the taxi driver deliver a bottle almost daily, and I understand the girls have to put her to bed at night. No, I'm certain. She has a serious drinking problem."

"Have you heard about mine?" Ruth asked.

They looked at her and laughed. It was a well-known fact that Ruth hardly ever touched a drop of alcohol.

A car came down the street. "That's Toby coming in from a flight. Can't stay long."

"You'll have to learn to make him wait a bit," Kim teased. "We women are going places these days."

"That's right," Janet added. "We may have a first woman governor in Alabama this coming election."

"That's only a front for her husband so he can continue to run the state," Ruth said. "Of course I'd vote for her, for the principle of it."

"Oh, talking of principals reminds me of some gossip going around about Ray Dowling." Meg hesitated, "It may not be true, but I've heard that Mrs. Dowling had an appointment with Reverend Richard about Ray's running around with someone."

"Oh, dear, how could a nasty rumor like that get started?" asked Janet.

"The day she had the appointment, Reverend Richard thought the hall was empty and left the study door open. In strutted your real estate friend, Mrs. Tooker. You know what she's like. She hung around long enough to hear them discussing the problem, and couldn't wait to tell someone I know."

"I don't believe it," Kim spoke tartly. "It's the type of gossip Mrs. Tooker is capable of starting. Maybe Ray wouldn't let her use the school auditorium for one of her club meetings, and she's striking back."

"I agree with Kim. Besides, Mr. Dowling is well-respected and his wife is sweet." Ruth nodded her head.

"I hope you're right," said Meg, getting up and stretching. "I have to get home. Thanks for the coffee and company, Jan."

Kim looked at her watch. "I have a yoga lesson with Lenore, so I'll be seeing you. Thanks, Jan, it was fun."

After Kim and Meg left, Ruth said, "I'd like to take yoga lessons. I wonder if Lenore would make time for me."

"If you want, I'll ask my cousin if she can take you."

"Is Lenore your cousin? I didn't know you were related."

"We're first cousins . . . in fact, our parents were killed together in an accident and we were brought up in Baywater. This was all one estate at the time. We lived in the mansion with Uncle Taurus. Baywater was a well-known landmark in its day and many famous people from all walks of life, whom Uncle Taurus met in his travels, visited here." Then she paused remembering those days.

Ruth pulled herself off the lounge. "I've enjoyed your hospitality, Janet. It was sweet of you, but I must go. You will ask Lenore about lessons, won't you?"

"Of course. And I'm so glad you came over."

After Ruth left, Janet took the tray and glasses inside and called Lennie to see if she could drop by. Later, as they sat on Lenore's sun deck, Janet told her about Ray Dowling and the gossip.

Lenore replied, "You know, Janet, I often wonder if we did the right thing developing Baywater. Maybe we should have sold the property."

Janet was surprised at her statement. "What do you mean? We've made a lot of money and there's still a lot more to make."

"I know," she responded. "But, the people aren't the best and there are things . . ."

Janet was indignant. "Perhaps Dan is rough, but the rest seem fine."

"Time will tell, but I think one day we'll be sorry and want to leave here." Her son appeared at the door and the conversation ended.

"I'd like to borrow a telescope, mother. Could it be arranged?"

"Ask Mark to pick you up one the next time he comes over. Consider it an early Christmas gift!"

"Wow, that's swell. I bet I can see over to Fire Island."

Janet grinned and Lenore shook her head. Then out of the clear blue sky he said in a wistful tone, "I wish I could go to college like other boys."

Lenore swallowed, knowing how much her son liked the academic world. She spoke slowly, "Rob, when the time comes, we'll make arrangements about that too. We can discuss it with Mr. Dowling and Mark and see what they suggest. Now, sit down and have a sandwich."

He was a tall, thin boy, delicately skinned; even with all the sun he enjoyed, he looked pale and wan. Although few hemophiliacs survived for many years past their teens, Lenore insisted that he continue living as though he had a future. Lately, he had been rushed to the hospital often and needed so much blood that the local citizens had established a blood bank for him. If he minded being deprived of all the fun the other boys had at the pool and on the tennis courts, he never mentioned it. He used his time reading, listening to music, playing chess, and studying. He was good in math and had a new interest, astronomy. He liked bird watching and Lenore thought of interesting him in taking pictures through his telescope, to add to his collection of bird photographs.

On their first Christmas Day in Baywater, Peter and Lenore surprised him with a gift of a magnificent German Shepherd. Roma was a devoted companion for him, and the dog was trained to summon help when he needed it. She never let him out of her sight and now sat a few feet away watching him eat, her eyes fixed on his every move; her big ears flickered back and forth at each sound she heard. He motioned to her and she came and took an offering from his hand, careful not to let her teeth scrape his fingers. She backed off and sat down licking her chops, resting in the sun.

The lazy afternoon stretched into early evening; the faded sun was dipping into the bay. Janet and Charles were invited to dinner with Lenore, Peter and Robbie, and after dinner, Mark Harrison came by and dropped off a book for Robbie. After a few hands of cards, the company left and Lenore went back upstairs and out to the sun deck. She looked up to the sky, the moon's thin light, the twinkling stars, and begged, "Please . . . allow my son more life, and let him . . . at least . . . live long enough to start college . . . like other boys . . . it means so much to him." She put her head down and went back into the mansion.

The last few spare moments of summer were pure gold dust, and the tyranny of time brought about a feverish activity, particularly in the young.

School was the executioner's axe for them; not being rich in time they squandered the days with reckless frenzy, purchasing each hour with the price of physical fatigue, opposed to anything which interfered in the last, lingering, warm days of pleasure.

Mothers prepared for tiring shopping to outfit their children for the fall term. Only Janet and Lenore were spared the hectic days in the stores. Labor Day announced the tolling of the bell, the final death of summer, and it was celebrated with a final barbecue for the season. Although they had been rarely seen since they had moved in, the Birklands attended. They had spent most of the summer on their cabin cruiser with their two children, Henry and Adele.

The Howells had moved in and there was a great deal of regret in the community. Linda had steady deliveries from the local liquor store, and Stephen was a drunken menace behind the wheel. They stayed away from the barbecue, perhaps, as Meg said, "because they can't navigate that far on foot." The two Howell girls, Sue and Marianne, weren't a problem, but Terry was another matter. New students soon discovered that he was a sadistic bully, but he fooled many adults by his nice appearance (the short brown hair, clear and steady eyes, a ready smile) and polite attitude. Parents were prone to judge youngsters by their manners, and Terry's were the best. But within his own group he terrified everyone. He was the unquestioned leader of the boys he traveled with; his reputation with girls was unsavory, and he was dangerous.

Peter arrived late at the barbecue. Janet had to admit he looked ill and she was more attentive to his needs than usual. Vinny Rufone spoke with Peter and Lenore at length, and Janet concluded there was something seriously wrong. The Birklands gravitated toward the Fosters, quiet people. Dan was too tired to be troublesome. He was eager to complete one house and close on another before bad weather set in. Janet had suggested he hold off finishing the second until spring, when the weather would induce prospects. Stan Rudowski and Dan seemed content to sit and talk about the building business.

Lenore had invited a couple she'd met earlier in the year, a former big-league baseball player, Russell Howard, and his wife Claudia. A serious injury

had taken him out of the world of sports, and now, after some analysis of the need for a sporting goods store in Sayr's Point, he decided on the location. Claudia was a genial, fun-loving woman and the life of the party with her dry humor and wit. They had two children, Edwina and Andrew, who were visiting with their grandmother.

Kim Brack brought along some of the young people from the Summer Theater. Thompson arrived later, concerned about a large fire raging in the nearby woods. There had been a rash of fires all summer, and this one was creating a serious traffic problem in the area. The Chief of Police, Rudy Mayer, stopped by the barbecue to question the youngsters and see if anyone of them could "shed a little light on this one," but they were non-communicative, refusing to involve their peers. The party went on late into the night, most of the participants oblivious to the threat outside Baywater.

CHAPTER 4
AUTUMN 1966
THE ABORTION

Autumn in Baywater was stunning. The huge maples showered the grounds with brilliant gold and crimson leaves that rustled crisply underfoot and whirled like colorful tornadoes in the fall wind. The Banshatas were busy digging up bulbs and protecting their shrubs from the cold. Summer clothes were packed away, and the lines outside were colorfully gay with fall and winter things. The wedding of the President's daughter was still the subject of discussion. The shocking incident of the Texas student who murdered his wife, mother, and fourteen other people, set them thinking about the conditions in the country. Out west, the daughter of one of the Republican leaders was murdered while the family slept. Nervous parents installed burglar alarms. Janet quarreled with Lenore about her carelessness in leaving the house unlocked.

The one-story with the iron railing front was completed and Janet went to see Mrs. Tooker to persuade her to step up the attempt to find a buyer. No one had shown any interest in the house and they were afraid they would have to carry all the expenses over the winter. Mrs. Tooker was sitting at her desk reading when Janet walked in. "What a pleasant surprise, my dear. Do sit down. Isn't it a lovely day?

Janet winced at the unctuous tone. "Crisp, but a little too cool. I don't like the thought of the coming winter, freezing weather and snow."

"Perhaps we will be lucky and not have too much of it this year," Mrs. Tooker said soothingly.

Janet sat down, looked straight into her eyes and asked, "Have you found

a prospect for the new house? We much prefer to have you as the agent rather than some stranger. We like to keep the business in the Sayr's Point community." Janet knew that statement would please an old-timer like Mrs. Tooker.

She bit on Janet's bait. "I see what you mean, dear." She pursed her lips. "We do have to be careful about outsiders coming into the community, and we want people who will fit in properly and not give us any trouble."

Janet smiled to herself, and Mrs. Tooker continued, "As a matter of fact, someone was in earlier this week looking for a place, however I didn't think she would be interested in a house, being a single woman, although money didn't seem to be any object."

"Who is she?"

"The head of student nurses at Brookview Hospital, and I'd say she's in her thirties . . . her name is . . ." she thumbed through some papers on her desk, "Ester Fine. I'll call her."

"Good, we're anxious to sell before the cold weather sets in." Janet stood up to leave, but Mrs. Tooker detained her.

"How's Charles? I haven't seen him in the village lunch room lately."

"He's been on trial. He's representing the Mainland Ferry Boat owners. One of the boats going over to the Grove hit a buoy, and a few of the passengers were hurt and they're suing. Charles said they had very minor injuries, but they want to battle it out in court."

"That summer crowd is an outrageous bunch . . . and the ones with the poodles . . . oh, dear . . ." and her broad hand touched her forehead as though she had a headache. When she spoke, her voice sounded as though she had pebbles in her cheeks. "I'm so glad they're gone."

"Well, they are good for local business and the season IS short," she emphasized. She walked to the door. "Call me soon with a buyer."

"I'll try. Drive carefully, say hello to Charles for me," and as an afterthought, "and that strange cousin of yours."

Mrs. Tooker's remark about Lenore bothered her as she drove to Baywater.

"Yoo hoo, where is everyone?"

"We're in the den Aunt Jan . . . Mother is in her room."

Mark Harrison was playing chess with Robbie as she passed the door, both deep in concentration; she didn't stop and went directly to Lenore's suite. Lenore was running her projector, but as Janet came in she turned it off and opened the drapes.

"I've been at Mrs. Tooker's," and she repeated the entire conversation.

"Can you imagine what life with her must have been like for that poor, weak husband of hers? Add Susan to that . . . The sweet peace of death must have seemed very inviting."

"He should have run away."

"Women like that never let their man go, their pride won't permit it."

Robbie's voice floated up from the lower hall. "Mr. Harrison is leaving."

"Coming," Lenore called back, and she and Janet went down.

"This son of yours gave me a hard time today."

"I swamped him," Robbie said excitedly, with a big grin spread across his face.

Lenore replied, "Maybe next time YOU'LL be swamped."

They laughed and Mark said, "I have to get to the auditorium and set up a film on new techniques in learning mathematics. I'm sorry to see summer end, it was an enjoyable one."

"How's your tennis partner?" Janet teased.

Mark blushed. "Meg and I are only friends. Besides, she's married, and . . . not my type. I'm afraid I'm going to stay a bachelor, but I do admire you women."

"When the right one comes along you'll feel differently," and Janet patted his arm.

"Be that as it may, until that time I still have my job, so thanks for your hospitality. Thanks for the game, Rob." He turned, walked down the hall and left.

"I'd better go. I promised Charles a Quiche Lorraine for dinner tonight." She touched Robbie's hand and said good-bye.

As Janet pulled out of the driveway, she saw Ann Rufone walking from the club and called out to her through her open window. "Hi, what are you up to? The club is closed this afternoon."

"I know. I was walking for exercise but I'm tired and could use a lift."

"Hop in, I'll take you home."

In a few minutes Janet had deposited her by her door, and Ann could hear her phone jingling. She hurried in and answered it.

"Hi," her husband's voice greeted her. "I'm on schedule with my appointments and should be home in an hour. What are we having for dinner?"

"What would you like?"

"I could go for a nice Italian dinner, if it's not much trouble."

"It's no trouble. I'll have it ready."

"Fine, see you in an hour."

She hung up her jacket in the closet, went into the kitchen and took some sauce from the freezer. Ann loved to cook and fuss in the kitchen. As she was making meatballs, her daughter Lucille came bursting into the room. "Hello, mommy, Mrs. Marshall sent me home . . . We were building an erector set, and Larry hit me."

Ann thought for a moment, then asked, "Did you knock it over?"

Lucille looked away. "Maybe the wind did."

"Wind? What wind? You were playing indoors."

"It was an accident and Larry got mad." There were tears in her eyes.

Ann knelt down and put her arms around her daughter. "Lucille, honey, you should have apologized and helped him put it together. That would have been the right thing to do. Remember that the next time you play with him." She hugged the little girl to her and kissed her on the cheek. Lucille smiled, relieved that she hadn't been scolded. "Better wash up. Daddy will be home soon and we're having your favorite . . . spaghetti and meatballs."

Lucille left the room and Ann continued cooking. By the time Vinny pulled up in the driveway, Ann had already set the table and was putting garlic

bread into the oven. He came in. "Mmm, that smells great. How soon will it be ready?"

"Just as long as it takes you to wash up and get back in here." There was a lilt in her voice. Vinny was in a good mood tonight.

He brought Lucille back into the kitchen with him and the three of them sat down to eat. As Vinny was reaching for his second helping the phone rang. "Probably service with some messages." He got up from the table and went to the desk in the den to take the call. It was Joe Banshata.

"Hi, Vin, did I interrupt anything?"

"My dinner. What's on your mind?" He was eager to get back to his second helping.

"I have to see you. It's important and private."

"Oh?" Vinny was alerted by the impatient tone in Joe's voice. He couldn't imagine what the problem was. Beatrice was away at college, Mary was alright and he'd seen Jenny outside when he came home.

"Look, I have to talk to you, and immediately. This is something that can't wait. Is it okay with you if I drive over and pick you up after dinner? We can talk while we take a short ride. I know you have hours at seven, but this won't take long."

"Alright, Joe, if it's that urgent."

"Thanks a lot, I appreciate it. See you in twenty minutes."

Vinny went back to the table and scarcely touched his food. What on earth could it be? Joe sounded disturbed . . . and it had to be important if he couldn't talk over the phone.

"Who was it, Vin?"

"An urgent appointment, that's all. I'll have to go." He decided to leave immediately and meet Joe, before Joe left his house. He didn't want Ann to see the car; then she'd ask questions. He gulped down his coffee, backed the car out of the drive and pulled up to Joe's house and waited. Joe had seen Vinny's car so he rushed out to get in; Vinny headed out of Baywater. "Okay, what's up?"

"Vinny, this isn't the sort of thing I like to discuss, and if Jenny found out I'd asked you about such a thing, she'd be furious."

"Get to the point, I'm in a hurry."

"I have an important friend, a professional man, and he has to find a doctor for a client. One who will do an abortion for her. She's in her eighth week. Do you know anyone who could handle it?"

"Good Lord, Joe."

"I heard through the grapevine that there's a doctor in the vicinity who does. Could you make the arrangement?"

"Forget it, Joe, I don't know who it is. Besides, I wouldn't want to get involved."

"I know it's hairy, but I want to help this fellow. A thing like this could ruin his career."

"He should have thought about that before." His voice was dry.

"Yeah, well, you know how it is. Can't you nosy around and see what you can come up with?"

"Offhand I can't think of anyone, but I'll try to find out and call you." He let Joe out by the gates and wiped the sweat off his forehead with his handkerchief. "That was close!"

Joe Banshata was equally upset. He went into his study and placed a call. "Hi, I asked that party about it, but no success so far."

"What the hell am I going to do? Christ, if my wife finds out she'll divorce me; and you know what that will do to my political career."

"You were a damned fool. I can't understand you; at least you should have picked someone out of town . . . I'll keep trying, as one 'goomba' to another."

"I won't forget it. Someday I'll return the favor."

Joe hung up and sat by the phone. He had hoped that Vinny would come through. There was someone else he could call. He had a close friend who would know where to find such useful information. It meant further involvement and it might cost, but there was no other choice. He dialed. "Listen, I need information, the client will pay. Where can we get a medic? The girl's in a family way and they both have families already. Understand?"

"Yeah. Meet me at the entrance of Sayr's Point Restaurant in an hour, and bring fifty dollars cash."

"What will I get for that?"

"A piece of paper with the name you want."

Joe relaxed and took a deep breath. This was better. He made another call. "I'll have something in an hour. Costs you fifty."

"Pay it, make the arrangements. Set the time and place, and she'll be there."

"Right."

Joe went into the kitchen. Jenny was making jello. "I have to take a run down to the plant and check the locks on the back loading door. Maybe I'll stop for a beer on my way." Joe was cautious. He drove to the cleaning plant and made the rounds, then drove to the restaurant, timing himself carefully. He went in, had a beer and chatted with the bartender. He met his informant on the way out. They shook hands and exchanged money for paper. As he passed, the man muttered, "You can make your own arrangements."

He got in his car, unfolded the paper and said, "That bastard!" He headed for a pay phone.

"What's up, Joe? I have patients waiting. If it's about that, I told you I'd make inquiries, but . . ."

Joe interrupted, "I paid fifty dollars for that doc's name. How could you try to put something over on me, your friend?"

At the other end of the wire Vinny blanched. He was stunned and couldn't imagine who had peddled his name to Joe. He had to cover; Joe sounded mad. "Joe, you can understand my position. We're neighbors and social friends, our wives are close."

Joe cut him short. "Let's talk business. When?"

"Ann is going to Meg's later on. Stop by the house at nine-thirty."

At nine-thirty precisely, Joe walked up to the door and rang the buzzer. Vinny let him in and they went into the den.

"Where?" he asked tersely.

"Parson's Village Motel. You know where it is?"

"About twenty miles west. When?"

"Tomorrow night about nine. Tell her to register under the name of Greta Haynes. I'll call to see if she's there and get the room number."

"How much?"

"Three hundred cash. She'd better be alone. Now let me ask you a question. Who is she?"

"What's the difference, Vin?"

"A lot of difference. I have to be sure she won't talk."

Joe walked to the phone and made a call. "It's set except the man wants to know who the girl is and if she can be trusted to keep quiet."

Tony coughed. He resented having to go through this. He was genuinely fond of Pat, but he loved himself and his career more. "Tell him it's my secretary, Pat. She'll keep quiet."

Joe whistled. "You sure mess things up! . . . Well, I'll see you in the morning with the details. Have the money. Three hundred plus the fifty I laid out, and tell her it's set for tomorrow night."

He turned to Vinny. "It's Tony Di Pasco, and the girl is his secretary, Pat. She's a very closed-mouth broad."

"Wow! Tony. Well, alright. Tomorrow night at 8:30 meet me in the parking lot at my office with a rented car, but not in my name. I'll drop you at a bar and pick you up when I'm through." He was surprised that Tony would have gotten caught in this stupid situation.

"Okay, I'll see you tomorrow."

Vinny sat a long time with his head in his hands. What a mess. He didn't dare cross Tony and Joe. Now that Joe knew about him, he had no choice. He'd have to go through with it.

❧

The next evening Joe Banshata met Vinny on schedule and handed him the three hundred dollars. "Have you got coverage, in case anyone asks where you are?"

"Yes."

"I'm not going to a bar though. When you're done, drive to the railroad station. Someone else will meet you, someone I trust with my life, although he won't know the situation. He'll drive you back to the office. I'm not taking chances on this thing fouling up."

That night Vinny called the motel from a pay phone. Pat was in room five. Vinny hadn't told her who he was, only that he was coming directly, and she was both relived and surprised when she saw it was Vinny. Somehow she felt better, but her voice trembled when she spoke. "I think I'm about eight weeks."

"No problem. This should be very minor. You'll be up and around by morning . . . but Pat, are you certain you want to abort?"

"Oh, yes, of course . . . Tony is very upset . . . He wants that nomination for judgeship so bad he can taste it . . . we can't take any chances. Once he's got the judgeship he'll get a divorce and we can get married."

Vinny turned away from her abruptly and spread a plastic sheet on the bed. He rummaged in his bag thinking, "That shit, promising her marriage." He knew Tony was pacifying her, to be sure she'd go through the abortion without causing him scandal and divorce, which could only hurt his career.

He gave her an injection to make her sleep. It would take him twenty minutes. He changed his shirt for a disposable one and slipped on a pair of gloves. He cleaned her out; everything seemed normal. He lit a cigarette and waited to be certain she was alright. Suddenly she began to bleed heavily. He gave her an injection, but it didn't subside. "What the hell should I do?" he thought. If he took her to a hospital he'd be responsible. How could he explain? The bleeding continued profusely. Cutting the placenta was dangerous enough, but this kind of hemorrhaging indicated she was a bleeder. He should have known something would go wrong. He took her pulse. It was faint. He was panicky and could only think of himself. Self preservation prevailed. He'd have to leave her. Maybe he could call anonymously and get an ambulance. No one knew he was here but Joe Banshata; Joe hadn't told Tony who the doctor was. Besides, maybe Tony would be glad to get rid of her, she might be a noose around his neck. Joe would say nothing; not incriminate himself. Vinny had done all he could for her and could see no reason to jeopardize his career and family life. Maybe it would look like she had tried to abort herself. He peeked out from behind the drapes. There was no one around; he

packed his equipment, put on his shirt and tucked the disposable top in his bag, then slipped out unobtrusively.

Back on the road he toyed with the idea of making an anonymous call, but he was afraid to stop; somebody might see him, and by this time, it wouldn't do much good anyhow. He was reasonably sure Pat would be beyond help by the time help arrived. He rationalized that he had done all he could, anxious to shed the guilty feeling that nagged him. Anyway, maybe it was justification and she was only getting what she deserved. If he found Ann playing around behind his back, he'd probably kill her. He held to the European belief that a wife shouldn't play around, but that it was a man's world and the same values didn't hold true.

Vinny, himself, indulged in his own carnal and strange desires and didn't see himself as weak or selfish. He gave in to his every whim and desire, regardless of cost. He had a lucrative practice, but his indulgences outside of his home kept him open to means of making money that a more scrupulous doctor might avoid. He was a lavish tipper and a big spender; the best restaurants and clothes, expensive women, and a big car. Ann went without a car and a fully decorated house, and had the impression that the Baywater style of living and taxes ate up most of his income.

When he arrived at the railroad station, a thin, wiry man was waiting for him. Wordlessly he indicated a car and drove Vinny back to his parking lot. Then he went back to the station, switched cars again and returned the rental. Vinny went into the building and called Ann to say he'd be home shortly. A patient came in, an appointment, his cover, and he knew he was safe. He was three hundred dollars richer and no one was any wiser. Too bad about Pat, he thought, but it couldn't be helped. Fifteen minutes later he went home to bed.

Back at the motel, Pat had regained consciousness. She turned her head feebly and realized she was alone. She tried to move but felt very weak and seemed to be bleeding far too much. She knew that her life was slipping away with every tick of her watch. Why had the doctor left her like this? Then it dawned on her. He had abandoned her so as not to

involve himself . . . not to ruin his career. Wryly she thought this was the very reason she was here, to protect a man's career.

She had strength and courage and wouldn't give in. She looked around, weaker now. The phone was on the table beside the bed. She struggled to stretch her arm out; it was inches away but her hand couldn't make the last few inches. Somehow she'd have to move, but she couldn't get her body to respond. "Oh, God," she thought, "I'm going to die here alone like this." She struggled frantically and managed to get a little closer, but the phone was still out of reach, her fingers barely touching it. Eternities of struggling made her bleed more and she felt the full impact of the situation. No one would find her till the maid came to clean in the morning. All sorts of thoughts tumbled through her tired mind. Perhaps it would be easier to lie here and let the warmth ooze out, the darkness engulf her, and have peace.

But she refused to do that. She had to hang on and try again. Minutes raced by; the phone mocked her, looming like a distorted shadow eluding her grasp. Her groping fingers touched the Bible and a heavy ash tray. With all her strength she pushed. Everything went tumbling: ash tray, Bible, phone; even the lamp tilted and crashed to the floor. Pat no longer heard anything; she was suspended in a cloud of darkness swaying back and forth as though she were in a cradle . . . the cradle of death, where neither pain nor disgrace, fear nor trouble, could reach her again.

The night clerk at the desk answered the buzz of the switchboard. No one was on the line, but he was sure he had heard the sound of something falling. He listened, but heard nothing and assumed someone had knocked over a phone, so he disconnected the lines from the board. Room five. Being curious and bored, he looked at the register card. That occupant was the young woman, Haynes, who had been jittery. He wondered if she was meeting a man here for the first time; that would account for her nervous behavior. Then he remembered she had a call earlier. He had worked these jobs long enough to know that peculiar things happened in motel rooms. He decided to investigate, took a pass key and opened the door a crack. If all was in order he'd slip away unnoticed. Although the bulb had shattered when the lamp had hit the floor, there was enough light from the bathroom to see

an inert shape on the bed in a pool of blood. For one moment he stood motionless in stupefaction, then ran back to the office and called the police and hospital to try to save Greta Haynes' life.

CHAPTER 5
FALL
ELECTIONS

There had been a brief spell of bad weather followed by the rift of Indian Summer. Mrs. Tooker had made an appointment with Ester Fine to show her the house in Baywater, and they arrived at a time when the children were in school, and the community was serene. Ester was impressed with the elegance of the homes distinctly placed on large parcels of property, the marina, club, pool, beach and tennis courts; but above all, she liked the one-story house with the decorative grilled-iron railing. Now as they walked around the pool area, Mrs. Tooker wondered about Ester's ability to finance the house, but thought it better to wait to ask until she was sure Ester wanted to purchase it.

Lenore observed this odd pair from her sun deck. It occurred to her the stranger might be the head "Administrative Nurse of Student Nursing" at the Brookview Hospital whom Janet had mentioned. As Lenore sat waiting for Ray Dowling and Mark Harrison, she watched the two of them meander and poke about, then finally depart. Then her thoughts turned to Robbie. The two educators were coming to discuss Robbie's college studies. Her prayers had been answered and Robbie was accepted for the fall semester. He had done superbly on his entrance exams and the dean had been impressed. She looked at her watch. "They should have been here by now," she thought, and glanced up the street once more. There was no sign of a car so she went inside and called the airfield.

"This is Lenore Akton." It was characteristic of her to use her professional name.

"Yes, ma'am. Want the plane?"

"Not today, but early tomorrow morning. Can you get it ready and check the brakes?"

"Sure thing. Where are you headed?"

"To Orange to take shots of the big parachute jump. Why?"

"No particular reason, but the weather is due to change and I don't want to leave the plane out overnight."

"I'll check conditions in the morning, very early, and if it's wet or foggy, I'll call you at home." As she hung up she thought how easily men accepted women flying these days. She remembered back to their first dinner party in the mansion and how surprised Charles had been to hear that she had brought her plane from California to Long Island. Apparently Charles didn't think a woman's place was in the air. She chuckled. But it was a great convenience being able to fly and penetrate remote areas for pictures and stories. Besides, she loved the freedom and peace she found in the air; it was her sanctuary. She took out her camera and checked her equipment.

Ray Dowling had arrived while she was on the phone. As he stepped out of his car, he saw Mark pull in the drive behind him.

"Afternoon Ray. Beautiful day, isn't it?"

Ray nodded. "Not many more like this left this year."

"Have you seen Lenore?"

"No, I arrived a minute before you. I was held up in a meeting with one of the teachers."

"Not Sally Kendrick?" Mark asked softly.

"What made you ask that?" Ray was startled.

"I know it's none of my business, but she does teach in your school and it's creating a lot of gossip. I've heard from some of the teachers that Sally announced you were getting a divorce and intend to marry her. There's isn't any truth in that, is there?"

"Yes, it's true. Ethel and I have been to see our lawyer. We've agreed on a settlement. I'm flying to Mexico for the divorce over Thanksgiving, and Sally and I will get married as soon as I return."

Mark was stunned. "Good Lord, Ray, do you think that's wise?

She's so young."

Ray was annoyed at Mark's comment. "As you said, it's none of your businesses. Please don't interfere."

Mark flushed and apologized. "I only meant to be helpful."

Ray backed down. "I understand Mark. You see me as a foolish old man. Well, perhaps I am, but I love Sally and don't want life to pass me by. I'm providing for Ethel, she'll never have to worry about support. And as far the community, they have to accept the fact that all kinds of people get divorced these days . . . even principals."

"I can see you've made up your mind emphatically, Ray, but . . ."

Both of them turned at the sound of footsteps scraping on the porch. Lenore and Robbie had come outside. Robbie saw the papers in Ray's hand and raced toward him. Roma had pushed the door open and now trailed behind Robbie, her tail wagging as she sauntered. "Are those for me?" the young voice called.

"For your mom." He handed Lenore the papers. "Fill these out, Lenore, and send them along with a check for eighteen hundred dollars to the college registrar's office." He turned to Robbie. "Now you're all set!"

Mark added, "I'll get your books for you tomorrow. The professors have agreed they will be available to give you extra help if you need it, but the dean said he doubts you will, having seen your entrance exams. You scored in the highest five percent . . . You will have to go in for final exams though, and you'll have to catch up on the two weeks you've already missed."

"Wow, when do I start?"

"As soon as you have your books. I'll bring you outlines of the courses and what you are to do."

"You're legally enrolled once the college has these papers and the check," Ray reminded them.

"I'll take care of it right away," Lenore answered.

They said their good-byes and Lenore thanked them for all they had done to make this possible, and Robbie, in a flurry of excitement, ran up the stairs into the house and yelled, "Wait till I tell Peter I start

college this week!" He left Roma barking outside the door, forgotten.

Lenore had never seen him so excited and her eyes filled with tears, her face glowed and her entire being throbbed in jubilation at her son's happiness.

∾⌇

Charles sat back in his chair and observed Ester Fine as she studied the legal documents. She was a big woman, tall and heavy, her short hair was severely cut and she was neatly dressed in a navy suit. She wasn't pretty and appeared to be aloof and mistrustful. When she had filled out her mortgage application, they'd discovered that she was a reasonably wealthy woman, and further investigation revealed she received a monthly check from California, and her brother was Dr. Morris Fine, one of the country's most prominent heart surgeons, a possible Nobel Prize winner.

"They seem to be in order."

"That's what I told you," said her attorney, Sam Bernstein, and he handed her his pen. She signed the documents slowly and methodically.

After some checks had been passed around, Charles stood up. "Welcome to Baywater, Miss Fine," and handed her keys to the house. Sam and the title searcher congratulated her.

Janet, who had been sitting in the corner, bubbled, "Let's have a drink to celebrate!"

"Sorry," said Sam, but I have another closing in an hour." He shoved some papers into his briefcase hastily.

The title searcher added, "Can't. I've got to run back to the office." The two men belted toward the door at the same time, but the young title searcher, out of respect for the older, balding attorney, stood aside and allowed him room to pass through first, then followed.

"I guess that leaves the three of us," Janet chimed. "Where shall we go?"

Charles stood up and buzzed his secretary. "I hate to disappoint you dear, but I have to drive over to Family Court and see a judge." His

secretary came in with some papers for him to sign. "You two go ahead and celebrate. You must have a lot to discuss. You'll never miss me!"

"Oh, fluff, Charles, we will," and she leaned close and gave him a kiss. "See you later."

"Thanks for everything," Ester added. "I'm sure the closing went smoothly due to your diligence, Mr. Henderson."

Charles' secretary smiled at Ester, and Charles grinned in appreciation of the fine compliment.

Once in the elevator, the women agreed to celebrate the closing with a drink at a new lounge on the other side of town. On the way to their cars, they discussed various topics, and Janet found Ester politically astute, well informed on current issues, and most enthusiastic about Laureen Wallace's victory in her party's bid for the governorship. As they entered the parking lot, Ester suggested that she follow Janet in her car. They crossed town and parked in the lot next to the lounge, and as they walked to the doorway, Ester asked if Charles was interested in politics.

"Since Charles has changed parties we've been attending a lot of political functions. It's going to be an exhausting winter if we keep this pace."

"Do you go with him all the time?"

"No, it depends on the occasion, but he wants me to go more often. I don't like them, and he gets so involved talking with people at these affairs that I'm left alone."

They walked into the lounge and went toward a table. Janet was surprised to see Meg sitting in a booth with a man; she didn't know whether to ignore her or say hello. Before reaching a decision, Meg noticed her and called, "Hi, Janet, come on over." Ester had sat down across the room and Janet motioned her she'd join her in a moment. Meg's companion was about thirty-two; he had red hair and a gentle smile. She had never seen him before. Meg was amused by Janet's puzzled

expression. "Janet Henderson, Reverend Richard's son, Kerry. Kerry is up from Virginia."

"Nice to meet you, Mr. Richard."

"The pleasure's all mine, and please, call me Kerry."

Janet smiled. "How's the church show coming, Meg?"

"We were just discussing it. Kerry is giving us some help while on his visit. You're coming to see it, aren't you?"

"I wouldn't miss it for the world!"

Janet indicated Ester. "Meg, that's our new neighbor, Ester Fine," then seeing that Ester was giving her order to the waitress, continued, "I'll introduce you another time. Nice meeting you, Kerry."

She went to her table and she and Ester chatted about the house, but Janet was distracted by the serious expression on Meg's face. She watched them, Meg and Kerry, for a moment and thought they looked as though they were locked in a "no time" capsule, that a clock had stopped for them; they seemed to be sharing a world of their own. Janet was alarmed. The intimacy of the scene made her uncomfortable. Kerry looked at Meg adoringly and Meg's attention to him indicated that she was not unresponsive. The waitress came to the table with Ester's drink, took her order and left, reappearing a few minutes later to serve her.

As Ester talked about drapes and asked about decorating ideas, wild thoughts tumbled through her mind. She knew Meg was a sensible woman and good wife, but she felt a strange discomfort watching her, and Janet found it difficult to concentrate on her own conversation.

Driving back to Baywater later, she rationalized that Meg liked to flirt, but Meg herself had once said she was "happily married." Janet scolded herself mentally for having had any ridiculous thoughts.

Back in the booth in the lounge, the serious mood prevailed. Kerry folded his hand over Meg's. "I'll be sorry to see the rehearsals end."

"Yes, me too. It's been fun, and you've been a good friend for me. I feel as though I've known you a long time, Kerry."

"Do you?" His voice changed. He squeezed her hand lightly and took her other hand. Meg looked down at the intertwined hands, a slow blush rose to her cheeks. She didn't want to meet his eyes.

"It's more than harmony and friendship between us Meg, I'm in love with you," he whispered.

Meg's voice trembled, "Kerry, we're both married, you shouldn't talk like that."

He continued, "In name only. I married a girl with whom I went through school, but we've both changed as we've grown older, and things haven't worked out. This last year's been intolerable. I go out drinking almost every night to get away from her."

"Oh Kerry, I'm sorry. But have you honestly put an effort into the marriage to try and make it work?"

"Yes, we even went to a marriage counselor. I've tried, but I've outgrown her. All she wants to be is a little girl all her life. I've tried, for my son."

"How old is he?"

"Three, let me show you," he reached into his wallet and handed her a photograph.

"How adorable. Don't you think he's worth saving the marriage for?"

"Naturally, Meg, that's why I've done everything under the sun to stay with her, but it's no good. We live in the same house. She goes her way and I go mine. And I'm not sure that's the right way to bring up a child. Dad thinks I'm irresponsible and drink too much. In his day people were taught to keep a marriage together at any price, but I can't accept that philosophy. It didn't matter that much before, there wasn't anybody else. But now that I've met you, I don't think I can go back to living with her." He cupped her face in his hands. "I love you."

Meg drew away. She was aware that Kerry had been attracted to her from the beginning, but she didn't now how to handle her feelings. "Toby and I have a good marriage and we have four boys. It's too late for you and me, don't you see? You should go back if only for your son's sake."

"Meg, you haven't denied that you love me. If you do love me, then we should be together. Going back is wrong for both of us."

"No, there's too much at stake, it's too late for us," she repeated.

She longed to tell him that her marriage was a big mistake, that all the responsibility of raising her sons was on her shoulders, that Toby was away so much and paid little attention to her when he was home, that she hadn't felt like this in years and that she returned his love. But she knew it would only give him added impetus to persuade her to leave Toby and break up her home.

"If you want to stay with Toby and raise your sons, I won't interfere, Meg, but I love you, and if you ever need me, for anything, at any time, my sweet, I'll never be more than a phone call away."

She appreciated his honesty. "Since we have to keep working on the play together, you can't let your feelings for me show, particularly in front of your parents. I have to go on living here and seeing them every week."

"Whatever you say, my dearest."

Meg looked at her watch. "Heavens! I have to go. Toby may be home and it will be difficult to explain where I've been for so long." She was frightened.

"I'll see you tomorrow then. Take care."

Meg speeded to Baywater. She wanted to take Sarah home before Toby arrived, but as she swung in the driveway she saw his car. She straightened her shoulders and opened the door. Toby was in the hallway and said questioningly, "I got home a few minutes ago. Where have you been?"

"At church, discussing the finishing touches on the play. I'll take the sitter home."

"Hm, how much did that cost?"

"Oh, you said you didn't mind my working at the church."

"I know, but I didn't think it would take up that much of your time. Take the kids with you. They're so damned noisy, and I need a nap. It was a rough flight."

She rounded up the children, took money from her bag to pay Sarah, and went out to the car. The boys were boisterous and at that

moment she wished she had daughters. She'd heard somewhere that boys were the result of an over-sexy, aggressive father, but Toby wasn't over-sexy. It was usually Meg who was the aggressor. Donald, the eldest at nine, was most like Toby. Lawrence was six and a nervous youngster, uncertain about everything he did, a trait he had inherited from her. Andrew was a happy, blonde three-year-old, and Kenneth a year-and-a-half-old baby.

She dropped Sarah off and returned to Baywater. Toby was sound asleep so she took the children outside. The older boys promised to play away from the bedroom window where Toby was sleeping. She put Kenneth in the stroller and took Andrew by the hand and proceeded down the street. As she passed the Rufone's house, she noticed Vinny's car in the drive and wondered what he was doing home early. Then she heard screaming voices and knew whatever the problem was, it had to be serious enough to bring him home to quarrel.

The door flung open. "You bitch! I've had about enough of you," and he leaped in his car and drove away, oblivious to Meg's presence down the street.

As she passed the Henderson's she heard Janet's voice calling, "Come on in and have a cup of coffee."

Meg picked up Kenneth and carried him inside on one arm, while Andrew tottered along holding her other hand. As they were undoing the children's outer garments, the phone rang and Janet answered it.

"Don't cry, Ann, maybe something went wrong at the hospital and he's taking it out on you. Have you tried talking with him? Maybe he wants a chance to unload what's on his mind." She was silent. Then, "I know, Ann. Charles comes home many a night in a bad mood because something didn't go his way in court or there was an unexpected problem. You have to expect these things when you're married to a professional man. Get hold of yourself, and if you feel like it, come by. Meg stopped in and we're having coffee." She paused. "All right. I'm glad you feel better."

After she hung up she answered Meg's quizzical expression. "Vinny's been out of sorts lately and keeps picking on her. She said he's drinking a lot. I hope it's only a temporary thing . . . Maybe some of his investments

went sour." She picked Andrew up and hugged him. "How are our beautiful boys today?" She swung him back and forth and he laughed excitedly. Then she sat down and took Kenneth in her arms. "What a good baby." In a few minutes she had given Kenneth back to Meg and put coffee and cookies out. She gave Andrew a glass of milk.

They talked about the Halloween party and Meg asked, "Why wasn't Ester Fine there? I was looking forward to meeting her."

"She's still in the process of moving, and perhaps she's not as sociable as we thought."

"Well, she missed a good party."

Janet giggled, "Yes, but I was afraid Dan O'Quinn would spear Kim for winning that huge basket of cheer."

Meg chuckled and added, "And that Roman gladiator costume wasn't cheap to rent."

"Trust Kim to pick the right costume, a shimmering mermaid."

"You mean a shimmering mermaid who almost landed in the pool. Good thing Charles and Thompson held Dan back from throwing her in."

As they laughed uproariously, Andrew began to whine. Meg dressed the boys in their coats and thanked Janet for the coffee. She left in a good mood and felt relaxed enough to be able to cope with an irritable husband.

The following weeks were busy ones, especially for Charles. He was devoting a great deal of time and money to the election campaign. He rarely came home for dinner and by the time he did get to the house, he was exhausted from a long meeting or speaking engagement. Most of the people who heard his speeches liked him and believed in him. His quiet, soft-spoken manner won the people over quickly and the Republican leaders invited him to introduce the candidates, or speak for them if they couldn't make an affair due to another engagement. While Charles neglected his practice, his sincerity in answering questions at local meetings and his verbal reasons for endorsing these candidates proved

to be an asset not only for the party, but for his practice as well. It resulted in new clients deluging the office, and his partners had to work nights to catch up on the amount of work that Charles' popularity brought in.

After elections were over and the celebrations ended, the victors went away to rest from the arduous campaigning. For Charles, however, there was little rest; his practice was very busy. Now he had awakened to the potential in politics as well. He ran into Tony Di Pasco in the lunchroom shortly after the election, and Tony rebuffed him. He knew that Tony was disappointed not getting a judgeship and was probably angry that Charles had assisted in an election that had defeated his team. No one was aware how bitter Tony was, having sacrificed his personal life for the hope of judgeship. He had been fortunate not to have been linked with Pat's death. Alfred, her husband, had assumed he was the father of the unborn baby and believed that Pat just did not want a baby as yet. Tony had lost Pat, his marriage had gone sour, and the disappointment of the judgeship had been a severe blow.

Meg's *First Thanksgiving* play at the church was a big success. After the curtain calls, they demanded her appearance on stage, and Reverend Richard and the children presented her with a large bouquet of roses in appreciation of her efforts. Although her eyes were bright and her smile broad, she felt a twinge of disappointment. She couldn't help thinking how wonderful it would have been to have Kerry there beside her. She missed him.

Janet and Charles spent Thanksgiving with Lenore's family, along with Mark, and Russell and Claudia Howard, whose children were spending the weekend at their grandmother's. After dinner, they had adjourned to the library for coffee and after-dinner drinks. Mark lit the fireplace, and soon the flames blazed bright hues of color into the air. Lenore went upstairs to see if Peter wanted anything. He was in bed early every night now, reading and watching TV before he fell asleep.

The library was mellow and comfortable and Janet poured coffee or drinks as Charles sank into a chair. Claudia was chatting with Charles. "You must have heard that the Dowling's divorce came through and Ray married Sally. Seems he hurried the divorce so they could be married before the holidays."

103

"Who handled it?" asked Janet.

"Tony Di Pasco," Mark informed them. "I think Ray was embarrassed about having Charles handle it, since you know both so well."

"Ha," snorted Russ, "from what I've heard, he figured that Tony might be more understanding about the 'other woman.' Ethel and the boy, Austin, are at the old house, and the poor kid is so humiliated that he won't see his father."

"That's not unusual." Charles rubbed the back of his neck. "Seventeen is a sensitive age."

"It's unfortunate," Claudia responded.

Mark stretched lazily. "Ray and Sally bought a small house in Sayr's Point."

"I wonder how that marriage is going to turn out." Janet was pensive. "What a surprise that was!"

Lenore had come back into the library and heard her question. "Not good, I'm afraid." Then she fell silent, oblivious to the quizzical faces turned to her direction.

Russ swung the subject to politics, "Say, don't you think Edward Brooke's winning is something? Never expected to see that, in Massachusetts of all places."

Charles answered, "He's the first Negro United States Senator in eighty-five years, an indication that changes are coming." He stood up and stretched his arms.

Mark replied, "People are becoming more liberal."

"Possibly," Charles yawned. "Would you mind if I went home? I have an early appointment tomorrow."

"Of course not, Charles," Lenore replied.

"Do you mind if I stay, Charles?" Janet asked.

"There's no reason to run off, and Mark can drop you off," Lenore insisted.

Charles agreed. After he left they chatted on, then Emma came in to see if they'd like more pie.

Russ stood up, "Sure, Emma, I'd love some!"

"You can't be hungry already!" Claudia wailed.

"I'll work it off tomorrow, don't worry."

"By then you'll have gained five pounds."

"Well, there's always tonight?" and Russ ducked as Claudia threw a pillow at him. He went into the kitchen with Emma and sat at the large oak trestle table next to Robbie, and they ate pie.

"I'd suggest if we can't fight him, we join him," piped Mark, eager to have another helping, and they got up and trooped into the kitchen laughing.

CHAPTER 6
CHRISTMAS 1966 TO EASTER 1967

Janet pulled the blanket closer about her neck, then checked the time on the clock on the night stand. It was almost ten a.m. and still cold. She wondered how Charles could get up at six-thirty to jog in such freezing weather. She shivered at the thought of it. The phone rang and she leaned over to answer it.

She lifted the receiver and said, "Hello."

"Morning, Jan." Meg's voice was strained, and she rushed on. "Toby called and said he has to take an extra flight. Somebody's out ill and Toby owes him a favor; he won't be home tonight or Christmas Day," she moaned in disappointment.

Janet slipped out of bed and placed her feet in her pink, furry slippers and grabbed for her robe. The chilly air made her shudder. "How awful Meg. It's unfortunate, but at least you have the children. Poor Toby will have to spend Christmas in a strange place by himself." She knew Meg was bitterly unhappy. "Where does he have to fly?"

"He's in Seattle now, and tomorrow night he has to fly to Atlanta, then back to Washington, then the next day on to New York."

Janet thought quickly. "We're planning to find a Christmas tree this evening," she fibbed, "then come back and decorate it. Would you and the boys care to join us, or do you have your own to do?"

"No, we put ours up early." Her spirits perked up. "I'd have to see about a sitter for the baby and Andrew. We could take Donald and Lawrence along if you wouldn't mind."

"That would be fine, Meg. Charles likes the boys and it will be more fun having them with us. Supposing we pick you up at seven?"

"You're a dear, Janet. Thanks a million."

Janet hurried to get into town before the stores were mobbed. She needed ornaments and trimmings for the tree, more gifts, and candy canes. A festive spirit filled her. It would be a real Christmas with children around the house. The stores were already crowded and Christmas carols were heard in the streets and stores. Most of the best toys were gone and she had difficulty finding suitable gifts for the boys. The day passed quickly.

Charles came home to an empty house and wondered where Janet had gone. He made himself a drink and relaxed for a while, then heard her car pull in the driveway. He opened the front door, and Janet stood there barely visible behind boxes. She giggled joyously as they began to slide out of her arms. "There are lots more in the car."

Charles noticed that her face was rosy and her eyes sparkled. "What's all this?"

"Ornaments, presents and Christmas candy," and she told him about Meg and the boys being alone for Christmas. "We're going to have our first big Christmas tree!" she announced.

Charles was delighted, and the tension between them of late fell away as they chatted excitedly about the coming evening and carried the packages inside. Janet prepared dinner and they ate hurriedly so they could wrap some of them.

At seven o'clock they stopped by Meg's house and waited for her and the two elder boys. Finally Janet leaned over and honked the horn, much to Charles' annoyance, but a minute later the door opened and the boys came running out, with Meg following a short distance behind. Charles opened the rear door and the boys climbed in.

"Are we going to help decorate your tree after we buy it?" asked Donald in a breathless voice, checking to see if what he had heard was true.

"You bet we are!" replied Charles. "Now move over so your mother can have room."

The car lights shone on Meg. The hood of the rich velvet cape enhanced the beauty of her face, and the swirling folds enveloped her body. After she stepped inside and pulled the door closed, Charles started the

car moving.

He headed toward the village, and once there they saw people bustling about, many still doing last-minute shopping. The streets were crowded with cars, and there was no place to park. Finally Charles found a parking spot near a large display and said, "Well fellows, let's go pick a tree!" and the boys jumped up and out of the car, following in Charles' footsteps.

Meg and Janet watched them as they moved from tree to tree, carefully inspecting each tree from all sides; the height, thickness, and merits of each, until finally they chose one. Charles paid for the tree and it was tied to the back of the car. They drove home slowly so it wouldn't fall off, and they sang Christmas carols en route.

Once back home, Charles moved the living room chairs to make a place for the tree. The boys opened the boxes of ornaments and lights, and it wasn't long before tinsel and tissue were strewn about the room. The three of them made a procedure about trimming the tree, carefully deciding which ornament should go where. Once in a while they turned to Janet and Meg for their opinions and suggestions.

Two hours later, tired but pleased with themselves, they sat back to view their efforts. The angel at the top presided over the cascading tinsel, glittering ornaments and tempting candy canes. Charles turned on the light switch and the tree came alive. Janet turned off the table lamp to enhance the glowing tree. The flickering lights and the colorful bulbs on the Christmas tree highlighted the fullness of its branches.

Donald stared in awe and put his head on his mother's shoulder. In a whisper that was barely audible he said, "Isn't that beautiful, mother?"

Meg folded her arms around the boy and laid her cheek against his forehead. She was wearing a ruby velvet dress and Janet watched them and thought of the Madonna and child, and the real meaning of Christmas.

Meg said, "It's almost midnight. I'd better get these two home."

Charles got their coats, and as soon as they were bundled up he and Janet brought in gifts for them to take home.

The children's eyes widened when they saw the packages. "Are these for us?" Lawrence asked.

"Yes darlings," Janet replied.

Meg kissed Janet and said, "Thanks for a wonderful evening. Thank you, too, Charles. You both have been very kind."

The boys piled into Charles's car, their arms clutching the gifts, and as Charles backed the car out of the driveway, Meg rolled the window down and called back to Janet standing on the porch, "Merry Christmas!" Janet waved and then went inside to the warmth of the house.

When Charles returned, he was in a jovial mood. "Let's stop by Lenore's and wish them a Merry Christmas." They drove by the mansion, but it was in darkness, so Janet suggested they go to Sayr's Point and attend midnight service.

Charles headed the car out the gates. The town was ablaze with lights and decorations, and people were still coming and going. Carillons chimed as they pulled into the parking lot behind the old white church. They hurried inside and found seats for the service. Most of the pews were filled, and at each pew there stood a tall, magnificently beautiful, gold candelabra decorated with red ribbons and evergreen. Through the soft glow of candlelight they saw many friends and business acquaintances.

The service began as the Minister stepped to the podium and announced the hymn, and the choir processional came down the middle aisle, their voices filled with the glory and spirit of this holy night. The service was short, and afterward the minister greeted all the worshipers individually and wished them Merry Christmas. On their way out of church, Janet and Charles chatted briefly with the minister, then stood on the steps of the old, white wooden building and exchanged season's greetings with their friends. Later, they returned to Baywater.

Meg was still awake when Janet and Charles drove by toward their house. She was staring out the living room window, her thoughts sad and blue. For months she had been saving a little money each week from her household budget in order to buy Toby a black sapphire ring he had seen and liked. Her eyes fixed themselves on the little red box with the gold ribbon under the tree. She thought disconsolately that the gift would mean less once the holiday ended. She sighed and looked down the street at the bright lights around doors and windows twinkling

merrily. Loneliness engulfed her. As a car came closer she saw falling snow reflected in the headlights. She went into the den and waited impatiently for the phone to ring, but Toby never called, and as dawn broke, she climbed the stairs to bed.

It seemed like only moments later that the children burst into her room, screaming with delight. They had taken down their Christmas stockings and were waiting for her to get up so they could open their presents. Meg pushed herself up, still exhausted, dressed and went downstairs. The children screamed excitedly as they opened their gifts. Then they gave her their gift, a woolly robe with matching slipper socks.

After breakfast they played with their toys, and as she picked up wrappings from the floor, Meg thought about Toby's gift. She wondered if she should leave the little box under the tree with the other gifts or put it under his pillow or in his jacket pocket. She decided that the jacket pocket would be the best place. He always put on his old sports jacket when he came home from a flight, and she could imagine his surprised expression when he'd find the box. She scooped it up and hurried to the hall closet. She pushed the coats aside and tried to slip the box into the pocket, but it wouldn't fit. She put her hand inside the pocket and pulled out a bulky paper, then slipped the box in.

She turned away satisfied, glancing briefly at an envelope in her hand. It was addressed to Mrs. Toby Marshall, 11 Paquit Road, Seattle, Washington, in Toby's handwriting. She turned the envelope over and noticed the return address to himself at the airline's office. She was puzzled, so she tore the envelope open; two thin sheets of paper fell out. She bent to pick them up and her eyes focused on the words, "Dear Corrine." Her hands trembled as she read, "I'm sorry we couldn't spend Thanksgiving together, but when the airline calls, I have to fly. I'll try to make it up to you somehow darling. I miss you very much. Maybe when I get a few days off we can go to Acapulco. I don't like being away from you any more than I have to, my pet. Can you forgive me? See you soon. Love, Toby."

Meg stared at the paper. "Dear God, what is this?" She picked up the envelope again. Who was Corrine? She had to find out. She called information.

111

The number was unlisted and she shook with despair. Then she remembered the time she had called Toby at the airlines and the girl had reluctantly given her an unlisted number. She went to her room and pulled open the drawer of the night table, fumbling for the address book. There it was. Palm 4-7655. The operator put the call through. The line was ringing and she was about to hang up when a woman's voice said, "Hello?" Meg was uncertain and confused. "I'm sorry, I may have the wrong number."

"What number do you want?"

"Palm 4-7655."

"This is that number. Can I help you?"

"I'm looking for a Mr. Toby Marshall. Do you have any idea where I can locate him?" She tried to collect herself.

"This is Mrs. Marshall, Mr. Marshall was called on flight and he won't be back for a few days. Is it urgent?"

Meg groped for an excuse. "I'm . . . from the lost and found at the terminal. Someone found a Gulf credit card issued to Mr. Marshall, and fortunately they turned it in."

"Oh, I see. You can mail it here if you like."

"No, if he's away, I'll send it to the airline's office and he can pick it up there. Sorry to have troubled you."

"That's alright. Thank you for calling." The woman hung up.

Meg sat and stared at the phone in bewilderment. Her mind, broken in bits and pieces like parts of a distorted jigsaw puzzle, whirled darkly; her body trembled and hands perspired. Concentration sapped her strength, but she tried to gather her wits and think clearly. Then slowly, gradually, bit by bit the pieces assembled and fell in place in an orderly fashion.

She began to understand many things; his indifference to her needs, his aloofness toward her and the children, the abrupt trips, the long days away. Yet he always had a plausible explanation. She was not suspicious by nature and accepted his word. He had been able to lead a double life, and cover his tracks. Obviously he was living with another woman, this Corrine. "God, what am I going to do? And what about the children?" She pressed her fist into her mouth to muffle a scream. How

could Toby create such a predicament? She had heard of insane situations like this, but to be involved in one yourself was an incredible nightmare.

The emotional impact was overwhelming. She trembled violently and slipped back on the bed. She was weak and limp and the words, "This is Mrs. Marshall, Mr. Marshall was called on flight . . ." rang over and over in her ears, blotting out every other sound. She shuddered, images crossing her mind: Toby turning away from her in bed, his reluctance to put his arms around her or kiss her when he left, the cool, distant attitude that prevailed when he came home.

She visualized him holding this other woman in his arms, making love to her, having breakfast together . . . her head ached painfully. She curled herself up tightly and buried her face in the pillow so the children would not hear the wracking sobs. Toby had said he liked to fly because he felt free, and now she wondered if he had meant free of her and the boys. She wept in self pity and knew that there was no way she could blot this ugly truth from her mind. She suffered grief for her children and felt a consuming hate for Toby and this Corrine.

Her sobs quieted down. She pushed herself off the bed, staggered into the bathroom and splashed water on her tear-streaked, swollen face. Carefully she applied makeup to hide the ravages of her weeping. She moved toward the door, mystified as to what she should do . . . then went back to the phone to call Charles for advice.

Robbie was closest to the phone when it rang. "It's for you Uncle Charles," and he held the receiver out for him.

He shook his head. "Who could be calling me here?" but he took the receiver and put it to his ear. He said very little, but listened intently; a worried expression crossed is face. He put the receiver down and said, "You'll have to excuse me for awhile, there is something I must do."

Janet wailed, "On Christmas day? Can't it wait?"

Charles grimaced, "Something urgent has come up. I'll be back shortly. I won't be gone long."

Peter walked with him to the door to let him out, and when Peter came back in the room Janet exploded, "I can understand being concerned about clients, but their bothering him here on Christmas day is going too far!"

"She probably called your house and when there was no answer assumed you'd both be here."

"She?" Janet raised her eyebrows. "Do you know who it was?"

"No, but her voice sounded familiar and she was upset."

Janet sighed, then the conversation turned to the weather and the latest news. Emma stalled dinner till Charles came back. He had to leave his wet shoes in the hallway and sit by the fireplace with his stocking feet near the heat. To forestall any questions about his errand, he said, "Think I'll go skiing tomorrow. It would be a sin to waste that five inches of snow outdoors."

The fire was warm and cast a glow through the room. The day was gloomy and though it was early, the house was dusky. The flames shot strange shadows on the walls and flickering lights danced across their faces.

"Another year is almost over," Peter sighed.

"And an eventful one, too," added Charles.

Peter spoke with effort. "Lenore, before Emma serves dinner let's open that bottle of Greek liquor the Howards gave us and have a toast."

Lenore went to the corner of the room and picked up an odd-shaped, colorful bottle from under the towering Christmas tree. Peter, meanwhile, took glasses from the cabinet. Once the bottle was open, he poured the liquid and raised his glass. "To Charles's venture into politics and Robbie's first year in college."

"And," added Charles, holding his glass up ceremoniously, "to our successful wives."

The women were surprised by Charles's compliment, and before they could say a word, Emma came to the door and announced dinner. They finished their drinks and followed her into the dining room.

It was a magnificent sight. The table was elaborately decorated with silver and gold arrangements. The candles cast a festive glow over the room, the silver gleamed, the crystal sparkled, and the mirrors reflected the flickering

flames of the many varied candles that graced the sideboard, breakfast corner tables and dining table.

They sat down in expectation of a sumptuous Christmas dinner, and Roma sat patiently beside Robbie in anticipation of her lion's share. Then Peter said grace.

Janet watched Lenore knit and count stitches. The spring sun was warm and the absence of the March winds allowed them to sit comfortably on the sun deck. Janet stretched her arms out, "That sun feels good, doesn't it?" Lenore nodded, not wanting to lose count of her work, and Janet continued, "This past winter was terribly long. I'm glad it's past, but Charles misses the snow."

Lenore looked up, finished from counting, "Yes, he did a lot of skiing this winter." She hesitated and added, "It's unfortunate that you don't like that either."

"What do you mean?"

"Well, it would give you more time with him if you learned to golf and ski. Those are his favorite sports and he does spend a lot of time at them." Then as an afterthought, "Dottie likes to ski, doesn't she?"

"Yes, as soon as the snow fell they were at Bald Hill."

"Who went to Pittsfield with him?"

"Dottie, but Mark went too, didn't he tell you?"

"We didn't discuss it . . . but I think you should discourage his seeing her as much as he does."

"Oh, Lenore, are you hinting that something's wrong? Not Charles . . . I suppose, of course, that after living with someone like Dan all these years she can't help but find Charles attractive and kind."

"Aren't you trusting, Janet?"

Janet answered her crisply and emphatically, annoyed at the discussion. "Maybe YOU'RE not trusting ENOUGH."

Lennie didn't reply, absorbed in her own thoughts. She looked up at the sky and gazed dreamily at a large passing cloud that momentarily obscured

the sun and chilled the spring air. Lenore put her knitting on the table and looked around. From the sun deck she could see the houses and hear children's voices. "I wonder if we did the right thing developing Baywater. It's changed so. Perhaps we should have sold the entire parcel. It's so different from the Baywater that we knew as youngsters." Then in a whisper she added, "I've often though about leaving Baywater, you know, but with Peter ill it's impossible." This was the first time she made any reference to his illness.

"What's wrong with him, Lenore?"

She looked away, "A chronic myelogenous leukemia. They're giving him drugs for it."

"Oh, no." Janet's voice was compassionate. "How long does he have?"

"We don't know. It depends on how well he responds to the medication. It could be year, or two, possibly three. It's ironic, Janet, now that he's really ill he doesn't complain. He sits there and waits."

The two cousins sat in silence, each absorbed in her own thoughts. The screen door opened and Roma came out, walked over and sniffed at Janet, wagged her tail in greeting and sat down, her anxious eyes on the door. Robbie came out carrying his telescope.

"Hi, Aunt Jan." He proceeded to set the telescope up on the tripod.

"May I look, Robbie?" And Janet walked over to the scope.

"Sure, let me adjust it for you."

Janet was startled, not only at the clarity of the scope, but the distance she could see. "I suppose you can see nearly everything that goes on around here with this thing."

"Yes, I suppose, but it would be a waste of time. Watching the boats is fun, but I prefer looking for birds in the weeds."

Emma brought out lunch trays with a message. "You have a call from Mr. Howard."

"Thank you, Emma, I'll take it in my room. You two go ahead and eat. Be right back."

Janet and Rob set the table closer to the chairs and began lunch. Robbie gave some tidbits to Roma, and they chatted about the telescope.

Lenore returned shortly, "Russ Howard's coming over soon. He needs

some pictures for his store." She sat down and proceeded to eat heartily. As she ate, they talked about Russ' sporting goods store and how well he seemed to be doing.

Lenore leaned back, finally full, pushed her tray away and picked up her knitting. They talked casually, waiting for Russell. Then they heard his voice. He stepped out on the porch. "Hello everybody . . . bird watching, Rob?" He was a tall, large-framed man, quite handsome.

Rob laughed. "Sure, and Aunt Janet's been peeking at Fire Island."

"Rob, I was not," she protested.

"Come and sit down. Coffee will be along in a minute." Lenore indicated a chair.

As he lowered himself into the seat, Janet said, "Lenore tells me business is good. I'm glad to hear it. Charles should be in to see you soon. He mentioned something about buying new clubs."

"Well, tell him I won't be in the store much next week, but that I've put on a new man who can help him. Claudia and I will be out looking for a place to live that's closer to the business. It's too long a haul going back and forth to the apartment every day."

Emma brought the coffee out to the porch. Lenore began pouring a cup and passed it to Janet as she asked, "Are you going to buy or rent?"

"It depends on what we find. Claudia wants space, I want to be near the store, and we both want to be close to the water."

Lenore spoke slowly, "Baywater is close, isn't it?" and she stirred her coffee. "How do you like the new house Dan is working on?"

Janet watched her cousin in disbelief. It wasn't like Lenore to be interested in the business of selling houses.

"How much is it going for?"

Lenore turned to Janet for an answer. "It could be anywhere from sixty-five thousand up, depending on extras."

"I'll talk to Claudia about it. I know she'd like living here, and the children would enjoy it. We'll let you know."

"There's no hurry, Russ. Dan still has a long way to go to complete it." Janet stood up. "You two have business and I have things to do. See you later."

As Janet left, Russ asked, "Any ideas for pictures?"

"I've got enough to paper your whole place. Let's go over them and you can take your pick." She led the way to her study, leaving Roma and Robbie on the sun deck. She called back, "Don't stay out too long. You might give Emma some help clearing up the cups."

"Sure thing," but he turned his attention to the telescope.

Meg had begun her separation and was in a quandary. It had been a cold winter and she had to keep the heat down low in order to conserve on fuel costs. There were many other worries and she was finding it difficult to manage by herself, make decisions, and be both a father and mother to the children. She was astonished by Toby's casual attitude when she confronted him with knowledge of Corrine and his duplicity. He admitted he wanted to be free of all the responsibilities of a family, so it was easy for him to agree that she have sole control over the children. He had visitation rights, but had never come to see them since the breakup. He had agreed to let Meg have his interest in the house and pay child support, but refused to pay any support for Meg. Charles persuaded him to pay for the divorce. (Meg would go to Mexico for that.) And after much discussion, convinced him to give her a small settlement, to which he grudgingly agreed.

He left Long Island and made his home in Washington. He and Corrine had been living together for more than a year and he had successfully explained to her that Meg wouldn't give him a divorce. He did not, now, reveal the facts of his separation, but instead told her that he wanted to be with her permanently. She loved him and accepted his words on blind faith, and he soothed his guilty conscience by buying her a Lincoln Continental for her birthday. His only communication with Meg was through Charles. Now Toby had little responsibility and was as footloose and fancy free as he chose.

While the separation was easy for him, it was difficult for Meg. She and the children had been betrayed and she suffered humiliation, even though her

friends were kind, understanding, and offered help. Janet spent time with her and frequently sat with the children so Meg could go out. The entire neighborhood included her in all activities and insisted that she attend the get-togethers at the club. Her mother had been appalled at the separation and insisted that she and the children return home to Virginia when the divorce became final, but Meg wouldn't hear of it, and confided to Janet that her mother implied that she must have done something wrong to drive Toby to another woman, which upset her further. Reverend Richard's offer of a part-time secretarial job was no solution. She'd have to pay a sitter as much as she earned.

On Palm Sunday she took Donald, now ten, and Lawrence, seven, to church while Janet stayed with the babies. It was chilly, so she wore her winter coat. She was sitting in the back pew waiting for the service to start when a hand touched her shoulder; she looked up into Kerry Richard's face. For a moment she was stunned, then she moved over to make a seat for him. The first hymn was announced and Kerry opened the hymnal and shared it with her. Their hands touched for a brief instant and her heart beat faster. There was a smile on his face and he leaned over and whispered, "I've missed you, lady."

Her eyes met his, she swallowed nervously, then returned his smile and said, "I'm glad you did." She was happy momentarily. She reflected on the day in the lounge when he had told her he loved her; she wondered if he knew about the separation and what she was going through. After services, he followed her outside and walked with her. She introduced him to the boys, who immediately engaged him in a discussion about skating, hockey and winter sports, babbling to him as though she wasn't there. It was apparent that the boys needed a man's companionship and interest.

Finally he suggested, "Why don't you fellows join your school chums?" He rumpled Lawrence's hair, then put his hat back on his head.

"Okay," and they raced away.

"How has it been, Meg?"

"Rough, Kerry," and she hesitated, not knowing what to tell him. Then the words came tumbling out and she told him about the separation and

coming divorce.

"Why didn't you let me know?"

"How could I? Besides, you have your own problems."

"Not as many as you might think. I've stopped drinking, been working hard, and became a scout leader. Can you picture that?"

"Yes, and you have a knack with children. I saw that when we worked on the children's play."

"What are your plans?" He took her hands in his and said softly, "I'm sorry you've had such a bad time, but I can't say I'm sorry you're though with Toby."

"The real shock was in finding out that I didn't know him at all, after living with him all these years. I was young when we met and impressed by him. You can't judge a book by its cover."

"Meg, real love is a rare commodity. When you find it you know it, and it's worth waiting for."

Meg blushed and pulled away. The boys came running back, and Donald addressed her in a grown-up manner. Now that his father was gone, he was the man of the house. "Janet is waiting for us. Shouldn't we get going?" Then he turned to Larry, who was jumping up and down, and exclaimed, "Stop that!"

"I'm cold if I stand still," he grumbled.

Meg said, "We have to go. Janet will be worried."

"Can I take you home?"

"I have the car, Kerry."

"Can I see you soon? I'll be here a few more days."

She hesitated, having doubts about the propriety of it, then she searched his face, and when their eyes met a tremulous smile touched her lips. She knew she needed him. "Call me."

"What are you plans for later today?"

"We have none. We usually stay home on Sundays."

"Well, this is a special Sunday." He directed his attention to the boys. "Do you both ice skate?"

"Sure we do!" they screamed.

"Suppose we all drive into the city and go skating at Rockefeller Center.

We can have lunch there and make it a day."

"You mean you'd take us all the way to the city just to skate?" Donald was flabbergasted. His own father wouldn't dream of doing anything like that, but then he rationalized his father didn't like sports.

Meg was uneasy. "I don't know if that's a good idea, besides, I'd have to find someone to watch the babies." She found herself wondering if it would look right.

Lawrence started jumping up and down. "Please mother," he begged, "can't we go, can't we, please?"

Their faces shone with excitement. She hated to deny them the fun they would have. "All right, providing I can find a sitter for Andrew and Kenneth."

Donald suggested, "Maybe we could take Andrew. He can use double runners or sit and watch, and that would leave Kenneth, and Aunt Janet loves him so much, I'll bet she'd want to mind him the whole day!"

"That sounds sensible to me," Kerry said, and a smile playfully crossed his lips.

"Alright, the three of you have convinced me! If it's agreeable with Janet, we'll go. Stop by in a half an hour and if everything's worked out, we'll be ready and eager." She was certain Janet would take the baby.

Kerry said, "Fine, I'll see you then."

He watched as they walked to the car. The boys bounced around her, jabbering excitedly. Kerry knew he loved her and wished he had known of her problems earlier so that he could have flown up and helped her through the agonizing period. He whistled to himself as he walked into the parsonage.

The half hour dragged by slowly and he found himself at Meg's door ahead of time. The boys were racing around exuberantly and practically threw themselves in the car. They were shouting and when Meg got in, she put her hands over her ears. "Keep it down, we'll be deaf before we get there."

They roared at that comment, then the noise subsided momentarily, but one joke from Kerry had them in stitches. The trip to town seemed short,

then they were on the ice. Kerry skated with the older boys for a while, and Meg stayed with Andrew, who was trying to master double runners. It didn't take him long to tire, so Meg sat with him and watched the skaters.

Kerry disappeared for a moment, then skated over to her with a blanket and some hot chocolate. "You look cold." He tucked the blanket around her and Andrew, and handed her the chocolate. "Your nose is turning red." She smiled. She was touched by his consideration and thoughtfulness.

They sat and observed the people on the rink. Their attention especially focused on one young couple rehearsing, and their grace and technique on the ice indicated many long, arduous hours of practice. From time to time a woman walked out on the ice to talk to them. Then they floated off in perfect rhythm and harmony and skated without interruption. Meg and Kerry sat and watched, and concluded the couple must be entering some contest, possibly the Olympics. Finally Kerry beckoned to the boys and they came over reluctantly, knowing they had to leave. Kerry helped them off with their skates and suggested they eat on the way home.

It was dark when they pulled into Janet's driveway. Janet saw the headlights and wrapped Kenneth in a blanket. The baby had fallen asleep and Charles carried him out to the car.

Meg apologized for being late, and Charles said, "It's no inconvenience, and we enjoy having him here." Charles and Kerry chatted for a moment, then Charles went inside and Kerry took Meg and the children home.

Kerry was supposed to leave in a few days, but he called his company and requested additional time. He decided that he wouldn't leave this time until he had a commitment from Meg. He felt that if he indicated he was serious about both a divorce and remarriage to Meg, he might be able to persuade her to make a decision. His father learned of his reason for staying in Sayr's Point and insisted that Kerry return to his wife in Virginia. Kerry refused and they quarreled. He only gave in on one point: he did call home to see if his wife and son were alright, but even while he was talking to his wife, his decision was crystallized. He knew that he would never continue in that marriage, regardless of Meg's answer.

Kerry phoned his attorney in Virginia and gave him instructions to begin

divorce proceedings at once, then went to see Meg and asked her to marry him. He told her he was willing to make any changes that she wanted, live anywhere, go anywhere, and he argued that he'd be a good father for the boys.

Meg was uncertain. "My world blew up around me. I'm still confused and hurt Kerry. I love you, but I need time to pull myself together."

She agreed to give the matter a great deal of thought, and on that note he made arrangements to go back to Virginia. Easter Sunday, after dinner, she drove him to the airport, waited till his plane disappeared from view, then returned to Baywater. She felt lonely and melancholy. The boys were full of questions as to why Kerry left, when he was coming back, and was he going to live with them. The pressure was unbearable and she was near tears as she pulled into the garage.

"The phone's ringing mom, shall I get it?" Donald took the keys from her and ran into the house. He raced out again in a few minutes and yelled, "It's dad. He wants to talk to Kenneth and Lawrence, too. Hurry up." The boys followed him inside the house, leaving her to cope with Andrew and the garage door. She went into the house slowly, not wanting to talk to Toby. It was ironic that he should call, now that she had to consider a future with Kerry. Her head ached as she saw her sons cluster around the phone.

CHAPTER 7
SPRING 1967
CHILDREN AND DIVORCE

Once the warmer spring weather arrived, the children spent more time outdoors. After school the boys met to play ball and the girls skipped rope or spent time watching the boys. One nice April day they stood for a long time till finally young Adele Birkland said, "Why don't we go over and ask the boys if we can play too?"

"They won't let us, they never do," sighed Kathy Quinn.

"We never asked them, did we? There's nothing else to do, and anyway, I'm tired of skipping rope. Come on, let's go ask."

Adele walked slowly in the direction of the game, the other girls following in the distance. "Can we play?" she called as she came closer.

"Go away, Adele, can't you see we're busy?" yelled George Rudowski. "Anyway, we don't need any dumb girls."

"Oh, come on, George, don't be so mean. You know we can do most anything thing you can." Adele was angry. She wasn't a tomboy, but she hated being called dumb. She glared at George.

"So you think you can do anything we can, huh?" scoffed George.

"Yes, I can run as fast as you can, swim better than you; I can fish and drive a boat too."

"Sure you can." George held his stomach and bent over, mimicking. "Bet you think you can climb a tree better or maybe even beat me bike racing."

"That would be easy, I always win races and I can climb a tree as good as you can."

"Prove it!" yelled one of the boys. "We dare you."

"Alright, I will!" Adele yelled back at him.

"Not any little ol' tree either! A real big one."

"There aren't any real big ones around here." George surveyed the premises.

"No, but there are some on the other side of the tennis court." Jerome Brack pointed, and their eyes followed his direction. Several large, old maples towered over the surrounding trees.

"That's nothing," Adele said. "I can climb any one of them."

"Okay, let's see you, you think you're so smart." The boys began pushing her toward the tennis court.

"Don't do it, Adele, you might tear your clothes," pleaded Lucille Rufone. "Besides, you might fall."

"Chicken!" sneered George as Adele hung back. They were at the base of the tree. Adele looked up and her mouth quivered slightly. She was frightened now. It was very tall and big, but she didn't dare quit.

They all watched her as she swung herself up the lowest limb. The boys laughed as she stiffened, trying to get herself over the branch. She made it and stood up, looking back at George, who was sneering. Gradually she worked her way up a little higher, clinging tightly as she moved. Her hands were clammy; she tried to swallow, but there was a lump in her throat; she began to bite her lips.

"Aw, is that as high as you can go? That's nothing. We go right to the top, and a lot faster too." George stuck his tongue out at her.

"I'm going higher, and you wait and see, I'll be at the top before you know it." Adele's voice was squeaky but she was afraid. She deliberately concentrated on moving slowly upward, feeling her way with her feet and clinging. The boys taunted her, daring her to go higher and higher. The girls begged her to stop and come down. Once her feet slipped and she almost fell, then she clung precariously to a limb. The girls caught their breath. They were frightened, but Adele regained her balance and stopped a moment to rest.

One of the boys yelled, "What's the matter, Adele, getting chicken? Thought you could do anything we can."

"I'm not chicken." She was almost in tears, but the voices goaded her on. As she neared the top a strong breeze rustled the early spring leaves and the tree swayed lightly.

"Hey George," said Jerome, "she's awfully high. She might fall. It's shaking up there." The group fell quiet. They were watching her.

"Come on down, Adele," cried one of the girls. "That's high enough."

George scowled. He hadn't expected her to go up that far and he felt a queasy sensation in his stomach as the top branches continued to sway. Adele was wearing leather soled shoes and could easily slip. "That's far enough, Adele, I wouldn't go any higher if I were you. Come on down," he called.

"I told you I can go farther than you can." Adele grasped the branches above her and pulled herself higher. The branches were thinner and they swayed in the wind. She wedged her foot carefully into a crotch of the tree and looked down to gloat. The faces below her were strained and tense. She was scared and hadn't realized how far she had climbed; the youngsters were a long way down. A terror of heights checked her, she wet her lips nervously.

"Please come down," pleaded Kathy O'Quinn.

"Be careful, Adele," Lucille screamed.

Adele tried to ease herself down but her foot twisted as she moved and stuck firmly in the crotch. She felt herself losing her balance. She was too far from a main branch to grasp it and in fear clutched the nearest one. She was petrified. "I can't move," she wailed. "My foot's stuck. I can't get it out."

"Twist yourself around a little. Maybe you can free your foot that way," called George.

"No!" Adele screamed, "I can't let go, I'll fall."

While the boys conferred, she looked down again. She was dizzy and nauseous with fright; her body tensed and her mind froze. She was stuck up there and there was no safe way down. "I'll come up and help you." George started up the tree; as he got higher, she screamed.

"No, no, everything's moving. Stop it, don't shake the tree!"

"I'm not shaking the tree. It's the wind moving the branches."

"No, no!" She was hysterical now, and George moved back down. The youngsters were frightened.

"We'd better get help," suggested Kathy. "I'll go get my mother." She and Lucille ran off.

George was guilty and scared. If anything happened to Adele, he'd be blamed. He wondered what his parents would do if they found out how he goaded her into climbing. Adele was crying in abject fear, her blouse was torn and her arms and legs scratched. The sun started to set and she shuddered. She didn't have her jacket on. Tears were running down her cheeks, dropping to her blouse, dampening it and making it feel clammy. She heard voices and peered down to see her mother and Ann Rufone.

"Adele, you come down here this instant," Marian Birkland commanded.

"I can't, my foot's stuck," she wailed.

Dottie O'Quinn and Meg Marshall arrived on the scene. "What's wrong?" Meg asked. "We were outside talking and heard yelling." Then, following Marian's anxious gaze, she exclaimed, "Oh Lord, what is that child doing up there?"

"I don't' know exactly, but she's stuck."

In the tree Adele wretched, and in seconds her blouse and dungarees were covered. She cried in humiliation.

"We'll have to get a ladder," Dottie suggested.

"Who's got one long enough?" Meg bit her lip.

They heard a voice calling. Peter was leaning out of a window yelling something. Meg ran over to the house. "I saw what happened and I've called the fire department. They'll be here shortly."

"Thanks, Peter."

A few minutes later the sound of a siren caught their ears. More residents arrived at the scene. Kim came out, Ruth Gordon with the Banshatas, and the two Howard girls. The firemen put a ladder in place and one of them went up to retrieve Adele. It was an easy matter getting her down safely. The firemen left shaking their heads and grinning as they drove away. Adele stopped sobbing long enough to tell her mother

what happened as the other mothers listened. Emma came out with a hot drink and a towel to wipe the tear-stained face. Marian sponged her vomit away.

Gloria Rudowski took her son by the arms and marched him home, scolding him along the way. The other youngsters followed meekly, not daring to disobey their mothers, and the group dispersed.

Marian smiled at her daughter, relieved she was safe. "Do you feel better now, dear? We'll get you home into a hot tub so you don't catch a cold."

"I'm alright, mommy. I'm glad to get down."

"I'll bet you are, and I don't want to hear of your climbing another tree," she said firmly.

"I won't, I promise," and they marched home, Marian leading Adele by the hand.

The following week it was quiet in the neighborhood. There was a subdued atmosphere; the children were being punished for the incident.

❧

The school bus spilled its occupants out by the gates as the moving van turned into the drive. The children followed the van down the street to the Howard's house, watching curiously, eager for some new excitement. Claudia shook her head. "I swear kids are the only ones who think moving is fun!"

Russ grinned, "We'll have plenty of help if we need it. They look ready to pitch in and help." He propped the door open and went down the walk to the truck to speak to the movers. The children stood in a small group across the street watching everything going on.

Andy ran after his father. "Mother says to remind them that all the boxes are numbered as well as the doors to the rooms where they go." Then the men started carrying in boxes and furniture. Russell followed them inside, but Andy saw the group of children across the street and waved, "Hi, I'm Andy Howard."

"Hi," they responded in a general chorus, then some of them moved

closer, gave their names and offered to help.

Andy ran inside the house and told his mother, but she suggested, "I think it would be better if you stayed out of everybody's way for the time being. Why don't you go outside and make friends with these children?"

"Okay, mom," and he raced back outdoors.

Two hours later the movers left and she looked around at the boxes and furniture. "What a mess! How can things get so dirty? Everything was clean when I packed, but look at these things now. And look at me, I'm a mess too!"

Russ kissed her on the tip of her nose. "All messes should look like you," and he put his arms around her and kissed her again. "Tell you what, you shower and dress, and I'll make up the beds. We have to be at Lenore's for dinner in half an hour."

"My gosh, I almost forgot."

As she went into the bathroom she heard him calling Andy and Edie. She put the shower on and stepped in, humming cheerfully. After she was done, she stretched out on the bed a few minutes while Russ washed and dressed. Then they went to Lenore's.

After dinner that evening, they strolled back holding hands. The children meandered behind, studying their new surroundings. Claudia sighed, "I'm going to like it here. So are the kids. I can't wait to soak in that heated pool."

"You should have a chance tomorrow. I told John to come here and give you a hand instead of reporting to me at the store." He opened the front door, then locked it behind them. Walking up the steps toward the bedroom he added, "I want you to be happy."

She smiled up at him. "I can practically guarantee that, my love," she answered as she closed the bedroom door behind them.

※

Meg sat on the edge of the bed in her hotel room looking at the Mexican divorce decree and the English translation that accompanied it. Memories tumbled through her mind; she reflected on the first time

she had seen Toby. She was at a party at a friend's apartment in New York (where she was working) when a good-looking young man smiled at her from across the room. She returned the smile and a moment later he was at her side introducing himself. After the party ended, they stopped for coffee. It was late when he dropped her at her door, and he made her promise that she would keep the next night free so he could take her to dinner and the theatre. They dated steadily for three weeks, and the following night he proposed. They were married within the month and she became pregnant almost immediately.

Perhaps, she thought as she sat in this strange room, if it hadn't been for the birth of Donald, they might have had time to get to know each other, had more fun and less responsibility. Perhaps, too, if she hadn't allowed him to pressure her into marriage so soon after their meeting, she wouldn't be sitting here now holding these papers in her shaky hands.

She conceived again and a second boy was born; then when she became pregnant a third time, Toby blamed her for the "accident," and although he did not want the child, would not consent to an abortion. After the birth of their third son, Meg suggested that he have a vasectomy, but he was outraged at the idea, a "mutilation" he had called it, and absolutely refused. So although they took precautions and counted days, she became pregnant a fourth time. She was continually miserable and uncomfortable carrying. Her heavy, swollen body made it difficult for her to run the house and mind three active children. And when Toby came home from his trips, she fought with him and they bickered constantly. She found it harder to cope after Kenneth's birth, and instead of being sweet and calm, she picked and nagged. She thought now that it must have been about this time that Toby had met Corrine.

There was a stillness in the room, and as she sat on the bed, she thought back to the events that landed her here and how Charles had been so kind and helpful. He had made all the arrangements for her and refused to consider a fee beyond the actual costs. She remembered how startled she had been when he told her the trip to El Paso would be a "group divorce" flight! "It's cheaper this way," he said. Once on the plane, she was amazed at the comradeship aboard and the different

attitudes that prevailed.

One woman kept repeating, "I don't want a divorce, but he insisted, so here I am!"

Another woman spoke bitterly, "While the kids and I did without things, that bastard was keeping a gorgeous blond. You should have seen the elegant place he put her in." She sniffed, then added in a hostile voice, "To even the score I hit him for every cent I could get."

Everyone within ear shot laughed, except two men who had little to say and kept to themselves. There was one extra passenger aboard, an elder, balding gentleman who accompanied a sultry brunette. They were planning a wedding in the marriage bureau next door to the court following her divorce. Meg thought, "Nothing like having your insurance with you!"

The attorney met them at the airport and had private buses waiting to take them to the hotel to freshen up; then on to a sight-seeing and shopping tour. Meg was aware that everything had been tactfully and carefully handled, and she understood that these "divorce" flights arrived daily from cities throughout the United States. She had found the whole experience incredible. You could fly to El Paso, cross the border to Juarez for a divorce, and return to El Paso, all in the same day.

She walked across the room to the mirror and studied herself in the reflection. She looked tired and drawn and noticed the lines around her eyes, found fault with her hair and features. This was no time to be alone. She needed reassurance. At least at home she had a phone call or letter from Kerry every day, but here there was no one to turn to. Kerry had his divorce granted. His wife had been reluctant to sign the papers, but when he told her he would leave anyway, she consented. She was young enough to start over and the alimony and child support he agreed to pay was generous. She realized that it would be an opportunity for her, that she could afford to take her time choosing someone more suitable to her way of life.

Kerry was happy in his new textile job. He was well liked, displayed an interest in other people's work as well as his own, and it wasn't long before the bosses noticed his talents, invited him to join them for golf

and hinted at possible advancement. Meg wondered, now that she was actually divorced, whether he would still want to marry her. Perhaps he would hedge, find excuses. This sometimes happened, and the thought made her shiver.

The telephone rang and she answered it. "Room service Madam, we're sending up a bottle of champagne, compliments of the house."

Meg thought, "They haven't forgotten a thing!" Then the line was disconnected. She stared at the phone. Who wanted to drink champagne? Why celebrate alone? She shook her head. Even the thought of going down for dinner dismayed her; she was in an emotional quandary.

There was a knock on the door and she walked across the room to answer it. As the door opened, she gasped and flung herself at Kerry, who was standing there holding a bottle of champagne. She buried her face in his shoulder and started sobbing.

He stroked her hair and said jokingly, "It's alright, Meg, I won't run away with your champagne." He led her into the room, put the bottle down and tilted her face toward his. "It's not very flattering having you cry when you see me. It's bad for my ego," he said teasingly.

Meg smiled, "Kerry, what are you doing here?"

"I decided to come and help you celebrate. I phoned Charles for the name of the hotel, and here I am. How I've missed you! Now, go find a couple of glasses while I open up this bottle."

Meg went into the bathroom, returned with two glasses, and Kerry said, "To our happy and long life together."

All her doubts and fears fell away. "Mmm," she murmured as she drank. "What a fantastic surprise."

"Honey, my watch says five o'clock. We can sit here and finish this bottle or go out for dinner and take on the town. What do you say?"

She brightened up, "Let's go! I can be ready in ten minutes."

"Fine. I'll meet you in the lobby. Here, let me pour you another one." He filled her glass, gave her a kiss lightly on the forehead, and was gone.

Meg was excited. She went to her suitcase, took out the best dress she had brought, drank another mouthful of champagne and hurriedly took a shower and dressed. It was a few moments past her promised ten minutes when she came out of the elevator and stepped into the lobby. Kerry

beamed. She had always been beautiful to him and now appeared more so with her faintly flushed cheeks and sparkling eyes. He took her arm and led the way to the bar lounge.

"Let's start with a drink here and inquire about a good restaurant." He held her hand and she could feel the depth of his love glowing through his eyes. The bartender recommended a fine restaurant, and after one cocktail they started out in the car he had rented at the airport. After dinner they went to watch a show at a nightclub, then Kerry insisted they drive across the border to Juarez because he did not want to leave "without setting foot on Mexican soil." The night passed quickly and merrily, and Meg felt complete being with him. She needed no one else, and felt that her life was beginning anew. It was almost morning when they returned to the hotel. Kerry said, "Meg, let's get married right away."

"Kerry, we can't! You know I want to marry you, darling, but . . ."

He sealed her lips with a passionate kiss. He wanted to make love to her. Meg felt a momentary qualm, but then, realizing she needed him as much, if not more, than he needed her, capitulated. They undressed and slipped into the large bed. Kerry was as gentle and loving as he had been persistent and persuasive with his letters and phone calls. In the morning he leaned over, kissed her and said, "Meg, let's get married here and now. I have my birth certificate and driver's license. There's no reason why we should wait."

Meg demurred for a moment then agreed. "Yes, Kerry, let's get married."

They dressed, had some breakfast, and drove to Juarez. They stopped at a jewelry shop, where Meg selected a little gold wedding band, then they went to the marriage bureau. Following the ceremony they talked and planned their future together. Occasionally Meg twirled the ring around her finger excitedly.

"I've been offered a new job as PR head at the Barrington Mills in North Carolina. It's too good to refuse. I can go ahead and find a house, and you and the boys can come down at the end of the month when school lets out."

"That sounds fine darling, but what about your own son?"

"Margaret has custody, but I have weekend visitation rights to see the boy. I can fly back to Virginia whenever it's convenient. Besides, I'm sure she'll be married within a year or so. She's not the type to live alone; she needs a man around the house."

"I'll have to sell the house. That may take a lot of time."

"Let Charles take care of things. I'm sure between him and a Realtor, they can sell it for you. Leave Charles the keys and let him handle it, but this time insist that he take a legal fee."

"Alright. I'll ask him."

He drove her back to the hotel to pick up her things and check out. They followed the buses to the airport and he turned the car in. He checked on a flight for himself and found one that was leaving an hour after hers. As she stepped through the gate at the terminal he called, "I love you, Meg," and added softly, "for eternity." There were tears of happiness rolling down her cheeks.

Once on the plane, she smiled to herself. Kerry had been surprised at the marriage bureau when he'd found out that she was two years older than he. She looked younger. But it didn't make any difference, he'd said. It proved she would always be young and beautiful as they got older. She touched her wedding band. Mrs. Kerry Richard. Some of the women aboard the plane congratulated her, some acted jealous, and some thought, "You can't tell about those sweet demure ones." She didn't care what anyone said or thought. She was happy! Then she leaned her head back and brushed any doubts from her mind. She was pleasantly tired and fell asleep with a smile on her face.

The July 4th weekend was hot and humid; the clubhouse and pool were the center of activity. Thompson Brack complained that the bay was as crowded as the highways. One afternoon Robbie was stretched out on a sun deck chair watching the fun. He didn't like to go down to the pool when it was crowded; he was afraid he might get hurt. Mark stopped by to see Robbie, and Lenore and Janet joined them on the sun

deck. They were watching Russ Howard teaching swimming to some of the youngsters in the pool. Kim Brack was lounging by the pool.

Mark said, "A regular sun goddess, isn't she?"

Robbie squinted, "She's almost unreal."

Janet remarked, "I can't get over Thompson's total lack of jealousy. Look at the men swarming around her."

Lenore laughed, "Like a moth around a flame!" Then changing the subject asked, "Janet, have you watched Russ teaching those children? He has a way with them. With his terrific personality I think he'd make a great recreation director."

"Yes, he's good with people," Mark added.

Janet perked up. "Charles mentioned that he thought things were getting a little disorganized around here. Perhaps that's what we need."

"Why don't you ask him?" Lenore suggested.

"Good idea," Janet said with a nod. They chatted leisurely, then Janet said, "Here comes Charles and the Rufones. Think I'll go down and join them and take a swim."

Mark stood up. "I'll go with you. I want to talk to Thompson about renting a boat." He wiped the perspiration from his forehead.

Lenore answered, "See you both later. I'm waiting for Claudia," and she poured herself another glass of iced tea.

Janet touched Rob's shoulder lightly as she walked by him. Roma wagged her tail, and Mark followed Janet inside and down the stairs.

As they approached the group of men she heard Charles say, "I don't have that much time, besides a boat is a lot of work."

Thompson replied, "It's a good buy Charles, and actually a boat isn't that much trouble, as long as you keep the barnacles off the bottom."

"And you have a reasonably good engine," scowled Ray Dowling. "Mine has been giving me trouble all year. I can't seem to get it running right."

"Take it to Cor, he's a good man on small engines," then he turned to Janet. "I've been trying to sell your husband a boat, but he says he's too busy and doesn't have the time for one. I failed to mention to him that he could have a small run about, so you could use it like Claudia does. In

fact, sometimes she takes Lenore out with her. I see them in the bay once in awhile, racing over to Fire Island."

"Yes, I know. They love it . . . I think they're crazy."

Thompson laughed, "They make a wicked pair! Lenore takes the wheel sometimes and hits the throttle. She loves speed, doesn't she?"

"I'm afraid to go with them!"

Mark chuckled, "She sure is a dare devil!" Then he turned to Thompson and discussed renting a boat for himself.

Ray Dowling stretched. "Have you seen Sally?"

"She's chatting with Kim," Vinny Rufone replied, and Ray went off in that direction.

Thompson turned to Vinny, "That boat's a good buy. I hate to let a bargain like that go to just anyone."

"Don't look at me, Thom. The only boat I'm interested in is the 'come along.' Easier and cheaper that way."

They laughed, then Thompson added, "Yes, there's a big difference both in price and the labor involved."

A shrill voice caught their attention. They turned their heads and saw Sally and Ray arguing. Ray walked away from her and yelled, "You're not only lazy, you're stupid!"

Sally ran after him, tossing her long red mane of hair about and screaming, "I don't know why I ever married a stubborn old man like you!" Ray stalked into the clubhouse with Sally behind.

Charles began a conversation in order to cover up the embarrassment created by the scene. Janet looked up and noticed Claudia and Lenore standing at the rail of the sun deck. She saw Claudia's lips moving but couldn't hear words. "I hate public scenes. People should do their fighting in private."

The group by the pool forgot the incident and resumed their activities. The balance of the day passed uneventfully. As Janet swam in the pool, she wondered if Meg was happy in Carolina; she missed her and the children. The Marshall house was empty; no one had shown any interest in buying it. She hoped Mrs. Tooker would find a suitable purchaser, one whom they would like as much as they had liked Meg.

The only incident that occurred the rest of the weekend was the disturbance created by Terry Howell and his friends. They had exploded fireworks late one night on the lawn of Meg's empty house and were jimmying the garage door lock when Vinny Rufone's car came down the street and scared them away.

CHAPTER 8

SUMMER 1967
MURDER AND INCEST

Ray was angry. "I told you to have Cor look at the engine. Why didn't you call him?"

"I forgot. Besides, I was tied up shopping and got home late."

"A fine time to forget." Ray tried the engine again but it was useless; they were stuck. He went to the stern, took the cover off, and after a short investigation got some tools out and went to work. "When I tell you, try starting it, but be sure you leave it in neutral." Sally moved to the wheel, her finger on the starter, and looked over her shoulder at him. "Try it now!" he yelled.

"Okay." She pushed the starter and nothing happened.

"Darn . . . I'll do something else."

He was leaning over the gunwale, moving back and forth. A thought occurred to her; here was a chance that might never come again. She moved her other hand slowly so that he couldn't see what she was doing in case he happened to look back.

"Try it again, it may start."

She pushed the starter, and the engine sprang to life; she put it in gear and gave it full throttle. The boat lurched, then the bow lifted as it leapt forward. The sudden motion pitched Ray overboard, head first. Sally turned the boat so she could watch him. The waves were a little higher now and she was confident that he couldn't swim to shore; it was too far. Ray struggled valiantly, waiting for Sally to come in closer and pick him up. Instead, she circled around him at a distance, and then it

139

dawned on him that it hadn't been an accident at all. She had done it deliberately and had no intention of saving him. He tried to see if there were any other boats close by, but the swells made it impossible. He knew he'd never make it to shore. God! What a fool he had been. Sally must have overheard him talking to Ethel on the phone, hinting at a reconciliation. But to kill him for that was absurd.

"Sally, help me!" he cried out. "You can't do this to me. For God's sake . . . please, help me."

She ignored him and headed the boat away. She felt exultant. Everybody would think it was an accident; they knew she couldn't handle a boat. He'd drown and she'd have everything . . . his life insurance, the house, the boat, car, stocks and whatever money he had. Better to lose him this way than hand him back to Ethel. Besides, he wasn't going to humiliate her like that.

She watched. He was struggling, then suddenly he vanished under the waves. She cruised back and forth to make sure he was gone. It had to appear as though she had tried to save him, so when she was convinced he wouldn't surface, she threw the life vests and cushions overboard. Then she headed west.

She knew nothing about the boat; she hadn't gone out with Ray often enough to learn how to handle it. The huge rolling ocean swells made her jittery, but she thought that someone would come along. "I wonder how long the gas will last. I'd better head toward shore." She was talking to herself nervously. Clouds began to sweep across the sun, cooling the air rapidly. She shivered from the chill in the air. There weren't any boats in sight, anywhere, and she was frightened. She wondered what time it was and how long she had been out there. The gray sky was ominous, the wind picked up rapidly and the wheel was beginning to fight her. She couldn't hold her heading and couldn't remember what you were supposed to do. The ocean seemed huge, empty; the boat was minuscule by comparison. Someone should have shown up by now. Where were all the fishing boats that came at dusk?

Suddenly, the motor quit; the gauge read empty. She was far from the shoreline and couldn't recognize anything. The whistling grew louder

and the deep mellow voice of the ocean gave way to a more menacing tone. The boat seemed to twist and slide as though trying to escape the hungry, gaping mouth of the waves. She gripped the wheel in panic. There was nothing to do except hang on. Rain drops splattered her hands and head, and black clouds rolled in to cover the gray sky. If one burst open she'd be wallowing in water. Her imagination amplified her fear. Would the boat sink suddenly? The rain came down harder and with the roar of the sea and the whistling of the wind, it created a mocking symphony of sound. Time was endless. A hideous flame tore across the sky accompanied by an ear-splitting crash. She shrieked. It seemed the shafts of lightning were deliberately dancing around her, toying with her own hurricane of terror, postponing her execution until she was reduced to a quaking, shivering mass of flesh.

"God help me!" she screamed, and an almost human wail answered her, "Sally! Please! Help me!" She tried to cover her ears from the artillery of thunder and lightning, but the violent motion made it impossible. Her anguished tears mixed with the stinging rain, and the ocean roared, moaned, splitting apart as though to make room for her grave. In her own guilty mind rose a hundred ghostly images of Ray, accompanied by the haunting monsters of the deep with their clutching, clammy fingers reaching for her, waiting to carry her to the eerie, seaweed laden world below. Her shroud would be the wind and rain, her eulogy delivered by the lighting, accompanied by the organ of the thundering clouds. Her mind could stand no more. She slipped to the bottom of the boat, alternately babbling hysterically and moaning incoherently.

Hours later she opened her eyes and heard voices. She was in the hospital. Someone had seen the small boat in trouble and the Coast Guard had found her. When she was able to tell her story, people were sympathetic and understanding. They believed that Ray had fallen overboard in the storm. Weeks later, back home again, she tried to resume a normal life, but the ordeal had left its mark. Ray's ghostly image rocked her bed, his voice on every sight of the wind. She couldn't bear the sound of the bay or sight of water. She sold the house and boat and left Long Island to do some traveling, but found that her constant companion was guilt. No one in Baywater ever heard from her again.

❧

"This summer has certainly been a hot one. I don't think the weather will ever cool off." Janet sighed. They were sitting in the shade of a huge maple tree. "It's so hot that nothing is stirring. Where's Robbie and Peter?"

"Peter's resting in his room; it's cooler there with the air conditioner on. And Robbie went out early this morning, bird watching with one of the professors."

"I'm bored. I wish we could go away for a few days but Charles says he's too busy to leave the office."

Lenore regarded her cousin soberly. "It seems that he's more occupied than usual lately."

"Yes, his practice is excellent, but what use is the money when you have no life together? Oh, here comes Robbie."

Robbie waved good-bye to the professor as he drove away, then walked toward them, dangling his binoculars. "Hi."

"Hello, dear," replied his mother.

"Hi, Aunt Janet . . . boy, am I hot. It's sizzling."

His aunt responded, "Yes, even the pool feels like bath water!"

"I don't see how Uncle Charles can walk around the golf course in that broiling sun."

Lenore gave her son a warning glance, but Janet's head whipped up suddenly. "Is Charles out golfing?"

"Yes, with Mrs. O'Quinn. I saw them on our way home. They were at the eighth hole. You can see that from the road. It's so hot, think I'll go in and wash up and get a cold drink."

After he walked away Janet exploded. "He told me he had to work all day! I wonder how many times that has happened this summer."

"I've tried to warn you, Jan, but you wouldn't listen."

"I'm sure there's nothing wrong." Janet, as usual, defended Charles. "But it bothers me that I hardly see him anymore. Perhaps his last client cancelled and he took the opportunity to relax, and I wasn't home when he called." Then she changed the subject, hoping to bypass a lecture from Lenore.

"Mr. Willoughby, the new owner in Meg's house, called. He had a few questions about the house and club activities."

"Is that the banker?"

"Yes, Charles knows him from doing closings at the bank and says they're fine people." She lifted herself from the chair. "I think I'll drive to the mall and browse around the stores. They're air conditioned. Want to come?"

"No thanks, it's too hot to go anywhere."

"Okay, I'll call you later."

"Bye." Lenore watched her leave. She stopped for a moment to talk to Joe Carter as he dug into his mail bag and handed her a letter. Lenore sighed. She was worried about Janet and Charles, but it was useless to try to talk to her cousin. Janet was blindly loyal where Charles was concerned.

Joe was almost finished delivering for the day. He was thirsty and tired, and the mid-August heat knocked him out. Luckily, all he had to do was deliver mail at a few more houses. He had left the truck at the gates and would pick it up on the way out. He had given Mrs. Henderson her mail, handed Mrs. Morgan hers, and he crossed the street to the club to leave some envelopes. He studied them, bills from the florist, an electric bill and some advertising. He wondered what special occasion there had been to order flowers. Joe was tall and wiry; the walking he did kept him thin, though he ate ravenously. As he dropped the mail at the club, he thought about the food served there. The best of everything, he'd bet.

Joe wasn't the serene, quiet man he appeared to be. Inwardly he was continually seething with rage and jealousy. He envied people at Baywater Estates. Every time he walked by the pool and tennis courts, he felt cheated. Even though everyone was nice to him and he received good tips at Christmas, he resented them. They all seemed very rich and would never know what it was like to live on a small salary like his, pay a mortgage and support a wife and two daughters. He particularly disliked Lenore and Janet, and the good fortune they'd had in inheriting this place; then being lucky to make estates out of it! He growled, "Some people have all the luck!"

He had been born in a cold-water flat in Brooklyn. His father became an

alcoholic and ran away with a bar maid and left him and his mother stranded. When Joe was sixteen, he dropped out of school and took a job in a chain food store in order to support his mother and himself. He was able to buy food cheaply, sometimes even steal it, so they were able to get by. They never heard from his father again, but one night the police stopped by and notified them of his death. It had been a heart attack. His mother cried, but Joe was glad the old man was dead; he felt his father had received a just punishment for walking out on them. After his mother passed away, Joe met Nancy, and they were married six months later. They moved to Long Island. Joe took night courses and received his high school diploma, then was fortunate to get a job at the local post office.

His next delivery would be the Bracks. There was plenty of mail for them, including some notices of insured packages for Mrs. Brack. He studied all the mail curiously before he stuffed it into the box. He was inquisitive and return addresses and post cards told a lot about people. Besides, it broke up the monotony of his job. He could fantasize about their letters, their lives, and their friends.

He heard a voice, "Is that you Jerome?"

"No ma'am, it's me, Joe Carter."

Kim came to the door. "Oh hello, Joe. My, you look hot! Would you like a cook drink?"

"That sure sounds good, Mrs. Brack." Joe knew he shouldn't stop, and if anyone from the post office found out, he'd be reprimanded. But his daughter, Amy, baby-sat for the Bracks, so if anyone asked, he could say Mrs. Brack wanted to talk to him about Amy.

"Well, come in, Joe, it's too hot to stand out there. I made some iced tea, if you'd like some."

"Anything cold would be fine, Mrs. Brack." He followed her into the house, and looking around he could see that Amy was right; it was beautifully furnished and very elegant. Once in the kitchen he stood watching Kim as she moved gracefully to the refrigerator, getting ice cubes and the tea. She stretched up to take a glass from the shelf, and his eyes greedily followed her body's movements. He had never seen her up close, and he couldn't help thinking that God couldn't have made a more beautiful creature than this,

and that next to her, Marilyn Monroe looked sick. She had a ready smile and a gentle word. She turned to him and handed him the tea. Joe tasted it gratefully.

"How's Amy?"

"Oh, she's fine, Mrs. Brack."

"Do you think she can sit for me tomorrow?"

"I think so, but I'll ask her." He finished his iced tea in almost one swallow.

"Would you like another one, Joe?"

"Oh, I don't think so." Joe was a little disturbed. Kim's nearness made his pulse beat faster. "It was nice though."

"Oh, I'm sure you can take a few moments for another glass. Don't be bashful, Joe."

"Yes ma'am, thank you."

Joe reached for the glass as she filled it, and his fingers touched hers. A ripple of excitement shot through him. He could feel himself beginning to sweat, and he hoped Mrs. Brack wouldn't notice. She seemed friendly though, and he began to wonder if there was something more in it. She went back to get herself a glass, and again he could see the breasts straining against the thin blouse. He had seen her from a distance at the pool in a bikini, and he began to imagine her naked. He wondered what she would do if he touched her. He finished his drink, running his tongue around the rim of the glass, imaging it running around her . . .

A voice cut through his thoughts. "Hi mom. Oh, hello Joe."

He hadn't heard the door open, and he startled guiltily. Kim's young son had come in.

"Hello, Jerome."

"Hi. What are you drinking?"

"Tea, but you may have some cold fruit punch."

"Okay, but first I'm going to wash my face with cold water. Be right back."

"I'd better be going, Mrs. Brack. Thank you very much for the drink. I appreciate it."

Kim walked him to the front door, and as he went out, she gave him that

beautiful lazy smile and said, "Any time, Joe. When you're hot and tired, just knock, and if I'm home I'll be glad to give you something cool."

Joe nodded his head, "Thank you again, Mrs. Brack." As he went down the walk, he moved uncomfortably. He wondered if she meant anything more by that; she seemed awfully friendly, but then you never know with these people, maybe she was being patronizing. He mulled that in his mind as he finished his route. He had some more work to do when he got back to the post office. Joe worked extra hours to make extra money, and the post office was cool. He was in no hurry to get home. The girls could take care of themselves pretty well.

When he arrived at the house, he found that Sarah had started making supper, and Amy was setting the table. He watched them from the doorway for a moment. Sarah met his eyes and looked away quickly, which made him angry for a moment. He went up and took a shower before dinner.

Later on in the evening, as he sat reading the paper, Joe thought about his wife Nancy. Even though she had to go to Georgia after her mother had the stroke, he resented her being away. He was waiting for a call from her, but he hoped she wouldn't make the call collect. The girls had done the dishes and wanted to watch television for a while, but he wouldn't let them; he wanted to read his paper in peace.

One of the girls called and invited them to the movies. Joe relented and let them go. As he sat and waited for the call, he thought about Kim Brack. Wouldn't you know it, she had to pick today to be nice to him. He kept seeing her stretching up to get those glasses and it aroused him. He kept thinking to himself, "Why the hell isn't Nancy here tonight? I could give it to her!" The more he thought about it, the angrier he became. Finally the call came, and Nancy said her mother would be well enough for her to leave by the early part of the following week. He was a little surly that she had made the call collect, and he scolded her for being so extravagant.

He settled down to watch TV for a while, but before his program ended, the girls came back and went to the kitchen for a snack. He could hear them out there giggling and joking. Feeling lonesome, he went out to the kitchen.

When he appeared, they stopped laughing, and Sarah watched him nervously. She was afraid of him. As he moved toward her, she backed away and said, "I'm going up. I want to do my hair. Good night."

He didn't answer, but watched her walk out of the room. She was sixteen and well-developed. He turned to Amy and reflected on the difference between his two daughters. Amy had always been thin and wiry like him, but now she was starting to bloom; her breasts were not little buds anymore, and her hips were beginning to round slightly. It wouldn't be long, he thought, and wondered about the boy who would be the first to savor her delicate taste. He resented the thought, and anger surged up in him again. Amy fixed him a sandwich and sat with him while he ate it. He remembered Kim wanting her to baby-sit and mentioned it. The phone rang. "Must be her now, you get it."

Amy ran to answer the phone, and he heard her talking. When she came back she said, "It was Mrs. Brack. She said she'd pick me up about eleven. She said Jerome and I could go to the pool tomorrow. She has to go to the hairdresser."

Joe grunted. "Okay, but mind you watch him good. I don't need any trouble because of you being careless at the pool."

"Oh, don't worry daddy. I keep my eye on him. Well, good night, think I'll go up."

Joe decided to have a couple of beers. The TV was being troublesome and he turned from channel to channel trying to find a clear station. He began to think about the cost of the trip to Georgia. The train would have been expensive enough, but in an emergency Nancy had to fly, and he resented the cost. She had no business to go. A woman belonged with her husband, besides he needed her tonight, and even if she would have been passive, it wouldn't have mattered because he could think about Kim.

A wave of desire swept over him. He went into the kitchen, drank another beer, took a few with him, and went back to the living room. There was a voluptuous girl dancing and he glued his eyes to the screen. He began to curse his wife now. Joe was demanding and had no qualms about slapping his wife if she refused him; he thought how he wanted some sex right now and began to see his wife's naked form in front of him. He

over to kiss him. He held her arms and said, as he pushed the spread aside, "Listen Amy, I think you're old enough to learn some facts of life." He forced her to sit on the bed and slid one hand up under her pajama top and began to squeeze her breast.

"Daddy!" she screamed, and Sarah came running into the room as her father began to pull Amy's pajamas off.

"Don't do it, daddy, take me instead. Leave her alone, please!"

Sarah pummeled at her father, and again he threw her to the floor. "Now you get out of here or I'll beat you to a pulp. Anyway, do you want me to tell your precious boyfriend how long you've been playing games with me? He wouldn't want you after that, would he? Now get out of here before I get up and beat you or tie you to a chair so you can watch. Get!"

He started to get up, and Sarah ran sobbing from the room.

Amy tried to get away, and he tightened his hand on her wrist till she winced. "Be a good girl, honey. You don't want to make daddy mad, do you?" He began to stroke her hair.

"No." She quivered and hunched her shoulder, trying to cover her nakedness. She couldn't understand the gleam in her father's eyes and the feel of his clammy hand. He stroked her breasts and she quivered.

"Now you lie down over here beside me and relax. You don't have to do a thing; there's nothing to worry about." He pushed her onto the bed and moved beside her.

"Daddy," she wailed, "what are you going to do? I want to go to my room."

"Not yet . . . I told you to be a good girl. You don't want daddy to beat you, do you?"

A sob was his answer so he said, "Sarah and I do this a lot, and you can see it hasn't hurt her. She likes it as a matter of fact." He stroked her entire body.

"Please, let me go," she begged.

"In a little while."

"I'll tell mommy."

"No, you won't. Sarah doesn't. And do you know why? Because I'll beat you both badly, maybe I'll even beat mommy." Joe's voice was

caressing and soft. He kissed her, whispering all the while. "It will make you feel good. It's time you learned to have a little fun. You don't have to do a thing, baby, daddy will do everything. You lie here like a good girl and you'll see." He leaned on top of her.

Amy covered her eyes with her hands and squeezed her eyes shut as she felt her father's weight bear down on her. She felt a very sharp pain, then revulsion flooded her. The body heaving on top of her, those horrible sounds and grunts coming from the lips of this creature couldn't belong to her father, but only to some disgusting strange animal. Maybe it was a dream and she'd wake up.

Joe didn't want to hurt her, she was his daughter, but he rationalized that it was only right he should break her in instead of some young twerp. Granted she was no Kim Brack, he thought, but Amy's slender body gave way to the lush image of Kim and he was in the mood tonight. Perhaps when he finished with Amy he'd bring Sarah in here. A man was entitled to some relaxation after a hard day's work.

Sarah, meanwhile, huddled on the floor outside the door. She could hear the bed squeaking, slowly at first, then faster as the grunts continued. She ran to her room and threw herself on her bed crying, "Poor Amy, poor Amy."

It was much later when Amy stumbled, shaking and retching, back to the room she shared with Sarah. Her sister helped her wash up and cleaned up the mess. Sitting on the bed, she cradled the sobbing Amy in her arms, crooning to her softly and rocking her back and forth till she quieted down. Neither of them could sleep; they spent the night planning and talking of their future. They knew they couldn't tell their mother. Since Sarah was still only 16, and Amy almost 15, they would have a long time to wait till they could safely leave home.

In the meantime, they decided they would have to be careful and make sure that they were never left alone with their father. Sarah had wanted desperately to go with her mother to Georgia, but money was short. Sarah decided to get a lock for the door; she would explain to her mother that they wanted to have privacy, counting on the fact that her mother would consider it a teenage whim.

The early gray light of dawn appeared, and Sarah persuaded Amy to lie down for awhile. Sarah then sat on the bed, her knees drawn up under her, watching her younger sister huddled under the sheet. She heard her father get up and go down for breakfast, passing by their door for a moment. She held her breath, dreading the thought of his opening the door, then she let out a sigh as he continued down the stairs. A short while later she heard the front door open and close; he was leaving for work and she breathed a silent prayer. Amy was muttering and whimpering, and Sarah lay down beside her.

The sound of a car horn startled them both awake. Amy sat up.

"Oh, it's Mrs. Brack and I'm not ready. Tell her to wait. Since we're going swimming I can put shorts over my bathing suit. I'll be ready in a minute." She began to pull her bathing suit on. "Do I look any different, Sarah?" she asked, her eyes brimming with tears.

Sarah hugged her, "No, dear, don't even think about it. I'll run out and tell Mrs. Brack you'll be right out. Put everything out of your mind, Amy."

Amy finished dressing and ran down to the car. She waved good-bye to her sister.

"How are you this morning, Amy?" asked Kim.

Amy mumbled something under her breath as she stepped into the car. Kim couldn't understand her, but it didn't matter. She was more concerned about her hair dressing appointment with Madelaine. She gave Amy instructions. "Jerome is at the neighbor's waiting for you. Make sure you watch him carefully while he's in the pool, and don't let him swim long. If he gets hungry you'll find ham and cheese in the refrigerator, and give him milk, not soda."

Amy nodded and Kim glanced at her curiously. She thought the girl was oddly silent, but then perhaps she was tired. She looked a bit peaked. "I'll be gone two or three hours." At the gates Kim stopped the car, "I think you can walk from here. I'm sure you'll hear Jerry long before you get there."

Amy tripped getting out of the car, caught her balance and said good-bye, then she walked slowly down the street. She could hear Jerome shouting. He ran out from the Rufone's driveway and came up to her

panting. "Mother said we can go to the pool." She didn't answer. He watched her curiously; she seemed strange, sort of sad, he thought. "Are you alright, Amy?"

"Yes, let's go."

"I have my suit on under my pants," he said.

She didn't reply. They started toward the pool, Amy walking slowly and Jerry running ahead of her, then waiting for her to catch up to him. He thought she looked strange but decided not to bother her about it. Once they were swimming, she would forget whatever was bothering her.

At the pool Jerome dove in and swam vigorously. Amy sat on the side of the pool and watched. A tear rolled down her cheek and she brushed it away impatiently. She felt dizzy and sick to her stomach, and her mind turned to the horror of the night. That horrible animal had been her own father! She wondered how long Sarah had been enduring his attacks. She thought of her mother and what she would say or do if she knew. She shuddered and grabbed at her stomach.

Jerome studied her from the pool, then called, "Are you alright, Amy? You look funny. Maybe you should go inside or sit under the umbrella."

Amy was stubborn. "No, Jerry, I have to watch you, that's what your mother is paying me for. Go swim for a while." She sounded cross so Jerome swam away.

She kept worrying, then heard a voice say, "It happened last night. Can you image?" The woman was sitting in a chair near her.

"Such a shame," said another voice, "and so young, too."

The first woman looked at Amy and, realizing Amy could overhear the conversation, whispered to the other. Amy turned red and shuddered. Could they be talking about her? She wondered how anyone would know unless Sarah had said something. "It must be me they're talking about," she muttered to herself, and she turned away so they couldn't see her face. In small communities everyone seemed to know everybody else's business. She trembled. If they were gossiping about her, they might tell her mother what they knew. What would her mother

say? Would she believe them? She could hear her father denying it, accusing them of having boyfriends in their rooms.

Her thoughts were wild. Sitting there, miserable and ashamed, sick at heart, she barely heard the voice behind her. Someone touched her shoulder and she jumped, then saw Dave Scarbough from the high school football team standing near her.

"Hi Amy. A penny for your thoughts. You must have been a million miles away. I called you twice."

"Oh, hi Dave." Her voice was thin.

"What are you doing here?"

"Watching Jerome Brack."

"Say," he said, dropping down beside her, "you look groovy in that suit." He grinned, letting his eyes run appreciatively over her body. "You sure do look good. How about a soda?"

She cringed. "I can't leave. I have to watch Jerry while he's in the pool."

"Don't worry about that. My brother Ted is swimming, and he can watch him for you." He called to his brother and asked him to keep an eye on Jerome for a few minutes. Ted nodded and he waved back in appreciation. Then he helped Amy up and ran his finger down her back as they walked over to the soda machine by the clubhouse. "You still dating Frank?"

"Yes, sometimes." She put her face down to sip her coke.

"Does he have an exclusive?"

"What is that supposed to mean?" she asked softly.

"Are you his girl?"

"I date who I want." She sounded bitter and he wondered why. Maybe they'd broken up.

"How about dating me? I'm not going steady and we can have a ball whenever you're at the club. You could be my guest and spend the summer here." He rolled his eyes at her and pulled the back of her bra. It snapped hard against her back when he let go, and it stung her body. "What about it Amy?"

She gasped and dropped her coke. His tone implied more than dating.

She pushed him and ran away screaming, "Leave me alone, Dave."

Dave went after her completely bewildered. He knew she liked him, she had always been friendly enough. "Amy wait, I didn't mean it," whatever "it" was, he thought. "Please, wait a minute, what's the matter with you?"

She looked back over her shoulder at him with an expression of revulsion and fear on her face. "Just stay away from me, you pig."

Everyone stopped talking, startled at what was going on. Amy became aware of their gaze and came to a stop. She didn't know which way to run. Ahead of her were all the people, their faces a blur now, and behind her Dave was coming closer. She twisted from side to side in sheer panic and embarrassment, not knowing where to go. She grabbed a ladder that was close and tried to get her feet up on the rungs. She missed some and skinned her knees as she frantically climbed up to the diving board before Dave could grab her. She was almost at the top and saw him starting up the ladder.

"You're rotten, like my father!" She was yelling hysterically. "I hate all you men. You're so dirty!" Her words ran together incoherently and tears streamed down her face. Several people started toward them and Dave began to turn red.

"Darn her, everyone's going to think I did something wrong." He saw the questioning, accusing glances.

Amy saw these same glances but thought they were directed toward her. She sobbed to herself, "They must know! What am I going to do?"

She ran to the end of the board. Dave yelled at her from the top of the ladder. He was coming closer. Someone from below yelled at her, "Young lady, come down instantly." The tone was commanding but gentle. People sensed that something was seriously wrong. The girl was twisting and swaying dizzily at the end of the board. Dave moved toward her, talking softly as he inched his way forward.

Amy froze. Her imagination was out of control and she could scarcely see through the stream of tears that clouded her eyes. She bounced the board and Dave made an effort to grab her, but missed; she convulsed and jumped, twisting away as she moved, completely off balance. She thrashed wildly in the air and then there was a dull thud as she plunged to the

bottom. Someone screamed. The board had struck her on the head. Everyone around the pool was motionless, their eyes wide in shock. Amy didn't come up; she was floating near the bottom of the pool, her arms hovering limply at her sides. Dave dove to retrieve her; two other boys helped and the three of them propelled her upwards. As her head surfaced, a gasp broke the silence. She gushed blood. Once they had her out of the pool, someone tried to staunch the ugly wound but saturated the towel instantly. Someone ran into the clubhouse to call an ambulance, then Vinny Rufone's house, hoping he might be there. One of the ladies covered Amy with a towel, and Dave whispered, "Amy, open your eyes."

Someone touched his shoulder and asked, "Young man, what did you do?"

"I didn't do anything. I asked her for a date, and she said something about men being rotten or something." The faces were questioning, and he repeated, "I didn't do anything, believe me, I asked her for a date. I wouldn't hurt Amy for the world," he sobbed.

The ambulance arrived and the men lifted Amy's body onto a stretcher and took her away. The news spread through Baywater and calls flooded the Sayr's Point switchboard. Janet called Madelaine's Beauty Shop and told Kim what had happened, suggesting they meet at the hospital. She told her she'd arrange for Jerome to stay with Emma till they got back.

Janet and Kim were sitting in the waiting room of the emergency section. Sarah came running in, her face white from the shock. "How is Amy? Can I see her?" Her voice was anxious, on the brink of hysteria, so Janet put her arms around the shaking girl to comfort her.

Joe Carter came in. "I heard about the accident and came right over. How is Amy? What happened?" He glanced at his other daughter briefly.

Janet answered, "I don't know. I wasn't at the club."

Joe turned to Kim. "I thought Amy was watching Jerome today."

"She was. They went to the pool, but I don't know anything more than that."

Joe lit a cigarette; his hands shook. In his own way he loved his daughters and now felt a twinge of guilt about the previous night. "Has the doctor come out yet?"

"No," Janet answered, and she looked down the hall. "Here he is."

A young doctor asked softly, "Are any of you relatives of the Carter girl?"

Joe stepped forward as Sarah turned her head. "I'm her father, how is she?"

"I'm sorry, I have bad news for you. The blow on her head not only fractured her skull, but it broke her neck as well."

Joe gasped, the color drained from his face; he scarcely felt the cigarette burn his fingers. Janet took it and mashed it in an ashtray nearby. Kim was stunned. Sarah hadn't moved. Joe asked to see Amy; Kim and Janet led Sarah to a chair.

Janet suggested, "You'd better come home with us, dear, your father will have a lot to do."

Sarah let them guide her out of the hospital, her eyes were dry, her face stiff and white. She moved like a zombie and murmured, "It's all his fault, all his fault."

Janet and Kim didn't understand her meaning, but thought she had heard that the kids were fooling at the pool. By now they realized that Amy had struck her head on the diving board.

Once back at Janet's they coaxed Sarah to lie down on the couch. Kim stayed with her while Janet phoned Emma to send Jerome there. They murmured softly, Janet stroking her forehead. When Jerome arrived he sat on the floor, his eyes big and round. Then Janet went to phone Charles.

She was startled when he replied, "That's terrible. But I hope there isn't anything wrong with that board either, because if there is, the club could be sued. Better check into it, and you'd better stop anyone else from using it till Dan checks it out. See if anyone saw the accident. I'll stop by Carter's on my way home and talk with Joe and Sarah."

"Sarah is here now. So is Kim. Amy was watching Jerome at the pool today."

"Has Jerome said anything? What about Sarah?"

Janet said, "The only thing Sarah said is that it's someone's fault. Jerome told us she hit her head on the board. Dave Scarbough was nearby."

"Well, find out what you can and take care of things at the club. I'll leave

as soon as I can."

Janet left Kim with Sarah and Jerome and walked to the clubhouse. People were sitting by the pool talking. They stopped chatting when they saw Janet and waited for information about Amy.

Her voice trembled. "Amy's dead. She fractured her skull and broke her neck. That poor child was so young and full of life, and now she's dead." Her eyes filled with tears.

Everyone had startled expressions on their faces. Janet was depressed; many things were happening and she realized she couldn't cope with them. She was crying.

Lenore put her arms around her. "Sit down, Janet. Relax."

"I can't. Charles said we have to check the diving board to see if there is anything wrong with it . . . the club could be sued. And he said we are not to let anyone else use it until Dan checks it out thoroughly."

"I've already been up on the diving board and it seems perfectly in order, but I roped the area off so no one can go up till it's checked further."

"Good. Well, I have to get back to the house. Kim is there with Sarah, and Charles should be home soon. I'll call you later." Her voice sounded weak and tired.

As she walked back to the house she thought that Charles was right to suggest checking the board and finding out the details. Joe was nice enough, but like so many other people, he might want to start a lawsuit to collect money. Once grief passed, people became mercenary.

When she returned home she'd found that Sarah had gone. Joe had stopped by to pick her up when he hadn't found her home. Kim had put coffee on.

"You know, Janet, there's something fishy. When Joe came in to get Sarah, she wouldn't go. She seemed to be afraid. We had to coax her to leave with him. When they went out the door Joe took her by the arm and she pulled away, sobbing, and ran to the car."

"That's natural, she was upset about Amy. They were close. Did Joe call Nancy?"

"He didn't say." Then she added, "Amy wasn't herself today. Both Jerome

and I noticed it."

"Well, you know girls in their teens."

They were sitting, drinking coffee and heard a car door slam. "That must be Charles. I'll get a cup for him."

Charles came inside, and without saying a word, slumped into a chair. He had an odd expression on his face.

"What's the matter? What's happened?" Janet offered him coffee but he shook his head wearily. Kim leaned forward as Janet pulled her chair closer. She leaned over and put her hand on his knee. "What is it darling?"

He lit a cigarette and said in a low, somber voice, "I stopped by the Carter's. Vinny was there. Sarah was screaming hysterically at Joe and they were arguing. Vinny wanted to give her a sedative, to calm her, make her sleep, but she wouldn't take it. She was screaming that she wouldn't stay alone with her father, that she was afraid of him. Vinny finally got her subdued, then sent Joe to phone Nancy so he could question Sarah. When he left, she told Vinny that Joe had attacked Amy last night."

"Attacked her, what do you mean, dear?"

He lowered his voice so Jerome, who was playing on the porch, wouldn't hear the conversation. "It appears that Joe raped her last night."

Kim said, "Oh God, no!"

Janet said, "Are you sure? I can't believe it."

"Yes, I'm sure. I heard her tell Vinny. I was sitting there listening. It seems last night was the first time he touched Amy. According to Sarah, he's been abusing her for some time. He had threatened to beat her if she had told, and last night he got drunk and went after Amy. The shock was too much for her. I called Dave to find out exactly what happened in detail, and he told me about the things she'd yelled at him about her father and men. Anyway, I doubt there's anything wrong with the diving board."

"Did Joe know what Sarah said?" Kim asked.

"Yes, he came back and she was still making the accusation, so Vinny had to call the police. Incest is a serous crime, you know." Then he cautioned,

"Don't discuss this with anyone. It will be bad enough when Nancy comes back, and once Joe is formally arrested and prosecuted, it will be in the newspapers. It's an ugly situation, especially for Sarah and Nancy. Of course, Sarah will have to testify against her father, and the whole thing will be another traumatic experience, telling it in a courtroom full of people."

Kim stood up. "I think I'd better bring Sarah to my house to stay till Nancy gets back."

Charles nodded. "That's a good idea."

Kim called Jerome and they left.

Janet was unable to control her emotions any longer and burst into violent sobs. Charles gathered her in his arms and drew her head to his shoulder. The room gradually darkened.

"I thought I understood . . . people. Who could have believed Joe . . ." She was tired and didn't complete her sentence. Charles helped her up the stairs and lay her on the bed. She was exhausted and fell asleep immediately.

CHAPTER 9
FALL 1967
ALCOHOL AND FEAR

Although a month had passed since the Carter tragedy, people were still discussing it. Joe had been arrested and let out on bail until the case came to court. Nancy refused to allow him in the house and he took a furnished room in town. No one wanted anything to do with him and he was miserably lonely. He was also frightened about the charge and what sentence the judge might pass.

Nancy and Sarah were living alone in the little house. Nancy had consulted with Charles about a divorce and had started proceedings.

Mothers became more cautious about their daughters and were relieved when school opened and they went back to a normal routine.

Janet and the women in the club sometimes went to the pool on weekdays. It was mid-September, summer vacations were over, husbands were back working, and children were in school.

"Has anyone heard about hurricane Beulah?" Kim looked up at the sky as she sat by the pool at the club.

"The last I heard, the winds had hit one hundred and thirty-five miles per hour, the damage was about five hundred million, and the deaths are listed at about fifteen; but I haven't listened to any news since this morning." Janet shook her head. "It's hard to believe the wind can blow that hard. I wonder if we're going to get any of it."

"Maybe the tail end. It left the West Indies and has struck southern Texas."

Ruth Foster came up to them. "Hi, want to walk on the beach awhile?"

161

"Sure, why not," Janet said, and Kim nodded.

As they started along the beach Ruth was complaining, "You know, my car isn't running right. It wouldn't start today."

"I have that problem sometimes, but it always happens when I'm miles from home with no service station nearby. Did you have anything important to get done?" Janet asked.

"No, I wanted to drive in and have lunch with Gordon, that's all."

As they made their way up the beach they saw Robbie sitting on a picnic table, deeply engrossed in his telescope. He barely heard them, but Roma nudged him with her nose and growled a subtle warning. He turned around. "Hi there. Am I in your way?"

"No," protested Kim. "But what were you watching so intently?"

"Some of the sailboats. What beauties!" Robbie gestured toward the scope. "Want to look?"

Kim moved to the telescope. She swung it around slowly. "Glory, you'd think you were only a few feet away."

Robbie looked again. "I can see everyone on the deck of the ferry, too. Hey, that looks like Uncle Charles in Mr. Brack's rental."

"What?" exclaimed Janet. "Let me see." She moved to the telescope. "I can't see him. Are you sure?" She stepped away.

Robbie peered intently. "He was behind the ferry. Sure, there he is, and Mrs. O'Quinn is there drying her hair."

Janet's face flushed and her eyes shone with anger. Ruth spoke softly, "I have to get back and get someone to look at that car." She walked away in order not to embarrass Janet.

"Bye, Ruth." Kim waved.

"Bye," Janet's distraught voice replied.

"What on earth is that?" Kim twisted her head. There was a roaring sound. Suddenly a motorcycle came into view and they walked toward the clubhouse eager to see who it was. It stopped a few feet from them, and they stared in amazement as Russ Howard pulled a helmet from his head. Then a second cycle whipped around the bend and spun toward them. The second figure pulled up, pulled off a helmet, and Lenore's red hair came tumbling down around her face.

"Lennie!" called Janet. "What are you doing on that thing?"

"Riding it, naturally."

"That's dangerous . . . you'll kill yourself. Where on earth did you get it?"

Russ answered. "It's mine. Stan Rudowski and I bought them yesterday and Lenore said she wanted to ride one, so I arranged for her to bring mine out to the house while I delivered Stan's."

Kim laughed, "Lenore, you're amazing. Where did you learn to ride?"

"In Europe. They're better than cars. Hi, Rob." She turned to smile at her son, who had walked over and was running his fingers over the machine.

"I've got to get back to the store, ladies." Russ turned to Lenore. "Thanks for helping me out. Just leave it by the garage." They heard the roar of his motorcycle, and he was gone.

Lenore watched him for a moment, put her helmet back on her head, tucking her hair in it, and said, "I'll be right back." She swung the machine around and whirled it toward the Howard's house.

Kim and Janet looked at each other in astonishment. Then Kim said, "Think I'll get a soda and go on home. See you later." She walked to the machine, got her drink and walked off the club grounds.

Janet turned to Robbie. "Are you sure that was Charles you saw on the boat?"

"Yes, Aunt Jan, I've seen him once or twice before."

"Alone?"

"No," Robbie answered slowly. He was embarrassed and added, "with Mrs. O'Quinn."

Janet walked away abruptly, very disturbed. First the golf and now this. She found herself wondering if he would admit to it or try to convince her that Rob was mistaken. She would talk to him that evening.

Charles was successful in convincing Janet that there was nothing but friendship between him and Dottie. He said that a closing had been postponed, so it was an opportunity for some relaxation, and without thinking he had made plans to rent Thom's little runabout in Sayr's

Point. He said he happened to bump into Dottie en route to the boat and on the spur of the moment invited her along. Janet tried to believe him but inwardly she was very distressed. Charles agreed not to go off boating again without telling her, so she rationalized there shouldn't be any reason for concern. Of course Charles was aware that the boating season was almost over, and by making his promise he hadn't sacrificed anything, but he had pacified Janet.

Meanwhile Baywater and its residents went about their normal, everyday lives. September flowed into October and it was getting cooler. Everything had calmed down in Baywater but Janet couldn't understand one thing. She wondered why the Rufone's front porch light was on every night. It disturbed her.

One particular evening after Ann had put Lucille to bed, Ann wandered around the house anxiously, one hand twisted in the pocket of her robe. Her brow was furrowed and there were dark circles under her eyes. She fingered a key, then took it out of her pocket for closer inspection. It was a motel key. Vinny must have forgotten to turn it in at the motel when he had left. Room fourteen. It had been five o'clock this morning when he had come home drunk again. She sat on the sofa to think. He had slept till noon then got up and went out. She hadn't had a chance to speak with him.

She was worried about him. The hospital had recently suspended him; his patient, an old lady, had been very ill and he had been summoned to see her. He had arrived at the hospital drunk, and before he could look at his patient, he had passed out cold. The old lady had died and Vinny had been held responsible, but since her case was terminal and she would have died within a few days, his suspension was temporary. He was forced to find another hospital way over on the north shore where he could admit and care for his patients temporarily. He kept coming home at odd hours, usually drunk, and if Ann was in bed asleep he would yell for her to fix his dinner, and sometimes he would slap her. It

wasn't late yet. She decided to lie down on the couch. If he came in screaming she might get him into the kitchen before Lucille woke up from the noise.

She thought of her five year old. How would you explain this to a child? Lucille knew that her father was different, and she cowered sometimes when she heard him yell at her mother, but Lucille loved him. Ann sighed and studied the room. They had been living here a year, and the house wasn't fully decorated. Vinny paid the bills and gave her a modest sum to run the house. She didn't understand what he did with the rest of the money he made, and never asked him. She rarely bought anything, and on the few occasions when she had needed clothes for herself, she cringed when she asked him for more money. He ended up thundering at her, insulting her, and "putting her in her place."

Basically she was an old-fashioned girl, brought up by an Italian family, and she accepted the fact that the man was the undisputed head of the house and earned the money. The woman stayed at home, always at her family's beck and call. She had tried to please Vinny, and it had seemed for a while that things were going well, except for their sex life. Perhaps he had a sex drive she couldn't understand that compelled him to drink and run around. She shuddered as she thought about sex; she couldn't discuss it openly, and even though other women talked about it, she felt it was too intimate and personal for conversation. Ann had tried in every way to please Vinny, but his insistence on oral sex, which disgusted her, caused many arguments.

She shook her head and wondered about these women he went with. Did they all please him? They couldn't have, because only a few months earlier he had taken some woman to motel, and shortly after they arrived, he had started to beat her. The manager had been called by the woman in the next room. When he opened the door with a passkey, he had found Vinny pummeling the woman mercilessly. When the manager tried to stop him, Vinny attacked him, smashed furniture, and passed out. The woman had run swiftly from the room, escaping any further involvement, but the manager had looked through Vinny's pockets, found his identification, and called Ann. She had promised to see that all the damages were paid, and persuaded the manager to keep the incident

quiet. She never questioned Vinny and tried to put the incident out of her mind.

She had fallen asleep but awakened when she heard the door slam. Vinny's voice was yelling harshly. "Ann, get my supper!" He stumbled into the living room and stood there, weaving back and forth. "Did you hear me, you bitch? Get my supper!"

Ann shook her head. She was bitter; he was drunk again. "Get your own, Vinny, we ate hours ago, it's almost . . ." Before she could finish the sentence, Vinny grabbed her by the hair and cruelly yanked her to her feet. She cried out in pain and tried to pull away, but he held her hair tightly. She took the key out of her pocket and threw it at him. "Here! You forgot to leave this at the motel last night."

"Oh, so you found it. I wondered what I did with it. So now you know! I had a good time last night, got what I wanted. There are some women who think I'm wonderful."

He let her go, and she smoothed her hair down as she walked into the kitchen. Vinny followed her, stumbling into her as he moved. She took food from the refrigerator, but Vinny kept getting in her way, laughing at her, pulling. Ann evaded him and put some food into a pan; Vinny came up behind her and covered her eyes. She stiffened. What would he do? His fingers strayed to her neck and she twisted away, picking up a knife from the counter. "Stay away from me Vinny. You've hurt me for the last time. If you ever hit me again, I'll kill you."

"Will you?" His eyes glittered with hate and his voice dropped a pitch as he recoiled slightly. "You know, Ann, someone came into my office today and said I'm God. Can you imagine that? Me, God? They should know that their doctor's wife wants to kill their God. Do you think I'm God, Ann?" He laughed as he moved farther away.

"No, Vinny, I don't think you're God. In fact, right now I don't even think you're a man. You're a drunk."

"I'm drunk alright. If I wasn't, I couldn't come here. Do you know that? Do you know that I don't love you? I don't like you. In fact, I hate you. I hate you."

Ann watched him warily. "I know you do, Vinny, but you're hungry now;

let me pass by and I'll warm your supper."

He moved away, then came the attack. He lunged at her and grabbed the knife with one hand, and with the other he slammed her violently against the counter. A pain shot into her back. Vinny was holding the knife at her throat now. "I have the knife now, Ann. Shall I kill you or shall I wait until you heat that garbage for me?" He waved the knife at the jar of sauce. "I don't want that crap, you make me fresh sauce."

"I can't, not at this hour."

"Hell you can't." He shoved her.

"Vinny, leave me alone or I won't make you anything."

She tried to pass him, but he grabbed her arm and twisted it saying, "Are you going to make me some fresh sauce?"

"No, I'm not." She was surprised at herself for standing up to him. He dropped the knife, picked up the jar of sauce and hurled it against the wall. Then he glared at her and stumbled out of the room muttering. She took a sponge and cleaned the mess. She was picking up the broken glass when she heard a sound behind her. She jumped, but it wasn't Vinny; it was Lucille standing in the room, rubbing her eyes and whimpering.

"Mommy, what's all the noise? I'm afraid."

"Oh, darling, you shouldn't have come down." Ann wiped the tears from her face. "Nothing's wrong, there was an accident. Go back to bed and I'll be up shortly."

Before the child could leave, Vinny returned to the kitchen, holding a rifle. Ann clutched Lucille to her as he came closer. He leaned over and squeezed her cheek. "Hi, baby."

Lucille smiled at him, unaware that he was drunk. "Hi, daddy."

"What's the matter, honey?" He crinkled his nose and she was amused.

"I couldn't sleep, I woke up. Daddy, can I watch television?"

Ann interrupted, "No, you can't, you have to go back to bed." She picked the child up and quivered as Vinny swung the gun toward her. He was very unsteady and she could see his knuckles turning white as he clutched the gun. "Dear God," she thought, "what if that goes off. He'll kill one of us."

"Are you trying to keep my daughter from me?" He took Lucille and said, "Come on, I'll put the TV on for you." He stumbled going through the door and Ann held her breath. She followed him anxiously. He switched on the light, placed Lucille on the couch and turned on the set. Ann swiftly sat down beside her daughter, who promptly put her head in her mother's lap and fell asleep.

Vinny stomped about, waving the gun and calling her names. He cursed her for not getting his super. Ann wished he would pass out, but he had worked himself up to such a state that she doubted anything would stop him. He sat down across the room and watched her intently. He sat so long that she sensed he was falling asleep, his eyes half-closed, his mouth half-open. She was startled when she heard his voice, low and dangerous. "I think I'm going to shoot you, Ann. Would you like to die?"

She made every effort to sound calm. "No, Vinny, I wouldn't like to die, at least not now."

He peered down the barrel at her and laughed raucously, "You look better this way . . . I could shoot you right through your eyes."

Ann didn't answer. Her mind was whirling with questions. "Why was he trying to punish her? Or was he punishing himself?" She didn't think that he would do anything crazy while Lucille was in her lap; perhaps if she stayed calm and ignored him, he would settle down. It was obvious that he wanted to torment her, but perhaps he'd have to go to the bathroom and then she could call the police.

He must have read her mind.

"Thinking of calling for help? I wouldn't do that. Are you willing to admit you think I'm God?"

He rose from the chair. There was a sudden muted explosion and a scream from Lucille. "Oh, dear God, you've killed Lucille!" She gathered the child up into her arms and rocked back and forth, whimpering, "My baby, my baby."

Lucille looked at her and pulled away. "What was the noise, mommy?"

Ann looked around, the hole in the wall to the side of them indicated where the bullet had gone. She didn't know if he'd missed them by accident

or if it was a stroke of luck that he was a poor shot. She raced up the stairs with Lucille and locked her safely in her room, certain that Vinny wouldn't purposely hurt Lucille. She tiptoed softly to the top of the stairs, and saw her husband standing at the bottom aiming the gun at her. Her first instinct was to flee and run to her bedroom, but she was sure he'd follow her and she'd be trapped. Perhaps if she walked slowly down the stairs talking to him she might soothe him. As she began to move he said, "Come down here and make me supper."

Ann stepped slowly and hesitantly. When she reached bottom he struck her across the face. "That's for not having my dinner ready. Now get out to the kitchen."

He pushed her forward and she took the momentary advantage. She turned and gave him a strong shove, then raced for the door before he could regain his balance. She had to get out of the house; maybe she could get to one of the neighbors, maybe Joe Banshata could handle him. Once outside, she started running toward the Banshata's when she heard his voice. "Stop right there. This gun is pointed at your back."

She froze in her tracks, her heart was pounding. He was walking toward her and was crazy drunk. He stopped, then as he started to move again, she ran to the shadow cast by a big oak. A shot ripped the night air. She knew her only hope lay in flight. Somehow she had to keep in those shadows and move from tree to tree. Vinny was twisting around looking for her. "Where the hell are you? Ann, come back here," he ordered.

She stood very still and tried to hold her breath. He began to mutter something about her and Pat, "both no good shits." She ran toward another tree, the shadows covering her. The rustling of the autumn leaves caught his attention.

"Ha, ha, now I see you," he called in a whimsical voice. He raised the rifle and aimed it in her direction. She cowered behind the tree.

"Please, Vinny, don't do this. I'll make you dinner," she begged. She was half hysterical with terror. She stared at the Willoughby's house across the street, praying for a light to go on, but the house remained in darkness.

Vinny was ranting at her. "I don't want lousy dinners and I don't want you."

She noticed headlights coming in her direction and she raced out into the road. Vinny started behind her. The bright lights of the car framed both of them. Vinny hesitated for a moment, blinking from the blinding lights. The car stopped and a door slammed. As Ann fell to the ground she heard Mark's voice, "Are you alright Ann? What's going on?" He helped her up and tried to make some sense out of her incoherent babbling. He had heard the shot, and seeing Vinny with the gun, realized that Ann had been the target.

As he moved cautiously toward Vinny, it became apparent that Vinny was drunk. He tried to sound casual. "Hi, Vinny, what are you doing out? Did you have to work late?"

Vinny was caught off-guard and began to mutter something about supper, and then Mark was beside him. "Listen, buddy, let me help you. You've just had a shade too much." He took the gun from Vinny's unresisting hands and put his hand on his shoulder. "Want me to help you into the house?"

Vinny snarled at him and mumbled, "I'm tired and going to bed." He walked off toward the house, listing side to side.

Mark put his arms around Ann. "Was he trying to kill you, Ann? Why?"

Ann collapsed into his arms, crying in agony. "He was crazy drunk; he took shots at me and Lucille and chased me with the gun. Thank God you came by."

"Shh, it's alright. Lucky I happened to leave the party at the club when I did." He patted her shoulder. "What shall we do? Do you want me to call the police?"

"No, I don't want any more trouble."

Mark put the rifle in his car. "I don't think it's good for you to stay in that house with him tonight. Where's Lucille?"

"I locked her in her room. Vinny won't hurt her, but I think I'd better see if she's asleep."

"I'll go with you."

The front door was open, and they stood listening for a few seconds. The house was still, and they crept up the stairs on tiptoe. Ann pulled a key from her pocket and unlocked the little girl's room. Lucille was sleeping peacefully. "Thank God she didn't see all of this."

They could hear Vinny snoring as they went back downstairs.

"I don't think you should stay here tonight. Is there anywhere else you could go?"

"Were the Banshata's at the party?"

"Yes, but they left earlier."

"I'll call Jenny and see if I can stay there." She went to the den and phoned.

"Ann, what's the trouble?" asked Jenny, hearing the shaky voice.

Ann gave her brief facts, and Jenny insisted she and Lucille stay at their house. "Do you want me to send Joe over?"

"No, Mark came by in time. He'll help me."

They took the baby and went to the Banshata's. After Ann put Lucille in bed, she came back to the kitchen. Joe offered Mark a drink, but he declined. It was late and he still had a lot of work to prepare for morning classes. As Joe walked to the door with Mark, Mark could only tell him what he'd seen and what Ann had told him, which still didn't fully explain what had happened or how it had begun. Back in the kitchen, Jenny tactfully avoided questioning Ann. She made cocoa and busied herself setting the cups and saucers out.

Mark left the Banshata's, shaken by what he had witnessed. He had always felt Vinny was fortunate to have a wife like Ann; now he realized how sad it was for her to have to live with a violent drunk like Vinny. It seemed to Mark that marriages were one-sided. One partner was the giver; the other was the taker. One would try to make the relationship wonderful and enriching, the other would tear it down and destroy. Perhaps that was why he had never married. He was angered by what he had seen and began to speed. If only he had been lucky enough to meet someone like Ann. Then he rephrased his thought. It was unfortunate that he hadn't met Ann before she had married Vinny. He shook his head abruptly and concentrated on his driving, unaware that he was pressing the accelerator farther and farther down, speeding faster and faster.

CHAPTER 10
ELECTIONS
"TWO AT A TIME"

Republican County Headquarters was jammed. The party had won the County Executive seat and the celebration was uproarious. The County Leader introduced Percy Harding, the new County Executive. The room was hot and Janet was perspiring. She hated crowds and noise and found the humid odor of bodies pressing and milling around her offensive. She continued to smile graciously, trying to convey an impression of exuberance. Harding's voice droned around her. "I'd like to thank all of you who helped us make this a victory. Without your efforts and support we couldn't have done it. I want to thank my wife, Martha, a real trooper, for her help."

The crowd whistled and cheered and some of the women close to Martha Harding hugged her. Janet saw tears glistening in her eyes, and a smile sparkled across her face. Janet spotted Charles in the crowed and waved.

Percy continued, "Hold it everyone, that's enough applause for the little woman, we don't want her to think she won this single-handed." The crowed laughed and he continued, "There's one other person who I want to single out and thank publicly. The man who directed my campaign, the man with brains and strategy who put it together. He gave up a good deal of his time, many of his nights, and more energy than I believed possible—my friend and yours, our co-chairman . . . and I want him up here to get the credit he deserves . . . Charles Henderson!"

As Charles walked up to the platform and shook hands with Percy and the County Leader, the crowd broke into a roar that drowned out the beating drum. The applause was deafening and Janet observed that her

husband basked in the attention. She had backed him in his political interests, but now she had the feeling it was a mistake, and that it would take him further from her. Holding his arms up, Charles subdued the crowd and spoke. He extended his hand. "Congratulations, Percy. I guess from now on I'll have to refer to you as 'Sir' and 'The Honorable.'" The crowd laughed. "I'm sure you'll agree that our new County Executive is one heck of a great guy." The crowd roared and clapped and Charles thanked everyone for their cooperation.

Once the rest of the victors were introduced, a small band of musicians marched up to the front of the room and led most of the people outside for a victory march. Charles stepped down from the platform to meet Janet and they stayed inside the building, waiting, till the conga line returned. Janet's head throbbed, and she whispered, "It's late and I'm getting sick to my stomach. Can't we leave?"

"I'm tired myself. I'll try to break away as soon as possible."

It wasn't much later that Charles headed the car toward Baywater, and as they drove through the gates, the serenity and peace they found there was a welcome relief after the noisy party they'd left.

"I can't wait to soak my feet in a warm tub." Janet wiggled her toes.

"What about a bite first?"

"That's a good idea. I didn't touch a morsel at headquarters. Say, look at that. The Fosters have their lights on. I wonder if they're watching the returns."

"Somehow I can't see Gordon having an interest in politics." He pulled the car into the driveway. "Am I stiff!" He stepped out of the car and stretched, then went up the front steps.

While Charles was searching for the key, Janet watched the Foster's house. Someone turned the porch light off, then the downstairs went dark. But she noticed the upstairs bedroom light reflecting through the light-colored drapes. She wondered if Gordon was taking the next day off from work. She knew they never stayed up past midnight during the week. Charles opened the door, and as she crossed through the doorway she forgot about the Fosters and thought only of having a bite to eat and taking a hot bath.

Ruth and Gordon Foster had been talking about the office and had

lost track of time. Gordon had obtained some new and prestigious accounts in the Hamptons, and his father had been impressed by his diligence and the steady increase of business from that area. Gordon had suggested they might be able to afford a long vacation in Europe next summer if business kept on this way. Ruth was excited. As they went upstairs to bed, Ruth clutched the invitation that had arrived in the morning mail. Now she sat on the side of the bed studying it. It had been written in very elegant script. Leslie Howard requested them to be at her New York apartment for a special cocktail party on December first.

"I don't want to go. I don't even know this woman or her friends," she balked.

"Look, honey," Gordon said patiently, "they're fine people, and it's good for business to show up. I sold many of them insurance for their summer homes."

"I know, Gordon, but ever since you've become friendly with them, I have the feeling that you're dissatisfied with Baywater and our style of living." She threw the invitation on the bed and walked to the dressing table to brush her hair. She could study Gordon's face in the reflection of the mirror.

"That's nonsense, Ruth. It's only that I've been working late on these accounts." His tone was sharp and expression exasperated. "What's wrong with being dissatisfied? I want to get ahead." Then his tone softened, "It would mean a lot to me if you would come. I want them to meet my wife."

Ruth sniffed and wondered about this Leslie. Whenever Gordon mentioned her name, his manner changed. "What's Leslie like, Gordon?"

He answered without thinking. "Very nice, on the ball, with it, with what's going on today . . . not like the people in the country towns."

Ruth noticed his animated expression. "Is she pretty?"

"Not pretty," then he laughed, "but all the men think she's a sexy bitch."

"Gordon!" She put the brush down and went to bed. Gordon had already slipped into his side of the bed and was leaning on one elbow. "Well, she's stacked where she should be, and slim where she should be, has a nice figure, dark eyes and long black hair." He paused for a minute thinking about

her assets, then added, "She knows what she's got! Everybody likes her. You will too."

Ruth didn't answer, thinking she hated Leslie already. No matter what she said, she knew that Gordon had made his mind up, and if she didn't attend the party with him, he would probably go alone.

"Alright, but I'll need a new dress, something suitable for an elegant cocktail party in the city."

Gordon was relieved. "Don't worry about the price, I want you to look special and make a big impression." He leaned over and switched off the light on the night table. "I know you'll have fun."

Ruth turned on her side, but it was a long time before she fell to sleep.

For days she searched for a suitable dress, but didn't like any she saw. Finally she called Kim and asked for her help. One afternoon they found a black sheath, very plain, no sleeves, with a jewel neckline. After she put it on in the dressing room of the store, Kim nodded. "That's it, it's perfect for you. If you have a nice pendant and good earrings to match, it will be lovely. And make an appointment with Madelaine to have your hair done the afternoon of the party."

The night of the party she studied herself in the bedroom mirror. The dress and jewelry looked elegant, and Madelaine had changed her whole appearance with a magnificent hairdo. She said aloud, "I feel like Cinderella going to the ball!"

Gordon grinned as he came out of the bathroom.

It was a long drive to the city and traffic was bad. A doorman took their names and called upstairs while they waited in the lobby. Ruth looked about; it was a beautiful and elegantly decorated building. Once they had been approved, the doorman escorted them to the elevator and pushed a button.

"What does Leslie do to live in such style?"

"Nothing. She inherited a lot of money from her grandmother, and she lives to enjoy life."

The elevator stopped and they stepped out into a small hall with thick carpeting. They could hear music coming from behind one of the

two doors; Gordon rang the buzzer as Ruth studied the fancy gold name plate. Someone opened the door, and a beautiful, dark-haired girl hurried over.

"I'm so glad you came, Gordon," and she gave him a peck on the cheek. "This must be Ruth." Her glance slid over the black sheath and hairdo, and she nodded with what appeared to be approval. Ruth couldn't take her eyes off Leslie's sequined sheath, cut so low that a bra would be impossible. Leslie puffed on her cigarette holder from time to time, and Ruth ruefully reflected how silly she'd look holding one. The woman continued, "I'm so happy to meet you, dear, Gordon is always talking about you."

Ruth thought, "I'll bet," but said, "It was kind of you to invite me, too." She emphasized the "too" and wondered if Leslie caught the meaning, but if she did, she wasn't letting on. Ruth sensed that Leslie was disappointed Gordon's wife was attractive.

Leslie waved the cigarette holder in the direction of the closet. "You can put your coats in there, dear." The dear was directed at Gordon, and a momentary flush deepened the color of his face, but Gordon followed her instructions.

The man who had opened the door sidled in toward Ruth and murmured, "And who is this lovely creature, Leslie?"

"Oh, Ben, these are the Fosters from Sayr's Point. Gordon and Ruth."

"Nice to meet you," he murmured as she shook hands with Gordon. "The name's Ben Klipp." He was tall, lean and handsome, and wore a fancy jacket over a turtleneck sweater, giving one the feeling that this was a casual, relaxed man. He took Ruth's hand in his, "I'm very glad to meet you." Ruth nodded, and didn't reply, flustered by her reaction to his suave manner and handsomeness.

Leslie took Gordon's arm and steered him toward the living room, smiling to Ruth as she asked, "Do you mind if I steal your husband for a moment, Ruth? There are some people here who would like to meet him. They need advice on insurance." She turned to Gordon, "You'll probably inherit them as customers." Then she suggested, "Ben, please get Ruth a drink."

As Gordon and Leslie passed through the doorway, Leslie called her maid over and whispered something. The maid looked over at Ruth for a moment, then disappeared.

Ben took Ruth's arm. "Don't worry about Gordon; Leslie is harmless. However, I'll have to thank her for allowing me this time with you. Let me get you a drink then introduce you around." Ben took two glasses from a passing tray. Ruth tasted the drink and shuddered. Ben laughed. "What's the matter, the drink's not to your taste?"

"I'm not used to anything this strong."

"What do you usually have?"

"Daiquiris, coke."

Ben put an arm around her, "My word, you are a real sweet country miss!"

"Perhaps not so sweet." Ruth answered and took another sip. She looked around. Leslie and Gordon had disappeared. She noticed that the entire room was done in a creamy color; the carpets a delicate beige, the rounded sofa and drapes matched, and above it all hung a magnificent chandelier that cast a hundred sparkling lights around the room. Even the baby grand piano was a soft ivory, backed by marvelous wall tapestries. At the other end stood an imposing fireplace with a marble mantle, and bookshelves. Nothing had been spared to create a palatial home. Opposite the door and slightly to one side was a built-in bar crowded with well-dressed guests who were chatting animatedly. Ruth was impressed with the splendor of the room and her eyes traveled about. There were long windows covered in beige-colored silk drapes, and she became aware of a staircase with a stunning, filigreed, wrought-iron railing leading to a balcony with doors apparently to other rooms above. The living room was two stories high. She had noticed a foyer leading off the reception room and wondered how many rooms there were back there. The apartment was low-key but elegant and comfortable. She was aware that Leslie must have inherited a small fortune to live in this style. She noticed a man and woman descending the staircase, giggling and whispering.

Another man detached himself from the bar and strolled over. "Well, Ben, I see you've found a lovely lady. How about sharing her?" His

voice left no doubt about his admiration, and Ruth glowed.

Ben laughed and shook his head. "Not right now, John, perhaps later. I want to get better acquainted with her myself." He took another drink from a passing tray and handed it to Ruth, taking her empty glass in exchange.

John chuckled and shook his head. "Fine, fine, but don't forget later . . ." The sentence drifted away and Ruth had become aware of an undercurrent between the two men; she interpreted it for a slight jealousy. She drank her drink, not wanting Ben or anyone else to think she was a country bumpkin. She wanted to appear that she could hold her own like the other women.

She had forgotten about Gordon, and a few drinks later she discovered that Ben was attentive and discouraged approaches toward her from the other men. He made her feel attractive and desirable. Ben indicated that he was a bachelor with no steady woman friend and was content with his life as it was.

"Would you like another?"

"Well, I think I'm getting high," but she held out her glass.

"Don't let it bother you. A bit of food will take care of that." He moved to the bar to get her drink. Several of the men glanced in her direction, and she could see Ben nod and make gestures that eluded her for a moment. She tried to cross the room, but her step was unsteady, her eyes slightly out of focus. There were fewer people in the room. She hadn't noticed anyone leave the party, and when Ben returned with her drink, she asked him about it.

"Leslie provides various kinds of entertainments for her guests . . . whatever they want. Sometimes she shows movies for their pleasure."

Faint clapping sounds intruded on her ears. "Where's that coming from?"

"The library. I suppose the movie is proving to be a success. Would you like to see it?"

"What . . . kind of movie?"

Before Ben could answer, another man walked by. "Hi, Harry, where are you headed? I thought you'd be at the movie."

"I've seen it and have an early day tomorrow, so I think I'd better go home." Ben introduced him to Ruth, and she heard him say, "Wish I could stay, but it seems everyone is ahead of me, anyway. So long."

Ben swung around and offered her a cigarette. Ruth didn't smoke, but she didn't want him to think she was unsophisticated. "I think that might be nice." He leaned toward her intimately as he lit her cigarette. Feeling awkward she asked, "Have yoush sheen Gordon?"

"I must be slipping. I thought I was making an impression. Leslie has him in tow, I'm sure, and has his best interests at heart."

The cigarette was making her dizzy and Ruth was slurring her words. "Thish is a bic 'partment. Ev.ry.one's dish..pearing.ng.."

Ben put his arm around her. "How about taking in the movie?"

"Oops, my head ish reel-in!" She stumbled slightly and Ben tightened his arm around her waist. "Ish think I'd besth sit . . ."

Ben half-carried her through the door to the library. He could smell her perfume; it was a light, delicate scent unlike the heady odors other women used. He found her delightfully naive and sweet, and he knew that she found him interesting. She was very different from the girls he was used to spending time with. It occurred to him that she was in the dark as to what kind of parties Leslie gave. He whistled to himself silently, "This might be a lot more fun that I thought," and lowered her into a chair.

Ruth rested her head back; she was on a merry-go-round. Her eyes were heavy and she could barely focus on the screen. She was dimly aware of strange sights, and thought she heard sounds of chains and screams. A voice said, "Hit me again." She shook her head. She must be dreaming; strange events crossed the screen. Her tongue wouldn't work. Ben moved closer, stroked her hand and brought it slowly to his lips. She lost interest in the film and assumed she must be drunk.

By the time the movie ended, Ruth was in a state of limbo. She vaguely heard the sound of applause and a voice calling, "Where's Leslie?" along with the answer, "With Gordon, naturally. We've been given orders to stay out of her bedroom tonight, remember?"

The first voice chuckled, "She's been waiting for this chance for

months," and a general laugh was the answer.

Ruth had difficulty following the voices, but she was upset. There was a thick, sweet odor around her and it made her dizzy. She wanted to ask what it was but the words wouldn't come out of her mouth.

Ben lifted her from the chair. "Would you like to rest, my dear?"

Her voice came from a distance; she could hardly speak, and with tremendous effort replied, "Yeah, I'm slee . . .py, find Gordon." Her voice trailed away and she slumped against him. She was vaguely aware of people coming and going; the maid came in, and Ben and the maid helped her upstairs. The maid left and Ben stood looking at Ruth for a few moments; she opened her eyes but couldn't see him, sighed and drowsed off.

Suddenly she felt a body near her. "Gordon?" Her head was reeling. She kept slipping in and out of consciousness. Hands were undressing her, stroking her body. She was in Baywater, in her own bed, and Gordon was making love to her. Lips were moving across her mouth, and a warm, wet tongue traveled over her body, and entered an area that Gordon never did. She felt distantly stimulated but couldn't respond, then everything disappeared and she entered a dark, gray world.

Ben was disappointed; he wanted her to enjoy it to the fullest, but it didn't really matter, he thought. This way he could do what he wanted. In moments he penetrated her, surprised at how small and tight she was. The door opened and a voice said, "Ben?"

"Not yet, John," and he grunted as he worked himself up and down. "Come in."

There were soft blue and red lights on. John moved beside the bed and alternately watched the bed and the mirrored ceiling. In seconds Ben had climaxed, relaxed to subside, then rolled off her. "Your turn, she's out cold. Nice and tight, made it harder to get there; have fun." Ben dressed and walked out as John, naked, mounted the still form on the bed.

As Ben went down the stairs, he saw another man enter the room he had left. He grinned thinking it was unfortunate she was out cold. He wondered how Ruth would like two at a time.

He didn't bother to say good-night to anyone. His party was finished, so he left the apartment. It had been a satisfying evening.

As Janet read Meg's letter, a glow of happiness spread across her face. Kerry and Meg had bought a new home, Kerry's job was going well, and they were "very happy." They had joined their local country club and Meg was having a gay time. She wrote that the boys and Kerry got along so well that Kerry was hoping to adopt them. Janet finished reading the letter and laid it down on the sofa next to her. She leaned back and thought that Meg's life was taking shape. She was convinced that Kerry and Meg truly loved each other and would stay together for the rest of their lives.

She thought about Nancy and Joe Carter, and how at the court hearing the judge had insisted that Sarah testify in detail about the night Joe had first raped her, how often he attacked her after that, about the night Amy was raped, and the terror Joe had instilled in them. Charles had been worried that Sarah might not be able to take the stress of the trial and lengthy cross-examination, but she behaved admirably and there was no evidence of any trauma. Joe had been sentenced to one year in prison, and after some persuasion from Charles and Nancy, he agreed to give his share of the house to Nancy and sign the necessary papers so she could fly to Mexico for a divorce. The newspapers throughout the county carried the story of the trial with pictures of Nancy and Sarah coming and going from court; the stories caused a lot of notoriety. Nancy came to realize that she and Sarah would have to move away; the faces of neighbors were either sympathetic or accusing, and they had received many crank calls. She put the house up for sale and once a buyer had been found, she and Sarah moved, leaving Charles the power of attorney to close and send her the proceeds.

Ethel Dowling and her son, Austin, were still living in the same house. Ethel had taken a position as librarian in Sayr's Point Public Library. The boy was bitter that his father had left home. Austin had enrolled in the same

college as Robbie Morgan and had been assigned to one of Mark's math classes. Mark had attempted to befriend the boy, but Austin knew his father had been a friend of Mark's; this disturbed him and he remained aloof. Austin did his assignments and studied hard, but he wanted no relationship with Mark, other than that of student and teacher in the classroom. This had been a disappointment to Mark, for he saw the boy's bitterness and felt Austin needed someone to talk with.

Stan Rudowski was busy finishing the new wing on the hospital. All the outside work had been completed before the cold weather set in, and the crews were busy working on the interior. The ground was frozen and Stan couldn't start any new projects.

The Birklands were busy at the stationery store. Marion helped around the holidays, the busiest time of the year.

Russ Howard's sporting goods store was doing a mammoth business. People drove from miles away to buy from him. He and Claudia were very happy and contented.

It was more than a year since Ester Fine had moved into her home. Janet had helped her decorate, but once that was finished Janet hardly saw her. Ester kept to herself and rarely attended parties at the club. She had visited her brother, Dr. Morrie Fine, for one week and had been disappointed when he did not receive a Nobel Prize. She was busy at the hospital, and on her days off she attended to errands such as food shopping, picking up and dropping clothes at the cleaners, and paying bills.

Ester was hungry and wanted a quick bite of lunch. Standing in the doorway of the restaurant she evaluated the situation, then walked to the nearest booth, took off her wet coat, and sat down. By the time the waitress had approached, she had decided what she wanted to eat and gave her the order. She had the day off from the hospital and was attempting to complete as many errands as possible in the shortest amount of time. She slipped her shoes off under the table. Her feet were damp from the pouring rain. She thought how mistaken the forecaster had been when he had predicted a very light snowfall. She was deep in thought when a voice reached her.

"Is this your day off, Ester?"

"Oh, hello Kim. Yes it is, and all I've been doing since morning is attending to errands." She noticed another woman standing beside Kim.

"That's unfortunate. Bad weather to be running around. By the way, this is Madelaine Nelson, my hairdresser . . . Ester Fine, a neighbor."

"Hello." Madelaine's voice was low and mellow.

"Nice to meet you. Would you both care to sit with me?"

"Certainly," replied Kim, and they slid in across from Ester. "Madelaine is usually closed on Mondays, but I had to have my hair done for tonight, so she was kind and opened the shop and did my hair." Kim's hair was hidden under a large turban.

"That was nice of you Madelaine. Do you have your own shop?"

"Yes, I've had one for two years, and Kim is a regular customer."

The waitress brought Ester's lunch, and Kim and Madelaine ordered. After the waitress had gone, Kim said, "We're going apartment hunting."

"Oh? In this dreadful weather?" She directed her attention to Madelaine, to whom she had taken a liking.

"Yes, I've been living in an old four-family that's going to be demolished soon."

"Apartments are hard to find, and terribly expensive."

Kim said, "I'll bet half of what you earn will go into keeping a small place."

"That's true, but what else can I do?"

"You're not married?" Esther queried.

"I was, but I'm divorced. It was a short marriage." Madelaine was turning her glass around and around. "Fortunately I have my own business, and although I run the shop alone, there's just enough profit so I can get by."

"Have you ever thought about having someone live with you to help share costs? It might ease your financial situation."

"I hadn't thought about anything like that. I had my mind set on my own place."

Kim thought for a moment, then said, "You know Maddy, that's an idea. In fact, for what you would have to pay for a small apartment,

you could share a nice house."

"A house? Where would I find a house?"

Kim fell silent. Ester was studying Madelaine intently. While not as stunning as Kim, the girl was very attractive. Ester guessed her to be about twenty-seven, with dark eyes and a rather voluptuous figure.

"Kim's right. For what it would cost you to keep a small apartment, you could contribute and live in a nice house. Bedsides, it would keep you from getting lonely." She hesitated for a moment, then added, "How would you feel about moving into my place? Of course that's rather a stupid question. You haven't seen the house."

"We hardly know each other; it might not work out."

"True," smiled Ester, "but we won't know each other until we become better acquainted. Suppose you stop by later. You can see the house and we can chat."

"That makes sense." Kim turned to Madelaine. "It wouldn't hurt, Maddy. I can drop you off, if Ester will take you home." Madelaine agreed with Kim's suggestion.

"Fine with me." Ester tossed some coins on the table. "Say in an hour or so?" She walked off leaving Kim and Madelaine to finish their lunch.

"I think that would be an ideal solution Maddy. Ester's house is large enough to allow you both privacy. It wouldn't cost you any more money, and you'd have a garage for your car. Baywater is lovely, and in the summer there's the pool, beach, and tennis courts. There's year-round parties at the club."

"How would my other Baywater customers feel about Ester taking me in?"

"The same as I do." And Kim told her about the other residents in Baywater, about the parties, then she broke off, "Come on, let's go. I have to get some pantyhose and do some food shopping, then I'll leave you at Ester's."

It was still raining when Kim left Madelaine at Ester's house. Ester took her wet coat and hung it in the hall closet, and after Madelaine followed her into the living room, she lighted a fire in the fireplace. They chatted casually

for a few moments.

"I've been living here over a year now. It's a delightful spot."

"Yes, Kim told me all that Baywater offers. Sounds marvelous."

"Come, let's take the grand tour. I have one empty bedroom. There wasn't any point in furnishing all of them."

"The house is much larger than I thought," Madelaine observed.

Ester opened the bedroom door and stepped inside. "If you move in, you could do what you want with this room."

The bedroom was large and had a nice view. She liked the house. It was decorated in traditional furniture, neat, but not fussy. Once they had gone through all the rooms, they returned by the fireplace.

"You haven't said much, Madelaine, don't you like it?"

Madelaine looked about and turned her gaze to Ester. "It's a lovely house, and big enough to permit privacy."

"That's true. Well, think about it. By the way, do you have any plans for dinner tonight?"

"No."

Ester's voice was deliberately casual. "Then why don't we go out somewhere?"

"Where would you want to go?"

"Anywhere you like. I'm easy to please."

"It would be fun."

"Good. You make yourself comfortable and I'll be ready in a moment."

Once Ester left the room, Madelaine wandered about. It wasn't long before Ester returned and they went out to find a restaurant. Dinner was relaxing, and they had a chance to talk and get to know each other. They discussed the house, the costs of sharing it, and Madelaine decided to move in the following Monday. Ester was pleased; Madelaine appealed to her very much, and she knew it could be fun having her in the house. After dinner Ester drove her home. She liked Madelaine more than most women and was certain it would work out. She whistled softly to herself all the way to Baywater.

The weather forecast had been correct. By the end of the week they had their first light snowfall. Janet tucked her nose under the blankets as the phone jangled. "Darn." She reached for the receiver. "Hello?" There was no answer. "Hello, hello?" The reply was a buzz; they had hung up. This made her angry. She wondered who would be calling at ten a.m. on a Sunday morning and hanging up. She turned to Charles. "Same thing again. That's darned annoying."

Charles mumbled, "Probably a wrong number."

She was disappointed that Charles refused to take the matter seriously, even though it happened often. She looked at the calendar clock. December 10th. She hadn't started her Christmas shopping. She lay back but couldn't sleep any longer. The call had disturbed her. After tossing restlessly she got up and went down to the kitchen. She made up a batch of muffin mix, and after putting the full tins into the oven to bake, went back upstairs to wash. She slipped into a colorful lounging robe, then went downstairs to take the muffins out of the oven. The phone rang again and she picked up the receiver in the kitchen, anticipating another annoying buzz; instead she heard Charles's voice. "Is that you on the extension? Dottie's on the phone."

"Oh, hi Dottie, what's up?"

"Nothing really. Charles promised one of the boys he'd lend him a book, so I thought I might drop by and pick it up, if it's alright."

"It's okay with me, if Charles wants . . . ouch . . . I have a hot muffin pan in my hand. Hurry down, Charles. See you, Dottie." And she hung up.

They'd finished breakfast when Dottie came over with Michael. The boy was delighted with the book, sat down and commenced reading it while the grown-ups chatted.

"How's Dan's leg?" inquired Janet.

"Not much better, he's still on crutches. He sits home drinking beer and watching TV, but at least I have a built-in sitter."

"Are you in shape for the skiing season? Been doing your exercises?" Charles teased.

"For weeks. With Dan home I'll be able to get on the slope practically

every day. I hope that leg of his takes another month to heal."

"Oh, Dottie, you can't be that mean," Janet chided.

"Not really, but he deserves a rest, so it's working out fine."

"Will you be going up to Hunter Mountain at all?" Charles asked. "Are they making snow yet?"

"I'll check with Russ. He had some travel folders for a day's trip. The bus leaves at six a.m. from the parking lot behind the store, and returns at nine in the evening. If Dan and Janet don't mind, we might go together one day."

Janet tossed her head. "Mind? Of course not." She winced remembering how Charles had taken Dottie boating, and she was convinced it was harmless. Skiing seemed innocent enough. "If you two want to get up in the middle of the night in freezing weather to take a ski bus tour upstate, go ahead."

After Dottie and Michael left, Charles said, "I wish you'd take up skiing."

"No thanks," Janet replied firmly.

A week later, the ski tour bus rolled away from the parking lot at six a.m. with Dottie and Charles aboard. Janet slept late, and when Lenore called she told her how Charles and Dottie had gone to Hunter Mountain.

"Aren't you being a little too broad-minded, Jan?" she scolded.

"There's a whole busload of people; they're not going alone."

"Well, come and have dinner with us. No sense being alone the whole day."

The day passed quickly. She had dinner with Lenore then went home to watch TV. She stayed up until ten-thirty, and feeling sleepy, went upstairs to bed. But she couldn't sleep. The bus had been scheduled to be back by nine. She started to worry. Perhaps there was an accident. All kinds of possibilities raced through her imagination. She decided to call Russ and was dialing the number when she heard the car pull in the drive. She went downstairs. "How was it?"

Charles brought a cold rush of air inside with him. "One of the best days I've had. Not too crowded, so we didn't have to wait in the towlines

very long." He took off his coat and gloves.

"Did Dottie enjoy it?"

"I guess so. Skiing is a singular thing. She didn't take the high slopes and stayed at the lower levels. She went her way and I went mine. I saw her at lunch though."

Janet smiled. They hadn't even skied together. At lunch there were probably a lot of people around. How ridiculous being suspicious. She turned and went back up to bed.

Christmas came and went. Janet and Charles spent the day with Lenore and her family. Peter wasn't feeling well and didn't stay downstairs very long. It was a short celebration and Charles and Janet returned home early. On New Year's Eve the club had a big party, and once the New Year had begun, the women were searching stores for after-Christmas bargains. Janet had been studying the newspaper for sales, and seeing some household items she needed, called Lenore to go shopping, but Lenore wasn't home. She decided to call Dottie. Dan was home recuperating, so Dottie might want to get out of the house.

"Do you have any plans today?"

"Nothing special, why?"

"I thought you might like to go shopping with me. They're having some marvelous sales, then we could have lunch later."

"I don't know. I was thinking about cleaning the children's closets today."

"Well, I suppose it's the kind of day to stay in, with this cold weather and new fallen snow. Charles is going to take advantage of it and go to Briar Hill for the afternoon."

"Thanks for inviting me, Janet, but I'll take a rain check if you don't mind. I should get at those closets."

Janet dressed warmly and drove into town. She finished her shopping then stopped for lunch. While she was eating, a thought struck her. She would surprise Charles and drive over to Briar Hill to watch him ski. She hurried home, changed into sports clothes, bundled her head into a warm scarf and drove to the slopes.

The colorful ski outfits dotted the white landscape and it was a while

before she recognized Charles. She yelled and waved vigorously; finally he saw her and skied over to her. "Well, hi. What are you doing here?" He was surprised to see her.

"Thought I'd watch you awhile, besides, the fresh air is good for my complexion. How's the skiing?"

"Nice. The snow is softly packed. Been here long?" he asked casually.

"No, I arrived a few minutes ago." She noticed a familiar figure racing down the slope and recognized Dottie's checkered sweater and brilliantly colored ski pants. Dottie skied up alongside Charles with a big swoosh.

"Dottie, what are you doing here? I though you had closets to clean."

"I did, but I decided that skiing would be more fun. How was lunch?"

"Fair."

"Did you get your shopping done?"

"Look girls, I want to ski. You two can gab. See you at dinner, Jan," and he skied off.

"I went shopping alone and finished early. That's why I came to watch Charles ski." Janet was miffed.

"I'd better get back on the slopes. See you later. Sorry about lunch," and before Janet could answer, Dottie had skied off, catching up to Charles at the towline.

Janet stood watching them. They were laughing and having a great time. Janet's temper flared. She never should have told Dottie that Charles was going skiing. How naïve of her. Their relationship seemed harmless at first, but now she wondered. She was furious. On her way home she thought about those calls. Whenever she answered, the person hung up; but whenever Charles answered the phone, there was always someone at the other end of the wire. Could it have been Dottie? And that excuse about the book . . . was Dottie using the boys to get through to Charles? She recalled the incidents on the boat. Robbie had said he'd seen them together several times. She felt desolate. She had made Charles her whole life. She did everything for him. It didn't pay, she thought, pounding at the wheel. What should she do? Make something out of it? No, that would make things worse. Perhaps she ought to play a waiting game.

During the next month she saw little of her husband. He was up early, spent the day at his practice, and most evenings were devoted to "important political meetings." On Saturday nights they attended political functions in the county, and Charles was usually busy talking to others and spent no time with her, leaving her at a table waiting. They had very little communication and she felt left out of his life. Whenever he had any spare time, he went to the slopes. She knew the mysterious calls were from Dottie and she wondered why Dan was so docile. Didn't he suspect anything? Two days earlier she had been at Lenore's discussing the problem with her and she'd noticed that Robbie behaved sheepishly. She remembered the incident on the beach and began to question him. Reluctantly Robbie admitted having seen Dottie and Charles on the golf course several times. It was then that she made her decision.

"Lenore, I'm going to Florida for a while. I haven't had any fun the whole year. Why should I stay cooped up when Charles is always out having a fine time for himself. February is dismal and cold . . . I think I'll go down to Palm Beach and think things out, evaluate the whole situation."

Lenore was silent, then said softly, "Do what you think is best, Jan."

"Don't tell Charles where I'm going, will you?"

"Not if you rather I didn't."

The trains were packed. She had been lucky to get a flight within two days due to a cancellation at the last minute. She took two suitcases and Lenore promised she would send anything else she wanted. She wrote a hasty note and left it on the kitchen table. "I'm going south for a while. I want to think about us and our future. I'll let you know my address as soon as I have one."

On the way to the airport she chatted casually with the other passengers in the limousines about the impending storm and garbage strikes in the city, but while they talked, she thought about Charles and her flight. She hated planes.

Once in her seat, the captain announced take off; she fastened her

seat buckle and gripped the arms of the seat as the plane rose. Her palms were clammy and wet, and she shuddered as the ground fell away. She felt the panic swell in her throat after one glance out the window, then shut her eyes, and her entire body began to tremble. She thought about her mother and father in that small plane.

A voice beside her said, "Would you rather change seats with me?"

"Oh, yes," breathed Janet tensely.

"As soon as we're leveled out we'll switch. In the meantime hang on to my hand, it may make it easier for you."

She turned to a very pleasant face with a gentle smile.

"Thanks," and she gripped his hand tightly. "What am I doing here?" she thought. She hated to fly and kept praying that the trip would be safe. Lennie assured her she had nothing to worry about, but she was terrified. Even the pills hadn't helped. She wished she had taken a train, but was unable to get a reservation. She swallowed once or twice, and to take her mind off her predicament, tuned her thoughts back to Baywater.

CHAPTER 11
FEBRUARY 1968
EXODUS SOUTH

Janet's flight arrived safely at the West Palm Beach airport. The trip hadn't been as bad as she had anticipated, and the gentleman with whom she had exchanged seats turned out to be a well-known songwriter. Janet told him about her days at the Julliard School of Music and her professional performances; and their common interest, music, made them fast friends.

He had inquired where she was staying so his cab could drop her off. When she admitted that she hadn't made any advance reservations, he suggested she stay at the Breaker's, where he was booked, and he called ahead to make a reservation for her. For the first two nights after her arrival Janet stayed at the hotel, but she preferred to live in a smaller place, something more intimate where she could do her own cooking; so he helped her locate a tiny apartment near Worth Avenue and the shops.

On Valentine's Day the doorbell rang, and when she answered it, a delivery boy handed her a huge box of chocolates. She anticipated that the card would be from Charles asking her to return home, but instead it read, "From your favorite songwriter." She was disheartened that Charles hadn't made any attempt to contact her, and she assumed their marriage meant very little to him. She wondered what he was doing and what was happening in Baywater.

That evening, while Janet pondered about Charles and Baywater, a big party was taking place. Russ Howard and Kim Thompson had arranged it. The club was lively and people were dancing and drinking.

Ester Fine had finished a drink and was toying with her glass. She was tired and depressed, and the snowfall hadn't helped her morale. It meant she would have to leave her house earlier in the morning to drive to the hospital. She glanced over at Madelaine. How attractive she looked in her red dress! Living together had worked out well for them, and the arrangement had been readily accepted by the community. Fortunately, Madelaine had no relatives nearby to bother her, and had no other friends coming to the house. She had adapted to Baywater's social life easily and gracefully, and it was her prodding that had drawn Ester to this evening's party. While Madelaine danced with Russ, Ester watched them and had an urge to dance with Madelaine herself, but she knew this was a "no, no." She went over to the bar to get another drink and saw one of the men cut in to dance with Madelaine.

"Will you look at that heavy snowfall?" Russ yelled from the door. "That's a regular blizzard."

They crowded to the windows but it was impossible to see out; the swirling snowflakes obscured everything.

The door opened and Claudia, covered with snowflakes, came in carrying a huge, heart-shaped cake; she was struggling and almost fell. "You know, if this keeps up, we'll be snowed in by morning."

There was a general murmur and a few chuckles.

"I hope not. I'm backlogged in the office," Charles scowled.

"You can always ski in, if you have to," chimed Dottie.

"Now that IS an idea. One thing for sure, if it gets much worse, we'll be out in the snow with sleds."

"Now that IS an idea," teased Dottie, and Dan grinned.

Someone went to the buffet to taste the cake and soon the table was surrounded with people as Lenore and Claudia served. One of the men threw another log on the fireplace. Sparks flew out, and the fire flared up. At that moment the lights went out.

"My gosh," Dottie's voice sounded panicky, "I wonder what happened."

"Let's look outside." Charles moved toward the door and opened it as a flurry of snow blew in. They all crowded behind him, straining to see outdoors, but the blinding flurry of snow prevented them from seeing anything.

"I'll go out and take a look." Russ donned his jacket and disappeared almost instantly.

Lenore lit candles and the gloom lifted as the colorful, flickering lights penetrated the room.

"The trouble is, if we have no power, we won't have any heat, either," said Charles pointedly.

Russ returned. "All the street lights are out. I think we'd better go on home."

There was a general chagrin. Then suddenly the lights flickered back on and came up bright and firm. The party resumed its pace, but gradually the festive spirit dwindled. Charles put on his coat to leave and the rest of them followed suit. Someone piped, "Let's get home and see how the kids are."

Lenore, Kim and Claudia put the food in the kitchen refrigerator and returned to get their coats. Russ draped Claudia's coat over her shoulder, looked down at her feet and said, "I don't think those little boots are going to do you much good in knee-deep snow."

"You can carry me," she suggested demurely.

"Oh, sure!" Russ heckled.

The joking and bantering continued as they left the clubhouse. Some of them had walked to the party so they continued home by foot. Their voices could be heard on the street as they struggled through the snow, but only the blurry outlines of their bodies were visible.

Madelaine and Ester trudged gingerly down the driveway, then suddenly Madelaine, caught up in childish delight, scooped a handful of snow and threw it on Ester's shoulder.

"Got you," she giggled. Then she made a snowball and threw it at Ester, who was ahead of her, and it caught Ester on the head.

"Do you want a snowball fight?" Ester bent down and packed a huge snowball. Madelaine ran clumsily but the snowball pelted her on her back.

The snowball fever attracted some of the others who had caught up to them, and in moments some of the falling snow was transformed into gigantic snowballs. They laughed uproariously as they threw them. One of

the women pushed her husband; as he fell, he grabbed her arm and they tumbled together. It wasn't long before everyone was rolling about, disregarding the cold. The trees and shrubs were cloaked in white capes of snow and heavy mounds bowed their branches to the ground. Old footprints were obscured and only small hollows gave evidence that a human foot had touched there. Silence surrounded them. As Madelaine tilted her head upwards, huge flakes stuck to her eyelashes. She stuck her tongue out in order to catch the wet, tasteless shapes. They melted instantly and she swallowed, then held out her hands to capture the exquisite forms.

"Madelaine, are you coming?" Ester called from the door.

"Yes, but isn't this a fairyland, a beautiful picture?"

Madelaine ran to the front door and went inside. Ester was taking hangers down for their coats. She suggested to Madelaine, "You'd better get into a hot tub now, in case the power goes out later. If this keeps up all night, we could be powerless for a couple of days."

"What about you?"

"I'll take a quick shower and get a fire going."

A little while later Madelaine went into the living room with only a warm robe wrapped around her. The fire was blazing merrily and an aroma of coffee attracted her attention. She walked into the kitchen. Ester was busy filling thermos bottles with hot coffee. "I'm going to load a lot of wood by the fireplace just to be safe. I put a canvas down so the carpet doesn't get soiled." After the wood was stacked, Ester rummaged about for candles and a flashlight. Once organized, they stood watching the falling snow. The lights flickered and then everything went black. Ester found her way to the flashlight and lit the candles.

"Won't it be awfully cold later? Where should we sleep?"

"By the fireplace . . . it would be the best spot."

Madelaine wondered about the heat. "Suppose we put the two couches there, and move all the chairs together to make a corner or alcove in front of the fire. That way we would block out any cold drafts and concentrate the heat in that spot."

"Good idea. I'll get the blankets." Ester disappeared with the flashlight and returned in moments with an armful of them.

Madelaine took the blankets and dropped them on the sofa. "I have two quilts in my closet."

"And there are two heavy quilts and large pillows in the linen closets."

Ester gave Madelaine the flashlight and took a candle for herself. They returned, placed the chairs together, the sofas together, took some quilts and hung them so that the cold air couldn't creep in under the furniture. They dropped the others on the ground, making a thick padding to sleep on, and saved a few blankets for covers. Once the pillows were in place it looked comfortable. Ester found her portable radio and put on the news station. While waiting for the weather information, Madelaine sat down on the padding. The enclosure was practical and the heat stayed in. She felt warm and drowsy. The news came on.

"Snow all night, and part of tomorrow." Ester repeated the forecaster's words. Madelaine yawned and Ester suggested, "Go ahead and sleep. I want to wait up for the late news."

"Okay." Madelaine yawned again, then wiggled down on the quilts and snuggled under the blankets. "Mmm, this is cozy." She was asleep almost instantly, lying totally still for a while, then turning and moving as though trying to get comfortable. Ester glanced at her as she slept. Madelaine's dark eyelashes lay against her creamy face like smoky feathers. Ester assumed the frolicking in the snow and the hot tub, coupled with the warmth of the fire, had tired her completely.

Time passed slowly. Ester read for a while, but the light from the fire and candles was too dim. Finally she turned the radio off. The deep stillness of the night was unbroken save for the crackling and snapping of the logs and the ticking of the clock. Ester didn't expect to have to go to work the next day, not with all the snow, but by force of habit she wound the clock and threw more wood on the fire. It flared up suddenly, and fresh heat rolled out toward the enclosure.

Madelaine turned on her back and brushed tendrils of hair from her face; her temples were damp from perspiration. Half asleep, she threw the blankets from herself. She had forgotten her pajamas, and with all her moving and turning, her robe had opened and fallen away from her body. She now lay almost naked. Ester studied her.

Flickering flames cast shadows of dancing tongues of fire that moved over her body, touching a breast delicately, kissing the pulsing throat, lingering pensively over the lovely mound that rose from silky thighs, twisting, turning and whirling, tossing a hundred caresses that lit on a velvet cheek and slid across rosy fingers. They hovered for a fragile moment, contemplating the snowy abdomen, then sighed deliriously to sink back down across the legs and over painted toes, before returning to the fire to replenish themselves and begin another sensual dance over the delicious body. Ester's eyes followed every flicker eagerly; her lips desired to share each caress, her hungry tongue longed to taste the warm, delightful flesh at every pause. Her hands thrilled in anticipation at every shadowy touch of the fiery reflection. She was jealous of the intimacy the dancing shadows so casually accepted. Her own desires were overwhelmingly demanding, but she didn't dare destroy the picture. She sat down slowly and waited patiently till the fire burned low again, then rose quietly to add more wood. The room elsewhere was cool, and as she eased herself back to the little island they had created, she realized that soon this would be the only warm spot in the house.

Madelaine murmured something and groped till she found the blankets; she drew them around herself, turned on her side and went back to sleep. Sparks from the fire shot past the fire screen onto the blanket. Ester got up and moved the logs farther back in the fireplace. She checked the candles. She looked at the clock again and decided to set the alarm. Then she lowered herself gently to the quilt and moved closer to the sleeping form.

Madelaine's back was toward her. Gradually Ester slipped her arm across the sleeping girl and drew her close. Ester drowsed contentedly, but the vision of Madelaine's body haunted her. Madelaine stirred and muttered something. Ester woke with a start; she realized that her hand had been stroking and squeezing Madelaine's breast lightly. The girl slept on and made no apparent objection. She began to caress the rounded stomach and slowly moved up and down the whole body, shivering slightly as the warm, silky skin passed under her palm. Madelaine twitched. Ester stopped for a moment, then again began to rub and stroke the girl, before

subtly rolling Madelaine on her back. She slid the blankets away to expose the silk she had been touching. Madelaine swallowed, and as Ester leaned forward, she could feel the quickening breath flow warmly by her throat. She was dimly aware of the seeking hands; it was pleasant and she gave herself to the feeling.

Ester put the heel of her hand between Madelaine's thighs and rhythmically pressed and released till the legs slacked and opened slightly. She wouldn't wait any longer; she was exultant, her mouth and tongue reached for the voluptuous body. Beginning at the corners of Madelaine's mouth, she moved slowly and lovingly, tasting, nibbling, licking the delightful skin, simultaneously using her hands to stir a fever pitch of excitement. A sound caught her ear, a slight gasp. She raised her head to see Madelaine's eyes open gradually. "Sh, sh, sh," she whispered, "just let me, love, just let me," as Madelaine's mouth parted slightly. Ester knew that this was now the time. Even if Madelaine wanted to stop her, it would be too late; her body was betraying her mind and she was reacting instinctively. Ester lowered her face, and this time she knew she would move past the dark, soft mound and bury her tongue deep into the warm moist beauty of this girl she loved. She had waited patiently for this chance; her heart was beating wildly, and she felt Madelaine's body rise and fall with the pleasure Ester was giving her. Only when Madelaine lay still did Ester move away, then she covered her with the blanket and gently gathered her in her arms.

Madelaine had never expected to thrill to a sexual contact with a woman, but she sensed the depth of Ester's love, and her own response had seemed natural; the results were undeniably satisfying.

Now Madelaine lay awake, bewildered by what had occurred; and Ester, secure in her victory, slept peacefully.

It was a dismal morning. The rain beat against the window panes and the March winds whistled through the eaves. Ruth contemplated breakfast, but the thought of food made her ill; she rushed to the bathroom and vomited.

"Darn morning sickness," she thought. Gordon wasn't awake yet; she went into the living room and sat by a window. She watched the children on their way to the school bus and speculated about the child in her womb. She thought about Gordon and hoped his mother wouldn't call again today; somehow she always found a way to blame Ruth for Gordon's behavior. He lately appeared very restless and high-strung, was always jittery, ate little, and slept poorly. He was tired and haggard looking. The night before, he had come home late, which seemed to be the usual thing. Ruth realized he must have driven to the city to visit Leslie. She hated Leslie . . . "that woman."

Her mind strayed back to the night of the party. She shuddered as memories came flooding back. It had been no secret that Ben had taken her upstairs. Nightmares of the events disturbed her sleep, but only later, as fragments became clearer, did she recollect that the nightmare had been real, and she had indeed been the recipient of more than one man's sexual advances. The man had admitted to it, and it was only after Gordon discovered she was pregnant that he turned on her hatefully. She heard him shuffling down the stairs.

"Do you want some breakfast?" she called.

"No, I'm not hungry." He watched her from the doorway. "Maybe some coffee though."

She went to the kitchen and he followed her. As she poured his coffee she studied his face. "You ought to have a decent breakfast, you hardly eat anymore."

"Leave me alone, Ruth, all you do is nag."

"I'm only trying to help, to look after you."

"Sure you do, like you look after yourself. You're a mess. Goddamn it, you're stupid; I leave you alone with some guy and you can't even take care of yourself!" He stood up abruptly and poured himself a second cup of coffee.

Ruth's head was spinning. She was enraged; it had been his idea to attend that party.

"Why don't you have the damned thing aborted? You're not too far, are you?" he asked.

"I'm three and a half months, but . . ."

"But what?"

"I told you before, I'm afraid. I don't want to do it. And maybe the baby is yours, Gordon. We could have tests done, if you want."

"You don't think I'm going to allow something like that, do you?"

"Well, since you don't really know . . . besides I'd like to have a child, and maybe it would be good for both of us."

"That's lovely. Every time I'd look at it, I'd wonder who the father was!"

Ruth turned away and brushed a tear from her eye. There was no use talking with him.

Gordon glowered at her. "You haven't told anyone, have you?"

"No, Gordon, no one knows. But I won't be able to keep it a secret forever!" She didn't tell him that she was ashamed for being naïve and stupid, and couldn't have discussed it with anyone.

"I've got to go to the office. I'm going up for a shower. Think over what I've said." He left the room, climbed the steps two at a time, and a few minutes later had the shower running.

Ruth bit into a cracker but couldn't eat it; food choked her. She put her head in her arms and leaned on the table, but even tears wouldn't come. She had to convince Gordon somehow. She went upstairs to their bedroom. Gordon was in the bathroom and left the door slightly ajar for the steam to pour out. She could see him standing there with a towel in hand. She caught her breath and froze on the spot. Gordon had taken a small case from the top of the counter and she could see a needle and syringe. He filled it carefully then shot the contents into his arm.

"Oh, my God!" she moaned in a whisper, and a wave of nausea overwhelmed her. She staggered away shaking. She wasn't sure she could believe what she had just witnessed. She had heard about drugs and the trouble they caused, but to imagine Gordon hurting himself like that wasn't possible. He wasn't the type. But then she hadn't believed he could ever have been the type to be involved with the Leslies of the world.

He came out of the bathroom. "Oh, Gordon." He made a disgruntled sound, walked past her, threw the case on the bed and commenced dressing. "My God, Gordon, what's happened to you? Is that what Leslie and her

crowd got you into?"

"They didn't get me into anything. With all my worries and problems I needed an escape valve. I'm sorry you found out, but it doesn't concern you!"

"Doesn't concern me?" she cried. "My God! She's certainly shown you another way of life. How could you be so gullible and stupid? Do you know what drugs can do to you?"

"Come off it. No one that goes to Leslie's is pushed into anything; it's there, and if you want it, that's up to you."

"I don't know you at all, Gordon."

"I guess not. Perhaps we never knew each other. Things change." He put his hand on her head. "I'm sorry, Ruth, but that's the way life is. We were different when we were young; we saw only surface things, not what's inside, what makes us tick. Perhaps we're disappointed to find someone behaves differently than we expected. I don't know . . . maybe you expected too much from me, maybe I wanted you to be more like Leslie. Anyway, dreams have a way of disappearing, and then we have to face reality."

"Some reality!" Ruth's voice trembled.

"Things aren't always what they seem to be, nor are the people. Look at the Hendersons."

She considered what he'd said, then asked, "Gordon, why don't we see a marriage counselor?"

"Don't bother me with that now, I have to go." Then he added, "We'll talk about it tonight. I'll come home early and we can thrash this all out once and for all."

She went downstairs into the kitchen to rinse the cups and saucers and heard the door slam. She did some chores and watched television, waited till late afternoon and called Gordon's office to try and persuade him to come home even earlier. She was anxious to talk with him but found out that he had not been in his office all day. She sat in the living room for hours waiting for him to come home. Finally, unable to keep her eyes open, she went to bed, lonely and frightened. She meant nothing to him. Their lives would never be the same, and she felt hers was through. It was pointless to keep on living.

The next day was cold and windy. While Ruth wrestled with her own problems, Lenore fretted over Charles and Janet. Lenore had driven into town to see Charles.

"He won't be long, Miss Akton. He's finishing an examination before trial." The secretary indicated a table. "There are some magazines, if you would care to sit and wait."

Lenore picked up a few from the table, sat down and began leafing through them. The door of the inner office opened and Charles ushered some people out. He said good-bye and looked around to see who was in the waiting room. "Well, what are you doing here, Lenore?" She stood up. Before she could answer he said, "Come in."

She followed him inside and noticed that the offices had been newly redecorated. She sat down without saying a word. Charles studied her closely and felt uneasy; it was most unlike Lenore to come to his office.

"Have you spoken to Janet recently, Charles?"

He turned red. He didn't like any interference in his affairs. "No, I haven't." Lenore's calm expression was no indication as to why she questioned him, and he was certain she would not be in his office unless she considered it critical. Perhaps Janet was ill, he thought, but he wouldn't ask.

"Have you called her at all?"

"No, I did not! She left me, or have you forgotten that? I refuse to ask her to come home. She'll have to come to her senses by herself. There was no reason for her to run off the way she did."

"Did you bother to find out why she left?"

"We won't go into that. Anyway, she may be happier down there."

"You may be right." Lenore leaned closer so he had to look directly into her eyes. "She is happier, but keep this in mind, Charles, the longer she stays away, the farther and farther she will get from you. I think you understand."

"What do you mean?" he asked angrily.

"There were things that bothered her, and you took her for granted."

"A man's wife should understand his problems and be there when he needs her."

"Janet leaned over backwards to please you. She never had any life

of her own . . . let me finish." She held up her hand as Charles started to object. "She hasn't said as much in her letters, but I think she has met someone else. It could be that she will make a new life for herself, and not return. Hasn't that thought ever occurred to you?"

He didn't answer, but busied himself arranging papers on his desk. He refused to admit that his pride had been jolted when he'd found Janet's note, or that he missed her. His explanation to others was simply that Janet had gone south to get away from the cold.

"Lenore, you should know that there wasn't anything going on between Dottie and . . . Believe me, she was just a companion, nothing more. Janet never wanted to share any of those activities with me . . ."

"That may be true, Charles, but Janet doesn't know that, does she? You spent too much time with Dottie; it didn't appear to be a casual relationship. Did you ever consider the embarrassment you caused her? It wasn't easy for Janet; everyone knew you were golfing, boating or skiing with Dottie. And Janet honestly believed that you and Dottie had a go-around behind her back."

"What?"

"You never made any effort to convince her to the contrary. Now perhaps she feels that she can get involved herself if she wants to, except that knowing Janet, you should realize it won't be a fling for her; she may decide to start a new life. She isn't the casual type, nor is she the type to stay alone for very long. The fact that you haven't bothered to contact her would increase her feeling of certainty."

Charles knew that he could have had an affair with Dottie had he chosen to; it was true he liked her company, but in his mind there was no excuse for Janet to leave him like that. He resented hearing the truth from Lenore and opened his mouth to stay something when the phone rang. "I shouldn't be disturbed when I'm in conference, my secretary knows that." He answered the call abruptly, listened for a moment, then his face became grave. "When did that happen? Alright, tell them I'll be right out."

He scanned Lenore's face. "That was Ann Rufone. It seems something happened at the Foster's. Ruth is dead."

Charles stood up. "She fainted in the garage with the car engine

running and the doors closed. She's been asphyxiated; I think we'd better get out there."

"I'll follow you in my car; you may have to come back here later."

When they arrived, the ambulance was taking Ruth's body away. The garage door was open and the car doors were still ajar.

"Where's Gordon?" Charles asked the small group of women standing out front.

Kim answered, "He went inside." Mrs. Birkland, Jenny Banshata and Mrs. Howell nodded their heads. Mrs. Howell clutched her afternoon cocktail in her glove.

"Who found her?" Lenore inquired.

"Gordon."

Charles went inside. He found Gordon in the kitchen splashing cold water on his face.

"Gordon, what happened?"

"I don't know exactly. We hadn't told anyone yet, but Ruth was pregnant. The only thing I can conclude is that she started the car and waited to get the heat going before she opened the doors. Or, she fainted."

"It's odd."

"What's odd?" Gordon's head came up quickly. He knew deep down inside himself that it hadn't been an accident, but there would be nothing gained by letting people know the truth, and obviously Ruth wanted her death to appear accidental.

"That she didn't hit the horn when she fainted."

"Well, I don't know what happened; I guess we'll never know now."

"Who found her?"

"I did. I came home early today so we could have the chance for a long talk. When I came in, she wasn't here so I went to see if her car was gone. I heard it running when I passed the door, then I found her. Ann Rufone pulled in the drive. Apparently she was coming by to chat with Ruth, unaware that Ruth was going out."

Charles said nothing. Something was decidedly odd, but he couldn't quite put his finger on it. The front door opened and Gordon's father and mother came in. They went into the hallway to greet them.

"Sorry son," his father said. His mother simply walked over to Gordon and put her arms around him, whispering something they couldn't hear. Then she went toward the kitchen.

"Ruthie's folks are on their way out Gordy, I called them." His father seemed a little shaken. Charles remembered hearing that they hadn't been very close to Ruth. "Such a nice girl, Mr. Henderson, we all liked her so much."

Charles nodded. "Everyone who knew Ruth couldn't help but like her." He paused for a moment. "I think I'll leave you alone. If I can be of any help, let me know. I'll call Janet and tell her. She was very fond of Ruth."

As he went out the front door, he noticed Mrs. Foster coming from the kitchen carrying a tray with a coffee pot and cups. The brisk March air was refreshing and he walked quietly to his car. He noticed that the little group had gone, and Lenore was nowhere in sight. He sat in his car for a moment, then looked at his watch. It was almost five; he decided to go home. He thought ruefully that had Janet been here, he would have gone back to the office. Perhaps Lenore was right and he had taken Janet for granted. Ruth's death affected him and he had the feeling that something had been wrong between Gordon and Ruth, but he realized it was too late to correct anything now.

The house was quiet when he went in. He missed Janet but wouldn't admit it to her or anyone. Ruth's death gave him an excuse to call her. He didn't have the number and called Lenore to get it.

When the phone rang in the little Palm Beach apartment, Janet, who was fixing hors d'oeuvres, called, "Will you get that, Bob? My hands are sticky."

The man walked over and lifted the receiver. "Hello?" There was no answer, so he started to hang up, then decided to give it another try. "Hello, anybody there?"

"I must have the wrong number, I thought this was Janet Henderson's number, I'm sorry..."

"Hold on, Jan is here, just a minute."

Bob called to Jan, "It's for you, darling."

"Who is it?"

"I don't know, some man." As Janet walked into the room he teased, "My competition?"

"What are you talking about, who is it?"

Charles could hear the exchange and was furious. He found himself angrily wondering who the man was. He was going to hang up, but he heard Janet's voice. "Hello?"

"This is Charles."

There was a pause as though Janet was trying to remember who Charles was. "Oh, hello Charles, how are you?"

"I'm alright, how are you?" His voice sounded stiff.

"I'm feeling wonderful. What do you want?"

Charles held the phone away from his ear for a moment, outraged; he wasn't used to this kind of treatment. Then he spoke softly, "I thought you should know that Ruth Foster is dead."

"Charles, what happened?"

"It seems she fainted when she went to start the car. She had the habit of letting it warm up before she opened the garage doors. Gordon found her. Ruth was pregnant, which may have had something to do with it."

"Dear me, what a shame! When did it happen?"

"A little while ago. I just came from there."

"I didn't know she was pregnant. Tell Gordy I'm sorry . . . I'll send him a note right away."

"Aren't you coming home for the funeral?"

"No, it's too far."

He could hear a voice mumbling in the background. "Who is that Janet?"

"A friend."

"Oh? Well, how come he answers your phone? Are you entertaining some man? What in the hell is going on down there?" His voice rose.

"Charles, this is a very special friend; besides, I don't think I have to explain anything to you. I've been away a long time and you haven't bothered to get in touch."

"You're still my wife!" She was infuriating him, reminding him

that he hadn't called before.

"I'm well aware of that, Charles, but I didn't think you were." He heard the voice rumbling again. "You're upsetting me, and I have to hang up. Something's burning. Thanks for calling about Ruth. I'll wire some flowers."

She hung up on him, and he stood holding the receiver in disbelief. This wasn't like his wife; that mysterious man down there must have something to do with her attitude. He reflected for a few moments, then called Lenore to ask her some questions.

"Did you know that Janet was seeing someone in Florida? Did you know about this man she's entertaining down there?"

"No, she never said anything specific, but why should you be so surprised? Janet's attractive, educated and talented, and far from poor. Besides, she has no children, no ties to hinder her."

"What do you mean 'no ties'? What do you think I am?"

She hesitated, then came on strongly. "A bit of a smug fool, Charles."

"Hold on, Lenore."

"No, Charles, you hold on. You have to admit you were in the wrong . . . you were foolish with Dottie, and you were ridiculous to wait so long before you got in touch with Janet. What do you expect her to do? Anyway, if you're that upset, do something about it!"

"I called her, that was enough." His tone was aggrieved. "She had a man with her."

"So?"

"She isn't returning to Baywater for the funeral. I think she wants to stay down there. What should I do? Call her again?"

"That would be a waste of time. You should see her and find out what each one of you really wants. You can't let anyone else do it for you. This is between you two."

"I'll think about it. Thanks, Lenore."

Charles sat down in the living room. He pondered the situation, then he decided to wait. He was sure that Janet would show up for the funeral, then he wouldn't have to swallow his pride and go to her.

Charles had been completely astonished when Ruth's funeral came

and Janet hadn't appeared. It had been a very cold day, and Charles was stunned by Lenore's strange expression as the casket was lowered into the ground. Gordon had asked him to thank Janet for her letter and flowers, and Charles had mumbled something; his thoughts were in turmoil. He finally admitted to himself that maybe Janet had not been happy with him, even though she had always supported his efforts and never complained about the endless political gatherings she attended with him. He realized that if she were left alone much longer, she might start a new life, one that would not include him. Charles would never give her a divorce, and he had to forestall any idea like that.

The earliest flight he could book on the day of the funeral was a dinner flight. He hadn't told Lenore where he was going and drove his car to the airport.

Later, the plane dipped down toward the Palm Beach airport, and he saw glimmering lights in the half dark of the early evening. The balmy weather was in sharp contrast to the cold, bitter wind of Long Island. He didn't blame Janet for not wanting to leave here; it was delightful. The cab deposited him at the apartment. He rang the bell but there wasn't any answer. His pride came to the fore. He wasn't going to let her find him hanging around waiting. He found a room in the heart of town, a last-minute cancellation. He unpacked and showered and decided to go out. The desk clerk had recommended the "Tabu," not far away, and he enjoyed the warm air and the pleasant walk.

The bar was crowded, but the bartender was friendly. In between drinks, he tried Janet's number, but it was fruitless, there was no answer on the other end of the wire. The drinks relaxed him. The band was good, and the dance floor was crowded. He moved to the end of the bar where he could see the dancers. He ordered a fresh drink and turned toward the dance floor when he saw her. She was radiant; the smile that lighted her face was one he hadn't seen in a long time. She danced in the arms of a heavy-set, half baldish man. Charles noticed that she had lost weight and the dress she was wearing was one he'd never seen before. It clung softly to every curve.

The music stopped; the man's hand stayed on her back, caressing her gently. Charles felt an anger rise slowly; she didn't seem to be objecting. The

music began and she flowed back into this stranger's arms as naturally as though she belonged. It was a rumba, and they danced it well together. Charles conceded that he should have taken the time to learn to dance well. Janet loved to dance, but, Charles reasoned, whenever they attended a political function, he had to talk to the other men and couldn't take time to dance. Janet's partner whispered to her, and she tilted her head back and laughed delightedly. He took her arm and led her from the dance floor through the crowd. As they passed the bar to leave, Charles stood up in their path.

"Hello, Janet."

She was startled. "Charles!" Her mouth opened in a gasp. "What are you doing here?"

He noticed the man's hand tighten on her arm and looked coldly at him. "I am Charles Henderson, Janet's husband, in case you haven't heard."

"Bob, Bob Sutton." His voice was equally cool. "Yes, I've heard."

Charles gazed directly at Janet. "I'd like to talk to you."

"We're on our way to a party and we're late as it is. How long are you planning on being in town?"

"As long as it takes to bring you to your senses."

Janet's face flushed. She was provoked.

Bob interjected, "Now look, I don't want Janet upset."

Charles was furious; this man acted as though she belonged to him, as though he were her husband and Charles merely a nuisance. He ignored him and addressed her again. "Can I see you tomorrow, then, alone?"

All right, Charles, call me about eleven, not earlier, we'll be out late this evening."

She took Bob's arm and walked away, leaving Charles standing by himself. He was enraged. She acted as though they were strangers. He watched them leave; Bob's arm around her waist, her face turned to him, sparkling. Charles stormed back to his hotel room. He went to bed but tossed and turned, then in the morning he arose early, walked around town for some time and stopped for breakfast. Time passed slowly for him; he was still smarting from Janet's attitude. Finally, close to eleven, he went to her apartment, wondering while he rang if that Sutton fellow would be there. Janet answered the door with a cordial greeting. She had made breakfast and

invited Charles to join her.

"No thank you, I've eaten, but I'll have some coffee with you." He sat at the table and waited for her to ask about his trip, but she spoke casually about the beautiful weather.

Finally she asked him, "Did you notice the nice tan I have?"

"Yes, Janet, but I didn't come to Florida to discuss your tan. I'd like to know if you've had enough time to think things over."

Janet placed her cup slowly in her saucer. "Yes, Charles, two months is a long time, especially when you're waiting for the telephone to ring."

"I'm sorry Jan, but I have pride. I don't think there was any justification for your walking out on me like that. You know I love you. I want you to come back with me."

"I've been doing a lot of thinking. After I met Bob, things changed. I feel young and appreciated. We have a great deal in common and like to be together. He has made me happy."

"What do you know about him? Has he ever been married? Where does he come from, what sort of background? This could merely be a sort of 'summer romance.'"

"Yes, he's married. He came to Florida for a rest, to get away from his wife. After we met, he decided to get a divorce; he's been to see an attorney here. I know a great deal about him, Charles. He's a well-known and successful songwriter. After he saw you here last night, he asked me to marry him."

"What? . . . What have you decided?"

"I haven't made up my mind. I'm not sure I'm ready for another try, at least not yet. I know I can't go on with you, not the way it's been."

Charles was stunned and felt he should explain. "You may not believe this, but there hasn't ever been anything between Dottie and me. She was fun to be with; we were good companions, that's all. I could have made love to her any time, if I wanted, but I didn't."

"That may be, but it's not important now. You embarrassed me, humiliated me, had no concern for my feelings, and you actually preferred to spend your time with her. You took my love for granted and regarded

it lightly. How can you expect me to return with you and pick up the same old threads?"

Charles touched her hand. "Please, Jan, I'm sorry I hurt you, I didn't realize . . ." He sensed that she was softening and pressed his advantage. "Try and see things my way, Jan. I promise . . ." The phone interrupted him; she drew her hand away and went to answer it. Charles felt he had made his point, but when she returned, he sensed that her mood had changed.

She said very determinedly and distantly, "No Charles, I can't go back." She began to clear the table.

"Did you have some plans?"

"Yes, Bob and I are going boating, and he wanted to remind me to bring an extra sweater so I won't get cold. You'll have to excuse me, he'll be here shortly."

Charles knew it was hopeless. The call had come at the wrong moment. "Damn him," he thought. As she went to let him out, he said, "I'll be at this number, room forty-eight, till early evening. I plan to take the dinner flight back. If I haven't heard from you by the time I leave, I'll assume you don't intend to come back." He tried to kiss her, but she evaded him and closed the door firmly behind him.

He checked with the desk several times before six, then took a cab back to the airport. He boarded the plane reluctantly. The flight back was choppy and rough; as the plane approached New York, he was nauseous. Reality rocked him and he became fully conscious of the situation. He had lost his wife. He was depressed and unhappy as the plane hit the runaway and rolled to a stop.

"Charles Henderson, Charles Henderson, go to the information desk." The loud speaker disrupted his thoughts. He hurried to the desk. "I'm Charles Henderson." The girl handed him a phone. It was Lenore. "How did you know where I was?"

"I called Janet; she's taking the eight-thirty flight from Palm Beach, same airline. Stay at the airport." She sounded overwrought.

"What's happened?"

"Robbie's in the hospital, there was an accident and he's

212

hemorrhaging. The doctors aren't certain if . . ." Lenore paused for a moment, there was a gasp, then she continued, "Can you wait for Janet's plane?"

"Of course, but she may not want to see me, Lenore."

"Don't worry about that. She's concerned about Robbie. She'll appreciate having someone bring her to the hospital. I have to hang up. I want to go back to my son."

She made every effort to sound calm and controlled, but Charles knew what she must be going through. She continued to amaze him, her composure in the face of a crisis was baffling. He knew Robbie might die; the boy was fortunate to have lived this long.

"I'm sorry, Lenore, we'll be there as soon as we can."

Charles hung up, tears stung his eyes. As he waited for Janet's flight, he reflected on the uncertainties of life; one never knew from moment to moment what would happen, how you would be affected. He was sad about Robbie, yet this misfortune might bring him luck; Janet was returning.

When Janet's plane arrived and she saw him, she began to cry. He took her in his arms and held her, stroking her hair. "Lenore called me as I got into the terminal. We'll go directly to the hospital."

"Is he . . .?" Her voice broke.

"I haven't heard, but Robbie has had accidents before and pulled through. Let's hope . . . Janet, I love you . . . Everything I do is for you. You're my whole life and I need you. Forgive me for being foolish and thoughtless."

She looked up at him, saw the tears in his eyes, as he continued. "Things will be different, I promise. Please come home," he begged.

Janet pressed her face against his shoulder. "Oh Charles, I love you too, that's why I've been so hurt. But, if we can't make each other happy, we should end it and go our separate ways."

Charles grasped her bag. "Let's go to the hospital. We can talk this out later tonight or tomorrow. We must think of Lenore and Robbie."

Janet clung to his arm as they headed for Sayr's Point Hospital.

CHAPTER 12

1968 TO SPRING 1969
GANG BOSS, THRILLS AND FLYING

Baywater's residents, and anyone else who knew about Robbie's crises, prayed for his life. Robbie lost excessive blood and had to have immediate transfusions. At one point, his being hung in the delicate balance of life or death. Janet and Charles had waited at the hospital with Lenore and left her only after the doctor assured them, "The crucial point has passed and Robbie's life was spared." The bleeding had stopped. Janet wondered about this peculiar hereditary disease that affected her nephew, and she wished for a cure to be found in time for Robbie to live a long and fruitful life.

Lenore's movements were curtailed through the end of March and month of April, but after Robbie was up and about, Peter encouraged her to resume her normal activities in spite of his own illness.

Friends and neighbors stopped by from time to time to visit Robbie and bring a gift. One day young Terry Howell and his mother came by for a visit, and although Lenore and Robbie were polite to them, they were relieved when the company had gone. Terry was unusually interested in Robbie's disease and the black and blue marks on his arm. Lenore sensed that the boy was odd.

April rains brought May flowers, and Baywater resumed its normal pace. Gardens were hoed, azaleas bloomed, and the pool and tennis courts were readied for the members' use.

Mark Harrison's car was frequently parked in Lenore's driveway. He had helped Robbie catch up on his assignments, and at the end of the semester he monitored his exams.

215

✑

Janet had remained at Baywater. Charles had convinced her that their lives would be different and he would make every attempt to save their marriage. He had been considerate and loving in the weeks that followed, and Janet knew the situation had improved. Bob Sutton had called, hoping to persuade her to come back to Florida, but she told him that although she would never forget his kindnesses and that he had given her a keener awareness of herself (for that she would always be grateful), her roots were in Baywater and she loved Charles. Charles and Baywater; that was where she belonged.

Charles had always wanted a son to follow his footsteps, and when Janet mentioned wanting to see a doctor about starting a family, he was enthusiastic. The doctor hadn't made any promises, but there was hope.

It was a hot day in June and the children's voices floated up to her room as they ran excitedly toward the pool. Janet sat on her bed dreaming about a beautiful baby, the son who would make everything perfect. As she dreamed, another event was taking place that would affect the lives of the Baywater residents.

✑

The driver looked into the rearview mirror, his eyes momentarily focused on the man in the back seat. "Boss, I got a call just before we left. You remember my two cousins Bruce and Patty Alieto from Bridgeport? You met them at my son's christening."

The man in the back nodded while lighting a cigar.

"The F.B.I. paid them a late-night visit."

The gentleman in the back took a deep puff. "Hell, what happened?"

"Lucky they built the houses next to each other with the tunnel in between. When they knocked on Bruce's, he ran down to the cellar and over to Patty's, then they got away by car while the Feds entered the house. They're holed up in Pennsylvania. Bruce's wife said they trashed the place, but she doesn't think they got anything special."

"Good, keep me informed," he replied.

The drive continued in silence, each in his own thoughts.

The limousine rolled smoothly off the parkway, slowed at the intersection, and turned onto Vet's Highway. The driver breathed a sigh of relief. So far they had been lucky. No one had followed them; the road behind them was clear. He had been nervous since they left the city, and thought it was foolish and risky to go out to the Southampton summer house. Lou Sbarglio was a target in the gang war that had erupted a month ago, but he was still the boss, and Al merely a driver. Orders were orders. Mario sat with Lou in the back seat, his eyes flicking constantly, watching traffic and studying Al as Al drove deftly in the light traffic; then he glanced at his watch. Ten a.m., the ride would take another hour, but at least the business traffic had subsided and it would be easier to watch the road. He stiffened slightly; a car was parked on the shoulder farther down.

Al muttered, "Flat," and Mario saw a man rolling a tire from the trunk. He was alone.

"How long has that car been behind us?"

Al looked at the mirror. "A mile, maybe."

Mario grunted, "Keep to the limit, Al."

He checked the speedometer and slowed down slightly. The car was still behind them, moving up steadily; another had turned from the intersection and was coming fast. His hands tightened on the wheel; he wondered if they were being followed. The light ahead turned red, and he deliberately slowed down so that both cars would have to pass him. The first one was a woman with a dog; the second car came abreast of the limo and two men inside were talking, ignoring everything on the road. "Must be late for work," Al thought as they sped by, going through the light on the yellow, moving well beyond the speed limit. Al had timed the light correctly and cruised on steadily. The car with the dog turned off, and the car with the two men was far ahead.

Another car turned in from the intersection and Al watched it carefully; one man alone, moving at a moderate speed. The car passed, remaining in the left lane. Al and Mario watched it for a few minutes, then relaxed; it was

probably going to make the turn east onto Sunrise Highway. Al wasn't sure where the turnoff would be, so he moved into the left lane. He checked the rearview mirror; nothing behind him. The car ahead made a U-turn across the divider and was coming toward them at a normal pace. The occasional trees on the grass divider obscured his vision; for a moment he couldn't see the car. Suddenly there was a shattering spray of sound as a barrage of bullets struck the car. Al momentarily lost control; the car swerved, and he fought to keep it on the road as Mario yelled, "Get down Lou," and pushed Lou to the floor of the car. There was a moment's silence, then Lou moaned.

"Christ, Lou's been hit! Where the hell did it come from?"

"Across the divider. The bastard that made the U-turn. There must have been somebody crouched down in the back seat that we couldn't see."

Mario helped Lou back to the seat. "Let me see, how bad is it?"

"Could have been worse, it's my arm. Did you recognize them?"

"I only noticed the driver, and I don't know him."

"How the hell did they know we'd be on this road?"

Mario growled as he inspected Lou's arm. "Set it up good! Must have tailed us from town, cut off somewhere and picked us up here."

"They had to know the area." Lou was gritting his teeth. "Stop a minute, will you Al?"

Al slowed the car gently and pulled off onto the shoulder.

"What do we do now, Lou?" Mario asked as he wrapped a handkerchief around Lou's arm. "This is pretty messy. You're going to need a doc."

"There's a book in my jacket pocket, Mario, get it for me."

Mario extracted the little book and handed it to him.

"My nephew lives near here in a place called Baywater. He can help me out. Hand me the phone."

"Why don't we just head over there?" Mario asked as he gave Lou the phone.

"Want to make sure he's there." Lou was calm, he ignored the fierce pain in his arm. "No use going back to town if we don't have to. Make a turn ahead, Al, and keep it smooth." He hoped Jenny wouldn't answer the phone. He had no time for conversation. Luckily he heard a man's voice on the other

end of the wire.

"Joe?" he asked.

"Yes."

"Uncle Lou. No time for explanations, Joe, I need a doc who can keep his mouth shut. I'm on my way over, be there in a few minutes. Jenny home?"

Joe took a deep breath, then lit a cigarette. He had known his uncle would call on him some day for a favor, but he wasn't prepared for it. He hesitated for a moment, then spoke slowly. "Jenny and the girls went to the city for the day. I'll open the garage door. Pull into the right bay. It will take a little time to find someone, Uncle Lou."

"I haven't got time, Joe, you understand?"

"Yes, I understand." He put the phone down and stared at it. Lou had taken care of him financially for years, allowing him to profit handsomely without getting his name involved. He had no choice, he had to help. Lou might be his uncle, but Joe didn't delude himself. As head of the "family," Lou's word was law, no matter how gently the request was phrased.

He tried Vinny at home. He wasn't there. Joe was glad; it would be easier to talk to him at the office. While he dialed he wondered how tactfully he could put it, and how Vinny would react. He wasn't terribly concerned about getting Vinny's cooperation, as he was aware of the greed that had prompted Vinny in doing illegal abortions. Pat's death left Vinny open to exposure; besides, Joe was cynically amused that Vinny would eagerly accept the money Lou would pay for services rendered. Joe would have no compunctions about using Lou's name to bring pressure on Vinny, if necessary, even though he was slightly disturbed at having to reveal the kinship. Vinny would be the only one aware of the front that Joe's business provided for the syndicate, and Joe was certain it would go no further.

When he had finished talking to Vinny, Joe went to the garage and started his engine. He didn't know what Lou's problem was but thought it expedient to be ready. He didn't have to conjecture for very long. Moments later the sleek, black limousine pulled into the next bay. Joe moved quickly to the

garage door and pulled it down. His face blanched when he saw the bullet holes on the car and the blood covering his uncle's arm and clothes. Lou and his boys switched cars. Joe drove, and they were on their way to Vinny's office in moments.

Meanwhile, Vinny paced the floor waiting nervously. He was terrified. On one hand the fear of getting caught plagued him; on the other, the thought of crossing Joe left him shaken. He had been frightened since Pat's death and had steered clear of anything illegal or unsavory. Although Joe hadn't said it outright, Vinny knew it was a gunshot wound. Treating it without reporting it could put him in jeopardy. He ground out his cigarette, realizing that he had no choice; he had to cooperate with Joe, otherwise Joe could get nasty and blow the whistle on him about the abortion. A knock on the door roused him from his thoughts.

"Alone Vinny?" queried Joe as he led Lou and Mario into the room.

"I gave my nurse the morning off. I don't have office hours until one." He looked at Lou's arm briefly. "Better come inside the other room. I'll have to take this bullet fast to make sure the arm doesn't get infected . . . You know I'm supposed to report this, could lose my license if I get caught." Then he added as he noticed the expression on Lou's face, "But don't worry, I'll forget you were here."

He led the way to the inner office. Lou studied the doctor as he sat down and removed his jacket and shirt. He didn't like the man's attitude and had some reservations about trusting him, but he reasoned that Joe must have been certain that he could be relied on. Lou had the impression that Joe had something on him.

"I'll wait outside with Al. Okay, Lou?" Joe asked.

Lou nodded and Joe hurried out to the car. Al had moved the car to the back of the parking lot. They sat waiting patiently.

Mario stood by the table watching Vinny work. The room was silent; Lou looked at the bullet as Vinny extracted it. "Give it to Mario."

Vinny cleaned the bullet and handed it to Mario to pocket. As Vinny was bandaging the arm, there was a sharp knock on the door. He stopped and looked from Mario to Lou. "Might be a patient."

"Don't answer." Mario's voice was steady and cold.

Someone tried the outer doorknob. It was locked. Inside the room the men waited motionless; whoever it was might go away if no one answered. As there was another pound on the door, a voice called, "Open up, Doctor. It's Officer Fallon. Saw your car. There's been an accident down the street and we need your help."

Mario's face tightened and he loosened his coat jacket as he stared at Lou.

Lou answered his expression. "Could be legit. Better check on it. Mario, you stand behind the door when the doc goes out and make sure it's okay."

Vinny was perspiring heavily. As he moved from the inner office door he thought, "My God! Why does this have to happen to me?" He was frightened but replied, "Be right there."

Lou was still on the table and Mario was standing near the outer door. Vinny glanced around; the door was firmly shut and no one would see Lou.

"What's the problem, officer?" he asked as he unlocked and opened the outer door.

"The ambulance is over in Sayr's Point picking up a heart attack victim and we need some help with the accident down the street. Spotted your car in the lot and figured you were here."

"I'll get my bag. Be right with you."

Officer Fallon entered the room to wait and glanced curiously at Mario, who had sat down and picked up a magazine, trying to appear like a waiting patient.

Vinny opened the door to his inner office, entered quickly, pulling the door behind him so that Fallon couldn't see inside. Fallon's eyes had followed Vinny to the door after his glance at Mario, then his eye caught a reflection in the mirror over the receptionist's desk; the face of the man on the table inside was familiar, but he couldn't place it. He knew Dr. Rufone didn't have office hours in the morning; he was momentarily puzzled, then assumed that it was a local resident who had come in by special appointment. That's why the face was familiar, he thought.

When Vinny returned with his bag Fallon asked, "Are you sure you can leave now, Doctor? If not, we'll just have to wait for the ambulance. Can't move them."

"No, no." Vinny mumbled, "Nothing that can't wait." Then he turned to Mario, "Mr. Gatto, you can stay here if you wish. I'll be back shortly."

He moved briskly out of the office as Mario, head down, replied, "Thanks, Doctor."

Officer Fallon opened the door of the patrol car and watched Dr. Rufone curiously as he got in. On the way to the scene of the accident, he radioed in and informed the desk that he was taking the doctor with him. Vinny was silent, but sweating. Fallon thanked him for coming as he stopped the patrol car.

Vinny mumbled as he hurried from the car toward the victims. Fallon's partner was kneeling beside a woman. He looked puzzled by the expression on Fallon's face. He rose and said, "What's up?"

"I'm not sure, but I want to go and take a look at something."

"Go ahead. I'll stay here. Another car will be along soon."

Fallon drove back to Vinny's office, his instincts signaling him to follow through on a hunch. Dr. Rufone had been jittery, and the face of the man on the table was familiar. It was obvious that he was being treated, but odd that the doctor should leave him abruptly. Things didn't add up. He analyzed that Rufone didn't have hours in the morning; perhaps it was an emergency, but the doctor wouldn't leave an emergency so casually. Another thing, the nurse hadn't been in sight and the doctor himself had answered the door. There had been that fleeting glance of the car in the parking lot with two men in it, and the car looked like Joe Banshata's.

Officer Fallon pulled into the lot and walked over to the car. It was empty and unlocked. He looked inside carefully, then ran his hand over the front seat; the cushion was dry but the back rest had a sticky, damp spot. Had to be blood. He stood up, took his cap off and brushed his hand through his hair. He was in a quandary. Joe was a fine civic man, well liked by everyone, and the first to contribute to the hospital and the policeman's

benevolent society. If a friend of Joe's had been injured and Joe had brought him in, Dr. Rufone would have mentioned it. Fallon didn't want to go back to the office. If anything was wrong up there, no one would answer the door, and he didn't want to break in. Perhaps the car had been stolen by some of the kids and left there, but that didn't account for Rufone's strange behavior or the nagging memory of the face on the table. He decided to drive over to the Banshata's; on the way he checked in to find out if Joe's car had been reported stolen.

Meanwhile at Vinny's office, the four men waited. Al and Joe had come back inside to see if Lou was alright; they were puzzled when they saw Vinny leave. Mario suggested getting out immediately. If Lou's arm had been taken care of, there was no reason to stay. Joe finished putting the bandage on and helped Lou with his coat. Al wanted to wait for the doctor's return, insisting that there would be medication for Lou to take. Lou finally shortened the argument by walking out the door. They all followed, and Mario moved in front of Lou as they started out the building. Fallon was just pulling out of the parking lot. Mario drew back and signaled the others to wait. When the patrol car was out of sight, they hurried to Joe's car and drove off.

Officer Fallon arrived at Baywater, and the Banshata house. He knocked on the door. There was no answer; he walked to the garage and peeked in. There was a strange car in the right bay. His call had informed him that there was no report of a stolen car corresponding to Joe's. He was fully alert now; there had to be something going on, and he had to find out what it was. He tried the door but it was locked; he cupped his hands around his eyes and looked in again more carefully. The limousine had holes in the rear left body, and the window was shattered. He was galvanized into action. It took seconds to force the door. Once inside he checked the license plates and inspected the car thoroughly. Blood on the back seat and the carpet, the shattered window, the line of bullet holes added up to one thing: a shooting. He raced back to the patrol car and called headquarters. Things began to move as soon as the license was checked. He was sent back to Rufone's office to report on the Banshata car and talk to Dr. Rufone.

Fallon called in to headquarters to say the Banshata car was gone from the parking lot when he'd arrived; then he went to Rufone's office. That face, he had seen it a hundred times—Lou Sbarglio, head of a N.Y. syndicate. But what was he doing in Vinny's office? How did he know Vinny? And where did Joe fit into the picture? He stood at the receptionist's desk, watching Vinny gulp down a drink.

"Why didn't you report a gunshot wound, Doc?" Vinny started to protest but Fallon went on. "I just came from Banshata's house; the limousine is there, the bullet holes are there, the blood is there, and we have a make on the car."

"Listen, Fallon, can't we forget his? What do you want?"

"That sounded like a bribe . . . Now, why didn't you report it?"

"I didn't have a chance. I had almost finished treating him when you came for me. I meant to report it, but with the accident I forgot."

"Doctor, you could have told me when we were in the car." Fallon went into the inner office, checked around, found the blood-soaked handkerchief that Mario had bound Lou's arm with, wrapped it, dropped it in his pocked and returned to the outer office. "You'll have to come with me, Doc."

Vinny stood up. "I told you I meant to report it."

Fallon ignored the statement and held the door open.

Vinny was ashen as they left the building, and on the way he sobbed, "Why does everything happen to me?"

The police had moved quickly once they received the initial call from Fallon about the limousine. They were at the Banshata house in minutes, and had picked up Joe's car on his way home.

Joe's connection with Lou triggered further investigation. Once the relationship was discovered, the police dug deeper and uncovered facts that proved Baywater's fine civic leader was nothing more than a hood. He ran the number rackets in the area, was the local shylock, owned bars under corporate names, used his big, successful dry cleaning plant as a front, and ran unsavory things in the county. What no one found out was that Lou had been waiting for some of Tony Di Pasco's "boys" to get choice political spots; perhaps a friendly D.A. who would shut his eyes for a fee.

Then Lou could take over on a larger scale.

Jenny was humiliated by the exposé and refused to leave her house or see anyone. Everyone who knew Joe was shocked.

Vinny had been suspended by the Medical Association. He drank more and more. One day, in a drunken state, he cried and ranted about Pat Seymour and how it hadn't been his fault that she was a bleeder; he hadn't meant to let her die. More facts came to light and it was known that Vinny had been the local doctor who had done Pat's (and some other) abortions.

Ann Rufone was bewildered and helpless. Since Vinny had been arrested there was very little money coming in. Most patients who had owed the doctor money weren't paying their bills since they knew he wasn't in any position to do anything about collecting. Vinny had little money put away for emergencies, and there were some medical insurances due him.

Neither Vinny nor Joe thought of engaging Charles Henderson as their lawyer because they knew that behind all of his ambition was an honest and forthright human being.

Baywater's residents didn't like the publicity that Banshata and Rufone brought the community. Even Janet and Lenore were disappointed in the men, and provoked at their actions.

Vinny and Joe were arraigned and released on bail, then in late July, along with Lou, were indicted by a grand jury. The trials were to be held in the fall, and in the meantime they were free on bail.

Ann was dismayed. Twenty-five hundred dollars of the money that Vinny had set aside for emergencies was used as a premium for a bail bondsman. The deed to the house was to be used as collateral for the fifty-thousand-dollar bail. She wept as she handed the deed to the house over to Vinny.

Vinny had expected Joe Banshata to help him out with money, or a good attorney. He was shocked to discover that Joe refused to have any part of him, nor would Joe intercede with Lou on Vinny's behalf. Vinny was on his own, facing a murder charge as well as his medical involvement with the shooting.

Lou had his usual attorney, provided Joe with another syndicate lawyer, and

made sure that Jenny and the children would be taken care of.

Ann Rufone was close to a nervous breakdown. Vinny sat in the house all day drinking and complaining that he had been cheated. She wasn't used to taking the reigns, and now Vinny left everything for her to do. Ann heard of a good lawyer in the city and went to see him. He agreed to take the case, accepted a five-hundred-dollar retainer, and advised her how much more he would need to go to court in the fall and try the case. Ann was wrought up, but fortunately she had one good friend, Mark Harrison, who called from time to time to console her. And when he heard about her financial problems, he offered to help her with Vinny's legal fee. Ann was grateful for his friendship; he was the one strength in her shattered life. Mark found her a job in the record room at the college and arranged for a sitter for Lucille. Ann's summer passed slowly and painfully.

Rudy Mayer, the Chief of Police, and his department received congratulations from officials and residents for acting as efficiently as they did in arresting Lou Sbarglio and his cohorts. Rudy was the invited guest speaker at a number of civic club meetings and was applauded most heartily. Both he and Officer Fallon appeared on a few TV news programs as well as local radio stations, and Rudy basked in the light of prominence. One evening, however, a tragedy occurred that would affect his own personal life; one he would never forget.

Terry Howell steered the stolen car toward the north shore. Carol was crying; Terry was angry at her. "Shut up, you bitch. It's your fault being careless. I can't find a doctor out here to do the abortion, so we'll have to go to the city." Terry was upset about her pregnancy; the last thing he needed was the Chief of Police breathing down his neck.

He was weaving in and out of the lanes. Carol cowered in her seat,

desperate and scared. She'd heard that only a week before he'd seriously beaten up another boy, but the boy was so frightened of Terry's twisted mind and what he might do to him later, that he would not reveal who had done this cruel act. She had heard about his other sadistic jokes and now realized how stupid she had been to be involved with him, that he was highly dangerous and probably mentally ill. The light in front of him was green and he let out a shout. There was nothing in front of him; he rammed the pedal to the floor. The car sprang like a hungry tiger, devouring the road ahead. He laughed crazily, confident he could hold the road.

Carol had been thinking about her father. She was more afraid of her father finding out than the abortion itself; her thoughts were interrupted by a siren.

"Damned pigs!" Terry yelled. He saw the blinking lights coming up behind him fast. He had just passed one exit but there was another one coming up soon. If only he could keep his speed going. Glancing up at the rearview mirror he was goaded by the sight of the red light getting closer. The "pig" was gaining on him. Another exit loomed ahead; he wrenched the wheel and took it, slithering, skidding and sliding madly to negotiate the turn. He didn't stop and remembered further on there was a little dirt road where he had taken some girl one night. Carol started to scream as he swerved and made the wild turn, then shut his lights off and continued down the lane. At the end he stopped and waited. The police car passed and they could hear the siren getting farther and farther away.

"We'd better get out of here, not safe." He started the car and headed south instead. He had lost his pursuer and felt ecstatic that he had frightened Carol. Maybe she'll lose the baby from fright, he hoped. He drove through Sayr's Point. No one was following them and he felt more secure.

He stopped at a liquor store and bought some gin. Carol was frightened and wanted to go home, but he convinced her to accompany him to the ocean beach where they could drink and have sex. He took the long Sayr's Bridge toward the ocean beach. He pressed his foot to the pedal for speed.

Carol was weeping softly, which annoyed him even further; he pushed the pedal down all the way.

Suddenly there was a strange glowing object of light above them. Bright colors flashed in the sky. There were some blue and white beams and the glow intrigued him. It didn't appear to be a plane, and it couldn't be fireworks that high up, he conjectured. Terry slowed down, confused. The object was in motion like a weather balloon, but it wasn't bouncing around. Although it had been moving quickly, it appeared to stop and hover over the bay. "Do you see that, Carol? What is it?" Terry was having difficulty concentrating on his driving.

She had stopped weeping and answered in a high-pitched voice, "I don't know. It looks like a huge, round sandwich with a dome." She was frightened. She hadn't ever seen anything like it. Suddenly the object flew away rapidly and was gone, out of sight.

"Wow, that was weird," Terry said, and he resumed his speed. He saw lights in his rearview mirror, coming down the bridge with speed. "Damn, the police must have followed us."

At the same time the object appeared from nowhere and was next to them, over the water, by the bridge road. Carol screamed. The object had been rotating and oscillating at once, yet there was an absence of sound except for the car motor and waves. The object dipped and spun around them.

"My God, what is that?" she screamed. The object appeared to be about forty feet in diameter, and maybe ten feet thick. Although there were flashing lights and beams, the middle part was all dark. Her body felt heavy and very, very hot.

Terry wasn't sure which phenomenon was more threatening . . . this huge object or the police car bearing down on them.

The object was getting closer; the lights distracted Terry from seeing the edge of the bridge, then suddenly something interfered with his motor. He lost control of the car.

Carol was screaming as it went through the guard rails and plunged into the deepest part of the bay. At the same moment, the object rapidly disappeared into the dark sky, in an instant.

Rudy Mayer, Police Chief, had seen the bright lights but assumed they were from a sea plane, as many of the well-to-do Fire Island crowd had sea planes to commute to and from work. He pulled up to the broken guard rail, got out and saw the car going down into the water. It was gone; he called headquarters for help.

It took two days for the barge with the crane to pull the car out of the water. There were several divers working, and when he received the call that they had retrieved a girl from the passenger's seat, he hoped it wasn't Carol, as she hadn't come home that night. Later, he sobbed as he identified his daughter's body, and was shocked to learn she was pregnant. The car she had been in was the one stolen, but they didn't find another body.

The Howells finally realized Terry hadn't been home in a few nights, called his friends, and were informed that Terry had been seeing Carol. An avalanche of information revealed he had often committed crimes, bullied people and behaved sadistically. Time went by and his parents conjectured that perhaps he had jumped from the car before it hit the water, drowned, or run away. Others who had seen the mysterious lights and object wondered if it was a flying saucer, and some others hoped, jokingly, that aliens abducted the nasty, cruel young man.

It was an agonizing summer, not only for Ann Rufone and Jenny Banshata, but for Rudy Mayer and his wife. Now they, too, had their own personal grief.

The leaves were tumbling and spreading gold carpets over the lawns and streets as fall came to Baywater. It had been an unforgettable summer for the residents, and most of them were glad to see it end.

Janet still wasn't pregnant, and she was terribly disappointed, perhaps more for Charles than for herself. The thought of having a child had exhilarated him and he had thrown himself wholeheartedly into supporting Harry Boyd, County Chairman, for State Leader. Charles was Harry's County Co-Leader and had spent many hours with Harry over political strategy. Harry was near genius politically, and truly cared about the state and the

welfare of the people. He had come from a hard-working family that taught him to work for his wages honestly, and stand by the institution he represented. Charles traveled around the state talking with many of the county leaders and committeemen; his own integrity and forthrightness convinced the men to support Harry.

In June, when Harry won, he had wanted to appoint Charles to a good post, but Charles refused politely. Since he had been busy politically all spring, Charles wanted to stay close to Janet for the summer; both of them were hoping she would conceive. When fall came, it looked as though she might never become pregnant, and once again he busied himself in the political campaign. He had been reelected as County Co-Chairman to the new leader who replaced Harry Boyd, and in November their ticket won; it was an amazing victory. Charles and Janet were enjoying the fruits of their labors over the years and their only disappointment was that they could not have a child.

Ann Rufone had tried to carve a new life for herself. She had taken Lucille and moved into an apartment in town. It had been difficult for her to leave the house, but she hadn't wanted Lucille to see her father in the condition he was in. His case hadn't yet come to trial. Vinny constantly bothered her by phone late at night, and she wasn't getting enough sleep. She changed her number and had it unlisted, but one night Vinny came banging on her door screaming threats until the neighbors called the police to remove him. Vinny was dangerous and capable of doing anything while he was drunk. Charles got an order of protection, and Vinny was told to stay away from her. Ann was worried that in his state of mind there could be another tragedy. She often thought back to the night he had almost killed Lucille and her with the shotgun.

Mark spent time with her; the girls in the record room at the college befriended her, but other than that she had few friends. Vinny's case finally came up in court and she was relieved when the trial ended; the tension had been unbearable. Vinny was convicted of manslaughter and received an eight-year sentence. Bail was immediately terminated and he was remanded to jail.

Vinny's lawyer decided they should appeal the case. After the proper

procedure, bail was again set pending the appeal. Vinny wanted Ann to bring the deed of the house to his attorney to use for collateral. Ann called Charles, telling him of Vinny's request and also that she wanted a divorce and was afraid that Vinny would refuse. When Charles heard about the appeal and the need of the house deed for the bail, he advised her not to give the lawyer the deed or sign the necessary papers unless Vinny definitely agreed and signed papers permitting the divorce.

"It wasn't enough," he said, "that she humiliates me and moves into town before the trial, but trying to force me into a divorce is too much!" His lawyer calmed him down and after talking with Charles, persuaded Vinny to sign the divorce papers, otherwise he'd have to stay in jail during the appeal. Vinny agreed. Ann signed her interest in the house over to him so he could use the house as collateral for the new bond, and she flew to Mexico for her divorce.

When she returned, Mark was waiting for her. He had minded Lucille during Ann's trip and was fond of the child. He was worried that Vinny might act on his threats somehow, and felt she would be safer as Mrs. Mark Harrison. When Mark proposed marriage, Ann accepted, and before Thanksgiving they became man and wife in a quiet wedding ceremony in the college chapel. Charles and Janet stood up for them, and a small announcement of the wedding appeared in the Sayr's Point weekly.

The year of 1968 had been an unforgettable one for the residents of Baywater. Janet was relieved when the church bells rang in the New Year. She and Charles spent New Year's Eve with Peter, Lenore and Robbie. During the evening, Ann and Mark, and later Russ and Claudia, stopped in for a toast before attending the New Year's Eve party at the club.

Peter's leukemia had progressed to the point where he had to have his first blood transfusion in February. Lenore and Emma saw to his needs and tried to keep his spirits going, but Lenore had most of the responsibility as Emma was along in years and had difficulty climbing the stairs.

Janet had heard from Meg. Kerry had adopted the boys, and their family was well and happy.

Ann and Mark Harrison, with Lucille, had moved into a dormitory apartment on campus and Ann was "housemother."

Gordon Foster had stayed on in Baywater, but he was considering selling the house and moving.

Jenny Banshata lived in the house with her two daughters. The older daughter had left the college she had been attending in order to come home and be with her mother and sister. She had enrolled in Long Island University and commuted to the school. Joe had been sentenced to one year in jail, but his attorney thought he would be out on good behavior in six or seven months. Jenny was well provided for by the syndicate, and they sent out a chauffeur for one day a week to drive her upstate to Greensborough Prison to visit Joe.

Dan had completed two new houses in Baywater. One was built on the lot between Janet's and Kim's, on the bay, and the other between Gordon Foster's house and the Clough's (formerly the old Rufone house, which had been sold at a foreclosure sale). Dan had been doing other home building in the county. One day he and Stan Rudowski announced they were forming a partnership and would become the county's leading building company. Dan was to be in charge of residential building and Stan would be in charge of commercial projects.

Kim was taking lessons in preparation for the summer stock theatre. None of the tragedies had affected her or Thompson personally; life was good to them. They spent some evenings at the club with Madelaine and Ester or the Birklands.

Over Easter holidays the new house on the bay was sold to the Elliotts. Mr. Elliott was a highly specialized consulting engineer to Graham Aerial Space Company. The Elliotts had two sons, ten and twelve, and appeared to be congenial and well-mannered to their peers.

The following week the other house was sold to the DeNicols, a middle-aged couple with three children. Mr. DeNicols was manager of a New York City Brokerage Firm and commuted to the city by train during the week.

Baywater's events and tragedies, although not completely forgotten,

became obscured by the passage of time and the excitement of new neighbors.

One of the most exciting pieces of information was that a blood clotting factor had been developed for hemophiliacs. Everyone who knew him rejoiced in the fact that Robbie Morgan would live and spend his years in normal fashion.

By late spring Baywater had resumed its normal pace, and the residents were anxious to participate in the summer fun.

CHAPTER 13

SUMMER AND FALL 1969
THE EXPLOSION AND FAREWELL

The telephone rang early Saturday morning at the Howards. Claudia reached over sleepily to answer it. They had been at Lenore's till late the night before.

"Hello," she yawned as she spoke.

A man's voice on the other end was crisp. "Good morning. Is Mr. Howard in? This is Christopher Lane, the writer."

"Just a moment." She leaned over and nudged Russell. "Wake up. Telephone. Christopher Lane, a writer."

As Russ took the phone she drowsed off again, almost instantly. When he had hung up, Russ shook her. "Rise and shine! We're about to have company."

"At this hour? Who on earth would want to visit us at eight in the morning?" She was peering at the clock alongside her on the night table.

"It's not a visit. That was Chris Lane, the writer. Seems he's doing a series on ex-athletes and what they've been doing since they left professional ball. He wants to do an interview of me. So, let's go, my love. I invited him for breakfast!"

"You're a beast!" she teased as she threw off the covers.

Claudia dressed and headed for the kitchen. She mixed buckwheat pancakes and took out some sausages. The food was on the grill when Mr. Lane arrived and joined them for breakfast. Later, the two men discussed sports and the other athletes Chris had interviewed, as well as what Russ had done since he left pro-ball. When Chris was finished with

the interview, Russ suggested, "Why not stay over? We have the room and you said you have no other special plans."

"Won't your wife object, Russ?"

"Claudia object? No, she'd love it! We have a heated pool and tennis courts, and there'll be a gang at the clubhouse after dinner, a great bunch."

"If you're sure your wife won't mind. I don't want to impose on her." He had found the interview very rewarding, liked the Howards immediately, and wanted to stay.

"If it bothers you, I'll ask her." He called Claudia from the den. She came in, drying her hands on her apron. "Honey, Chris has nothing planned for the weekend, and as long as he's here . . ."

She interrupted, "Why don't you stay with us, Chris? We have loads of room and you two can take a swim in the pool . . . and . . . what's so funny?" The two men were laughing.

"Nothing. You just repeated what I said, that's all."

Chris agreed to stay. He and Russ walked around the club and pool, later took a swim, and then as guests of the Birklands went on their boat for a spin. Chris enjoyed the day and was looking forward to the evening at the club. At dinner, a usually jubilant affair, they discussed the people Chris would meet that night; then Russ and Christ spent a short time going through some of Russell's pictures while Claudia changed clothes.

"The best ones are at the club, Chris. But if you see anything here you want for the article, take it."

After Claudia joined the men, the three of them had drinks and started to the club.

Once at the club, Russ showed Chris some pictures of his "days of glory," as he put it.

Chris studied them intently. "Say, these are great. Who did them?"

"That's some of Lenore Akton's stuff. Pretty good, aren't they?"

"Lenore Akton? She did these?"

"That's right, she did a few pictures of me when I was big time. She's done some things of me since I came here, too."

Christ tugged at his arm. "Since you came here? How's that possible?"

"What the hell, she lives here, next door to us . . . in the old mansion.

Why the big surprise? Do you know her?"

"Know her!" exclaimed Chris. "I worked with her for years; we were one of the best teams going. I'll be darned! Gee, I'd love to see her!"

Russ chuckled. "That won't be hard. Here she comes now."

Chris looked up. Lenore was walking across the room toward Janet and Charles. "She hasn't changed much," he thought, "still calm, cool and serene."

Janet was speaking to Lenore, explaining about Russell's guest. She turned and saw Chris, and her face paled for a moment. Then she moved toward him. Chris ran to her, caught her up in his arms, and spun her around. He set her down. "Lennie, it's great to see you!" He kissed her lightly on the cheek.

Janet's mouth fell open. She had never seen anyone behave so familiarly with her cousin and Lenore didn't seem to object.

"Hello, Chris! It's been a long time." She was smiling in a way that was new to those around her. "I'm fine. How are you? And how is your wife?"

"My wife? That broke up ages ago. How's Peter and Robbie?"

"Robbie is fine now. They've discovered something for hemophiliacs recently, and he might make it all the way."

"That's great, Lenore. Is he here too?"

"He's at home now. Perhaps tomorrow, if you're going to be around . . ." She didn't finish the sentence.

"I'll be here. I'll come by early if it's alright with you and Peter. How is Peter?"

"Peter is quite ill, Chris. He rarely leaves his rooms, but I'm sure he'd be delighted to see you."

"Let me get you a drink. Same as always?"

"Yes, thank you."

As soon as Chris went to the bar, Janet walked over. "Who is he?" Her tone was filled with intrigue.

"That's the writer I used to work with, overseas. I wrote you about him." There was a sparkle in her eyes.

Janet rolled her eyes. "You never told me he was good-looking. I want to know the story."

Lenore burst out laughing. "There's no story, you're imagining things."

"I'm not imagining that he likes you, or that glint in your eyes. Oh, here he comes." Janet changed the conversation.

Lenore indicated Janet. "I see you have already met my cousin."

"I met the lady, but I didn't know she was your cousin. Seems attractive women run in the family."

"You mean Lenore never told you about me?"

For a moment he was puzzled, then he asked, "Are you the one she grew up with?"

"That's me!" And he laughed. She could see they wanted to be alone. "Would you two excuse me? I want to talk to Claudia for a minute. See you later."

As Janet walked off he turned to Lenore. "What are you doing out here? Are you still working? How come you never wrote to me? I wrote several letters to you when I returned to the states but you never answered. Why?"

"You'll have me out of breath. I'll tell you what you want to know, later, or perhaps tomorrow. Come on, I want to introduce you to the rest of the people."

The balance of the evening passed in casual pleasant conversation. After the party, Chris volunteered to escort Lenore to her door.

Russ grinned and indicated they would be up fairly late. "There's no rush. I imagine you two have plenty to talk over."

When they were finally alone, Chris asked, "Lennie, why didn't you ever write me?"

"I'm not much of a letter writer; besides, I was busy . . . I'm sorry about your marriage not working out."

"That had been a mistake from the beginning. We were both so young. Marge didn't like my traipsing around the country, and she didn't want to come along."

"But you've never married again?"

"No, that one experience was enough for me. I met a lot of girls, but it seemed as though I couldn't see life their way. You know, Lennie, I've thought about you a lot."

They were at the house before Lenore answered him. "I'm glad you have."

"We had a lot of fun together, except that you were such a tyrant."

"A tyrant? Oh, Chris, when you first started working with me, you weren't dry behind the ears. I had to keep you working."

"Well, I was scared of you in the beginning, you were so intense. But I didn't realize until a long time later that I never got along with anyone any better than I did with you. We had the same ideas and it was easy to get the drift of what you were after."

Lenore's mind traveled back to the days that seemed so far distant. He continued, "I'd like to see you again."

"I'm usually here. Peter is seriously ill, leukemia, and he doesn't have much longer."

"I'm sorry to hear that. Would he mind my coming over?"

"I don't think so, in fact, come over tomorrow and visit a while. He'll be glad to see you."

"Fine, good night Lennie." He leaned over and kissed her gently. "It's been wonderful. Brings back a lot of memories."

She slipped inside the mansion and watched him saunter down the drive, then she walked up the steps slowly to see Peter.

"Can I get you anything, Peter?"

"Nothing." His voice was muffled. "Did you just get in?"

"Yes, I walked to the club, and guess who I ran into? Chris Lane. He came here to do an article on Russ Howard. He's staying the weekend and would like to see you, if you're up to it."

"I think so, I'll try. It must have been a pleasant surprise."

"Yes, it was. Like old times."

"You miss working, don't you? All that traveling and excitement?"

"I've always been a restless person."

"It won't be much longer, Lenore. With the new discovery for Robbie's disease, he'll be alright; and my time is running out."

"Don't say that, Peter. I'm not waiting for something to happen to you."

"I didn't mean it like that, but I know it hasn't been easy for you all these years."

"I haven't complained, have I?"

"No, and sometimes I think it would have been better if you had. You keep everything inside. You have been very patient, and I appreciate it, my dear."

Lenore touched his shoulder. "Ring the buzzer if you want anything. I'm going to bed. See you in the morning."

Peter smiled and watched his wife walk from the room. He tried to shut out the pain he was suffering. He wondered how much longer he would continue to linger and suffer. He took another pill to dull the edge of his pain, and tried to fall asleep.

The following months were serene in Baywater. Lenore and Chris spent a lot of time together. He would drive out from New York whenever he could. Robbie was indulging himself in all the activities he had been denied for so long. Peter had failed rapidly during the summer, but was adamant that Lenore continue her life as usual. There was little to do for him, except see that he had his medication when he needed it, and Emma and Robbie saw to that when Lenore was out.

Russ Howard bought a yacht, and Charles, Janet, Lenore, Chris, and occasionally Robbie, spent some weekends and evenings with the Howards cruising in the bay.

Charles had resigned himself to the fact that Janet would never bear a child, and he attempted to fill the gap in her life by spending more time with her.

The end of summer was marred by one indiscreet incident, and Janet was convinced it would be impossible to ever know her neighbors.

Reverend Richard had taken a group of youngsters to Fire Island on a field trip. During their stroll they had spied some unusual birds. Reverend Richard handed out binoculars to them for closer study. He scanned

the brush looking for the birds, then swung the binoculars out across the bay; as he turned he saw Thompson Brack's boat. He paused to watch what was happening on-board and was appalled at what he saw. Thompson was engaged in a deeply amorous situation with a young man, a handsome member of the college swimming team. The minister was shocked and hurriedly focused the attention of the youngsters away from the water, disturbed they might inadvertently catch a glimpse of the activity on-board the boat.

After they returned to the mainland, the minister related the incident to Charles and asked his advice. Charles felt it had some effect on the community, but by and large there wasn't much to be done; the young man was at the age of consent. He further suggested that public knowledge of this could only hurt Kim and the child. However, he couldn't help but believe that Kim knew of her husband's double life. Charles recalled seeing Thom leave late in the evening on many occasions.

Janet was appalled; she'd always thought that Thompson was refined, and that he and Kim had a good marriage. Perhaps, she thought, this explained Kim's absorption with herself.

Rob walked into the room. "Are you going into town?"

"Yes, why?" his mother asked.

"I'd like a new jacket, and there are some books I have to drop off at the library."

"We'll go as soon as I find out what Emma wants, besides the duckling."

"I thought Emma was at the O'Quinn's."

"I'll drop her on the way."

"How is Mrs. O'Quinn?"

"Fine, but it will be a day or two before she's up. Emma can prepare everything for them today, and the children can help tomorrow. The new baby is cute and the children are excited about him."

Lenore left the room and went into the kitchen. Emma was moving very slowly. She was old and frail but pride wouldn't let her admit it. She handed a list of groceries to Lenore and asked, "Does Mr. Peter need anything before we go?"

"I'll look in on him now. Rob is coming with us. You call when you're finished at Dottie's."

While the old lady walked carefully to the door, Lenore went up to Peter's suite. "Peter, are you awake?" she asked softly.

"Yes, but I'm exhausted." His voice was barely audible. "Are you going out?"

"For a short while. I have to get some groceries. Will you be alright alone, or should I ask Rob to stay with you?"

"No, no. I'll be fine." He turned his head as Lenore moved the phone to the bed.

"If you need anything, call Claudia. Chris is on his way over; he may be here before I get back."

She leaned toward him and stroked his head, a gesture she was not frequently given to, as Rob stuck his head in the door.

"Ready mother?"

"Coming."

Peter smiled weakly as he watched them leave. He heard the door slam faintly, and there was no other sound but the soft ticking of the clock. Agonizingly he fumbled under the pillow for the pills that would deaden the pain and help him sleep. His mind drifted to Lenore and Robbie, then to Chris Lane. He felt sure Lenore would not be left alone after his death. Robbie's future was assured. His decision to make astronomy his career pleased Peter. He was happy that Robbie would be able to go off to college in California this school year and not have to remain in Baywater and be exposed to Peter's prolonged suffering.

He began to drowse, listening to the gentle ticking beside him, and only roused to partial consciousness when an explosion rocked the house and smoke and flames engulfed the mansion.

Lenore had completed her shopping and was headed to the bookstore to pick up Robbie when an eerie feeling engulfed her. The red light at the intersections seemed to burst into a shimmering circle of light. She tried to dispel the strange feeling, but an urgency to get home filled her mind.

As they drove out of Sayr's Point, Roma, who had been curled up on the back seat, began to whine. Fire sirens hurled their wailing voices into the crisp air.

"Hurts her ears," Rob spoke as Lenore raced toward the gates of Baywater. There were cars and people surging through the streets. A glow was visible and there were rumblings and explosions that tossed debris high into the air. Robbie was startled. They couldn't see what house was burning, but once inside the gates, he realized it was their home.

Lenore screamed to the policeman directing the traffic, "Let me through, let me through. I live there."

She jumped out of the car and raced toward the house. The intense heat drove her back and her voice was almost inaudible in the roar of the flames. "Oh my God, Peter!"

She fought the hand that grabbed her as she tried to run to the house. "There's nothing you can do. They tried to save him, it was no use."

She faced Claudia and Russell. Claudia was crying. "We called the fire department immediately, and Russ tried to get inside the house, but he couldn't."

Robbie was crying, "Was it the fireplace?"

"No. Gas," replied Russ.

Lenore stood frozen in horror as the house began to scream and groan in its death throes. Her eyes fastened unblinking on the scene before her, her body rigid as Janet fought her way through the crowd to stand by her. Janet's face was wet with tears as she put her arms around her cousin. There was no response from Lenore, no movement, no sound. She was rooted to the ground in stoical silence; nothing anyone said seemed to penetrate. In the end they all stood by helplessly. Charles and Chris Lane appeared. A momentary lull in the fire opened a frame to reveal a part of the staircase, and the magnificent faces carved on a section of wall were exposed for a second before erupting into a violent writhing of flame. All the priceless antiques that Taurus had collected in his world travels were consumed by fire. There was little the firemen could do. The wood in the house was old and dry; the men concentrated on keeping the fire from spreading as sparks shot noisily around, and flaming

debris attacked the clubhouse, the trees, and the roofs of the other houses.

Chris shook Lenore. "Lennie, it's me, Chris. Are you alright?" When she didn't move, he took her chin and forced her to turn and face him. "Lennie, are you alright?"

Slowly recognition replaced the blank stare in her eyes. "Peter," she whispered, "dear God, Peter's in there."

Christ looked questioningly at Russ. Russ shook his head.

"I left him alone." Her voice anguished, she kept repeating, "I left him alone."

Charles suggested to Janet, "Get a doctor, she's in shock."

Claudia said, "I'll call. Who should I get?"

"Dr. Warren. He was looking after Peter."

While Claudia hurried way, Chris outstretched his arms around Lenore and pressed her head to his shoulder. They stood silently until there was nothing left but a shapeless mass of rubble, smoldering ash, and gray smoke spiraling in ribbons. Gradually the crowed thinned and people began to move slowly away, looking curiously at the cluster around Lenore.

Charles said, "We have to take Robbie and Lenore away from here before the firemen start searching for Peter's body."

He walked up to Lenore. "Lenore, I think it would be a good idea to take Rob away from here."

"Please mother, can't we leave?" Robbie began to shake.

Lenore nodded, and the group moved toward the Henderson's house as the police and firemen began the search. Dan O'Quinn brought Emma back; Dr. Warren arrived and gave Lenore and Emma some medication. Roma, unaccustomed to the confusion, whined incessantly and followed Robbie's every move. Janet had her hands full; the neighbors and friends began a sympathetic procession to the house and the phone rang repeatedly. Claudia had the chore of answering the calls and questions. It was early morning before Russ and Claudia went home. Emma was put to sleep on the sofa in the playroom; Robbie and Lenore slept in the guest rooms. Charles and Chris were the last to retire. They sat soberly discussing the tragedy and Lenore's future.

A few days later, Lenore moved into a motel in Sayr's Point, refusing to accept Charles and Janet's hospitality any further. They understood that it was difficult for her to remain close to the scene of the fire. There had been nothing left; her clothes were gone and her photo equipment had been consumed. After the funeral, Rob went to California to attend college. Roma was left with Janet and Charles, and Emma moved back to town. It wasn't much of a surprise when Lenore announced that she would resume her career full time and leave with Chris for South America. He had decided to try new facets in writing and wanted Lenore to marry and accompany him. Once again Janet and Charles "stood up" for a wedding. Chris and Lenore took a week for a short honeymoon in New England.

Charles and Janet were reading in bed one night when the phone rang. Charles leaned over and answered it. Harry Boyd's voice was at the other end of the wire.

"Good to hear from you, Harry. What's up?"

"Charles, before you say no, I want you to think this one over carefully. Will Brice, the attorney and Chief Counsel for the Federal Trade Commission, had a heart attack late this afternoon and died an hour ago. It's a big job, Charles, and we need a man of integrity to fill the position. Would you consider it?"

For a moment Charles couldn't speak. The Federal Trade Commission . . . that was a big job and something he might like.

Harry continued, "Of course you'd have to live in Washington for the balance of the term, and if everything went right, I'm sure you could be appointed again."

Charles started to speak, he had a frog in his throat and it took him a moment to clear it. "I'll have to talk this over with Janet."

Janet looked over, thinking this must be another invitation, then she saw the flush in his cheeks, and her eyebrows went up quizzically.

"Do that, Charles. Remember, we need someone of your stature and integrity for the job. By the way, I've never thanked you enough for all your help to me and the party. Think it over and call me tomorrow about your decision."

After Charles hung up the phone, he told Janet about Harry's offer.

They stayed up late that night discussing the pros and cons of the position. When Janet knew it was something Charles would like to try, she suggested he do it. It meant giving up his practice locally and leaving for Washington immediately. Janet would stay in Baywater for the time being, and they'd see each other on weekends until they made a decision about the house; then she would join him in Washington. Roma would keep her company and watch the house.

Janet realized a new turn was beginning in their lives and she hoped it would be for the best. It was decided that Charles would call Harry Boyd the next day with his acceptance.

EPILOGUE

The sleek, black limousine sped through Sayr's Point toward Baywater Estates, rolled through the gates slowly and was welcomed by the massive lions poised on the concrete, forever a symbol of the success of the heirs of Baywater.

Lenore could see the lapping waves between the houses, and then felt a blast of cold air when the driver opened his door. She wondered about Taurus, Uncle Taurus, whose calm, serene and magnificent Baywater had been intruded upon by two orphaned young girls. Was there eternal life after death? Had Taurus witnessed all that had transpired?

The driver placed Janet's bags in the trunk as she stepped inside the limousine. The house looked deserted, the shades pulled down; Roma was away in California with Rob. Charles had flown back to pick up Janet's car piled with the belongings they would need in their new home in Washington. The rest of the clothes had been packed and the new tenants, who would be renting the house, agreed that the boxes could be left in the attic until such time as Janet and Charles wanted them.

The driver started the car and the limousine rolled down the road, leaving behind the charred ruins of the old mansion, the clubhouse, and one by one the homes, events and tragedies that had shaped Baywater.

Each wondered what the future would hold. What was to be their new legacy . . . happiness, love, challenge, tears? As the car passed the gates, Janet squeezed Lenore's hand, and each turned toward the strong faces of the beasts. For one lingering moment, the two cousins' thoughts turned to the distant past. Memories crowded their minds, even reaching to the day they had been brought here to live.

Baywater, the once tranquil refuge in their lives, which had given solace to the two young, shattered hearts, was lost to them forever. Now, a different Baywater lived.

The driver pressed down the accelerator and they sped toward the airport, where Chris was waiting with crates and luggage. He and Lenore would see Janet's flight off to Washington, then fly to South America.

What was Baywater? Would anyone ever understand the secrets of Baywater . . . strengths, weaknesses, beginnings, endings, where all kinds of love and lust had occurred?